# SONGDOGS

# SONGDOGS

*a novel*

## Colum McCann

*Metropolitan Books*

Henry Holt and Company ▪ New York

Metropolitan Books
Henry Holt and Company, Inc.
*Publishers since 1866*
115 West 18th Street
New York, New York 10011

Metropolitan Books™ is a division of Rowholt
and an imprint of Henry Holt and Company, Inc.

First published in the United States in 1995 by
Henry Holt and Company, Inc.
Originally published in the United Kingdom
in 1995 by Phoenix House.

Library of Congress Cataloging-in-Publication Data
McCann, Colum.
Songdogs: a novel / Colum McCann.—1st American ed.
p.    cm.
I. Title.
PR6063.C335S66    1995              95-19931
823'.914—dc20                       CIP

ISBN 0-8050-4104-4

Henry Holt books are available for special promotions
and premiums. For details contact: Director, Special Markets.

First American Edition—1995

Printed in the United States of America
All first editions are printed on acid-free paper.∞

1   3   5   7   9   10   8   6   4   2

*The author wishes to gratefully acknowledge the help of the
Irish Arts Council for a 1993 bursary to write this novel, and The Tyrone Guthrie Center in
County Monaghan, Ireland, where part of this work was written.*

*For Allison*

# SONGDOGS

*Just before I came home to Ireland I saw my first coyotes. They were strung on a fencepost near Jackson Hole, Wyoming. An eruption of brown fur against a field of melting snow, their bodies hanging upside-down, tied to the post with orange twine. Two neat bullet-holes had pierced their flanks where brown merged white. They were foot-dry and rotten with stench. Muzzles and paws hung down in the grass and their mouths were open, as if about to howl.*

*The hanging was a rancher's warning to other coyotes to stay away from the field. If they trotted nearby, a paw raised to the chest, an ear cocked to a sound, a tail held in motion, the rancher would bullet them back to where they came from. But coyotes aren't as foolish as us – they don't trespass where the dead have been. They move on and sing elsewhere.*

# TUESDAY

## *the law of the river*

I sat on my backpack, behind the hedge, where the old man couldn't see me, and watched the slowness of the river and him.

Not even the river itself knew it was a river anymore. Wide and brown, with a few plastic bags sitting in the reeds, it no longer made a noise at its curves. A piece of Styrofoam was wrapped around one of the footbridge poles. Some oil boated lazily on the surface, throwing colours in the afternoon sun.

Yet still the old man was fishing away. The line rolled out, catching the light, and the fly landed softly. He flicked it around with his wrist for a minute, slumped his head when he finished each cast, reeled in the slack and rubbed at his forearm. After a while he went and sat in a red and white striped lawn chair under the branches of the old poplar tree. He turned his head in the direction of the hedge, didn't see me. Leaning backwards in the chair, he started fiddling with the fly on the end of the line, put the hook and feathers in his mouth, blew on them, trying to fluff out the dressing.

3

His overcoat hung in an anarchy around him, and his trousers rode up past the ankles of his green wellingtons. When he stood up to take the coat off I was shocked to see the lineament of his body – as thin as the reeds I used to make holy crosses with during February winters.

The afternoon wore on and he left the cork handle propped in lazily at his crotch, leaned down and spat on the ground, wiped some dribble off the bottom of his chin. Every now and then he tipped his hat upwards to the swifts that scissored in the sky, then stared at the line lying in the water, amongst the rubbish.

A long time ago, back in the seventies – before the meat factory came – he would bring me down in the morning and make me swim in the fast water, against the flow. He was a good swimmer, a strong body on him, powerful shoulders, the neck of a bull. Even in winter he'd climb into the water in his red togs, plough away, his arms making windmill motions. Wisps of wet hair stuck to his balding scalp. The current was strong enough to keep him stationary. Sometimes he could stay in one spot for an hour or two, just swimming. He'd let out big shouts while my mother stood on the riverbank and watched. She was dark-skinned, almost bog-coloured, like the land. Blue work gloves that migrated to her elbows. Bags under her eyes. She would stand and watch, sometimes waving, every now and then fumbling with the colourful flag of elastics that kept her silver hair together.

I stayed in the river by hanging on to the roots of the poplars. Seven years old, I could feel the tug in my armpits, the water skimming over my face, my body sweeping away. The old man kept moving his arms against the current. When he'd had enough he let himself be swept a little stretch downstream, to the riverbank curve. I'd let go of the root and be carried along after him. He'd reach down, catch me, drag me out by the waistband of my togs. We'd

4

dress, shiver together on the muddy bank, my mother calling us up for breakfast. The old man would give a nod to the river. It was the law of water, he told me. It was bound to move things on.

But, watching him this afternoon, I thought that if he tried swimming nowadays he'd just float around like all that shit and rubbish in the reeds.

When evening fell the eastern sky was the colour of nicotine, merging into red in the west. A few thin clouds slashed along through it. He took out his cigarettes, tapping the bottom end of the box with his palm, opening the lid, flipping it upwards with his thumb, a studied patience in the movement. Reaching into his overcoat pocket he got some long kitchen matches. Even from a distance I could see that his hands were trembling, and he lit two matches before the cigarette took.

He blew the smoke up to the swifts, lifted the rod again. Ran his hands lovingly along the glass pole, flicked it back for one last cast. A pile-up of line hit the water noisily. The river skipped. It was an instant of concurrency. The sunlight caught the droplets and coloured them as they rose, and it struck me then that the old man and the water are together in all of this – they have lived out their lives disguised as one another, the river and him, once wild with movement, churning new ways, violently ripping along, now moving slowly down towards some final, unalterable sea.

A russet-haired woman who only wore one sleeve on her dress gave birth to my father on a clifftop overlooking the Atlantic, in the summer of 1918. She was known in town as a madwoman – she kept one arm inside the dress, tucked down by her waist – and nobody was surprised by the circumstances of the birth. Spindrift blew up on to the cliff, and purple wildflowers were exploding in shapes that might have made her think of bombs erupting in far-off Flanders. She had just received a letter saying that her lover had been fed to the guns of the Great War – he was a local man who had furrowed inside her seven months before-hand, then stepped his way out from Mayo into a British army uniform. Perhaps she flapped a crazy dance of grief after slicing the umbilical cord, unsurprised by the shock of black hair on her baby's head, the rude red lips, the very white skin, the squash of his ears.

He was found by two Protestant ladies who lived together in a giant house near the edge of the sea. The ladies were out on a Sunday stroll when they saw the bundle of skin amongst some trampled flowers. One of them took off her petticoat and carried him home, wrapped in it. The madwoman, my grandmother, was nowhere to be seen, although a trail of her clothes, including the one-sleeved dress, led inland towards the mountains.

The Protestant ladies raised him in a house of fine china teacups, radio broadcasts, scones privileged with spoonfuls of clotted cream. They sat him by a grand piano, licked their fingers and combed his hair back, an unruly cowlick growing long at his forehead. His clothes were ordered all the way from Dublin, beautiful white shirts that he destroyed running through the bogs, tweed trousers that were ripped on sea rocks, gorgeous blue cravats in which he wrapped stones to fling upwards at curlews. They baptised him in the Protestant church with the name Gordon Peters, and years later – beaten up in school for the name – he repaid them by urinating on their toothbrushes.

Still he loved them in a strange way, these old ladies with scintillating bottle-green eyes. He came back from his long walks with bundles of flowers that he'd plucked from the sides of dark pools, purple flowers that nodded to one another in expensive vases on the dining-room table. He called each of them 'Mammy,' bounding home with stones from the beach, telling stories of dolphins that had leaped alongside him, the length of the strand. A friend of his, Manley, emitted a high-pitched squeal that he claimed attracted dolphins, and they spent days together on the beach, shouting, eyes seaward. The ladies brought packed lunches down to them, spreading their long dresses on the rocks, watching their adopted son.

He must have been a curious sight in his belted blue coat, my father, eyes very dark, a history of mischief and sadness already written in them.

At the age of eleven, when he was told the story of his mother, he renamed himself Michael Lyons, a name that was common among many of the locals, a name that could have belonged to his own father. He stood on the edge of the cliff in his short trousers and spat out over the ocean to soak Britain with phlegm for the pointlessness of his father's death. At the time he didn't realise that his spit was aimed westward – at Mexico, at San Francisco, at Wyoming, at New York – where in later years it would truly land.

The ladies came along the seaboard and each took one of his hands, swinging him home between them – a chairoplane of freckles, kicking small brown shoes up into the air.

In the spring of 1934 the old Protestant ladies decided to take a boat out to bring some food to islanders across the bay. My father wasn't with them – he was out slingshotting curlews in the bogs, his body awkward now with adolescence. The sun was pouring down turmeric over the perfectly calm water. The ladies stepped off the dock into a currach, white parasols above their heads. They began to row, the oars creating concentric ripples on the sea, the dock receding from them. Nobody knew what happened next – one of the ladies, Loyola, had been a skilled boatwoman by all accounts – but maybe she leaned over to look at a porpoise, or a floating shoe, or a starfish, or a discarded bottle, then tumbled in. Maybe her friend went after her in a fit of pure love, the parasol taking flight, a grey-haired woman in a white lace dress, with her arms outstretched, breaking the surface of the blueness with a dive. In the water they might have suddenly looked at one another and remembered the essential fact that neither of them could swim. The parasol drifted on the water's surface and I imagine the two ladies going down together to the ocean floor, holding hands, regretting that the boy couldn't join them in the seaweed.

Their bodies were found washed up on the strand, with seals barking loudly by some nearby rocks.

The Protestant ladies were buried in a quiet graveyard near where the river tumbled into the sea. In their will they left my father everything they owned – the house, the land, the china, the sad toothbrushes staring him down from a porcelain cup. He was sixteen years old and he sat at a giant mahogany table in the living room, contemplating the thud of empty house around him. Gardeners and housekeepers came by to do their work, rapping at the brass knocker on the door. They whisked their caps off and nodded gravely to him when he opened up. He gave them their wages, but asked them not to come back, said he would do the chores himself, that he'd continue to pay them every week from the inheritance. They moved down the gravel driveway, casting suspicious glances backwards. Grass began to grow long over croquet hoops on the lawn. Mallets were lost under leaves. Curtains were left open to shafts of sunlight, discolouring the furniture. My father's shirts and vests carpeted the corridors. He started sleeping outside, on the verandah, too many spectral voices in the upstairs rooms. The house seemed alien to him, but by day he wandered around it, opening drawers, tapping walls, scrawling 'Michael' in the dirt on the windowpanes.

It was a camera that woke him. He found it in a large red box under one of the beds, forgotten. It had belonged to

Loyola, but she had never mentioned it to him. Opening the silver snaps, a pandora of dust arose around him, and he lifted the parts out on to the bed. It was an old model with a dickybird hood, glass plates in perfect order, wooden legs sturdy, lens unscratched. A hand-scrawled note left instructions. He spent hours putting it together and carried it downstairs, stepping along the corridor of scattered clothes, out to the front lawn. He hailed the sky with his new discovery, roaming around the grounds, practising, looking at the long grass through a box-view, opening and closing the shutter, wiping every fleck of dust from the body, reinforcing the tripod legs with wedges of wood. He called the camera 'Loyola' and at night he carried it to the verandah, stared at it through his insomnia. He didn't know it then, but the camera would burst him out on to the world, give him something to cling to, fulminate a belief in him in the power of light, the necessity of image, the possibility of freezing time.

He ordered more glass plates and developing equipment from Dublin, built a makeshift darkroom at the end of the lawn, took the camera apart once a week, cleaned it with the flap ends of white shirts, put it back together again meticulously, polished it with a soft rag dipped in diluted vinegar, careful to rub the cloth in one direction, to avoid staining. In the cold winter months he stuffed clothes and old towels in the box to keep the equipment from freezing. During summer he put it in the shadows and draped it with a large white tablecloth.

I can imagine my father back in the thirties, roaming around, darting his head in and out, like a swallow, from the black hood of the camera. He carried it along dark roads built eighty years before, by famished men from the poorhouses. They were narrow roads, bits of sea-blown spray landing on them, winding drunkenly away from the cliffs towards the mountains. And drunken men walked along them, sometimes rows of men, like weeds in motion through the decade of the Great Depression. Rain soaked the soil, battered the land, flung rainbows over the bay. Storms squalled across the water, sometimes so strong that they carried slates and beams and occasionally the whole roofs of houses through the air.

His friend, Manley, had a motorbike that my father used to borrow. Leaning the Triumph around tight corners, along piers and through village greens, a scarf flying out at the back of his neck, my old man became famous locally.

Along the backroads of Mayo he caught black and white images of old women head-bent on the way to mass; flowers reaching up above black puddles; sheep huddled in the ruined shells of old cottages; packets of cornflakes fading in the windows of shops; fishermen down by the docksides warming their hands over oil drums; a middle-aged tinker resting outside an old caravan, spreadeagled, plucking at the crotch of his pants. It was a world that had seldom seen a lens of any sort, and my father moved around it, taller now, his body filling out, sleeves rolled up, drama in the exhibition of himself. The quiff of hair bounced around on his forehead. Veins rose, eskers on the back of his hand, blue and well defined. He could cock his arm and dance an easy muscle. Girls outside the dancehall watched him and wondered.

The owner of the dancehall – a man with a face like a hagfish – wouldn't allow any cameras inside. Still, my father was quite content to hang around, smoking, waiting for Manley to emerge, looking for opportunities to use Loyola. Eighteen years old, and the world back then was a fabulous place to him. He could have bitten off pieces of the universe and spat them on a big glass photographic plate. Outside the dancehall he sometimes took pictures of young women smoking for the first time, new hats cocked sideways, daring lipstick smudged upwards to thicken their lips. Sometimes the girls would try to get him to come in and dance, but it didn't interest him, dancing, unless he could take a picture of it.

Once he got caught trying to take photographs of the church housekeeper in the outhouse behind the priest's place. The door was left open, revealing the housekeeper with her skirt hitched high around her hips and her knees ajar. My father had hidden in a clump of bushes but didn't have time to take a single picture. The priest, a former hurley player, discovered him and knocked him to the ground with a single roundhouse, opened the back of the camera, held the glass plates to the light as if reading the holy scrolls. He gave a thunderous sermon the next week, passages from the Old Testament about graven images, feverish words flying around the pews. My old man slouched at the back of the church with his hat on. He tipped his hat a little when worshippers went up for the Eucharist. From then on, there was a dark, but almost heroic shadow following him in town. A swagger out the door of the church, a bit of spit aimed at the sky with missionary zeal, a bravura in the sway of his shoulders as he walked.

With his inheritance he set up a small studio in a disused cow barn at the end of a country lane. An ancient barn, it was strewn with animal shit and pieces of lumber. The carcass of a calf had been left to rot in the corner. He took it outside, burned the bones, slopped the barn out, nailed the boards down, festooned the walls with photographs, and waited for customers, leaning against the doorway, bored, smoking. Sometimes Manley arrived, touting his shotgun, wearing unfashionable ties and suits of outstanding vulgarity – clothes my father had lent him money to buy. Manley hung out at the barn, talking of new books he had read. He was championing anarchy at the time – said it was democracy brought to its fullest form – and pounded his fist in the cause of the late Sacco and Vanzetti, who had been executed in the States over a decade before. Manley dreamed of making his way to Spain, perhaps to join the International Brigade. My father nodded to the tune of Manley's rants, all the time looking down the road for customers.

News travelled late to Mayo. Papers arrived late. Ideas arrived late. Even flocks of birds sometimes arrived late. There was something about the heaviness of the soil and the weather that inspired torpidity. He knew that the locals would come to his barn if he did something unusual, so he soon announced that the portraits would be free of charge. After that a small trail of people came in and out – guiltily and secretly, down along the high brambled lane, into the building, where he hung a white curtain from a wooden beam. Ripples of light came through the slats of the walls, falling in peculiar shapes on their faces – gaunt farmers uneasy in their old Sunday suits, grandmothers with fingers over rotten teeth, policemen in hats, a boxer in billowy shorts, thumping his glove against his chest, the local butcher with a flower in his lapel, girls with safety pins in the undersides of their dresses. There were even some young women slouching in bony but salacious poses.

My father had rescued an old *chaise* with three legs. When the women reclined on it, their hair swooped towards the floor. Manley, giving politics a rest, let a licentious tongue hang out as he peeped in through the barn slats. They weren't lurid, the photos. They had a stodginess to them, as if the old man forced his hand too hard – unlike the ones he took of Mam years afterwards, fluid and sensual. Most of the women never saw their photos. But decades later, when he was somewhat notorious, he had them printed at a press in France. The book caused a minor uproar in town, giving one of the local councillors a mild heart attack when he saw a portrait of his aunt with her left nipple visible under a thin linen blouse.

The swifts moved with a disregard for space, some of them darting up for insects on the air, others swerving down towards the sea, or simply moving back and forth, whipping the evening sky. He looked up at them, as if envious, as if he might burst his way upwards himself, join them in a mockery of flight. They were bellyfull with insects as he rose stiffly out of the lawn chair, grabbed his fishing rod, put the flyhook in the lowest eye, and walked away from the river, through the muddy soil up towards our house.

He used the bottom end of the rod as a stick as he lurched, his dark overcoat open and hanging, cigarette smoke churning from his mouth, a blue bucket in his right hand. At the doorstep he leaned his rod against the wisteria, and slowly kicked off one of his boots. A stockinged foot trembled with cold on the concrete. He coughed into his fist and let some spit out into the hole at the bottom end of the drainpipe, bent down, stubbed his cigarette in a puddle, swiped at some midges in the air.

I lifted my backpack, stepped out from behind the hedge, and walked across the yard. Cocking his head sideways like a curious animal, he closed his right eye, fumbled in his coat for his glasses.

'Jesus Christ,' he muttered, 'if it isn't yourself.'

I held out my hand and he leaned his shoulder against me, smelling of earth and tobacco and bait. He moved to place his foot against the bottom of the door and shoved it open, coughed, threw his coat on the rack.

'Christ, that's some fucken monster you've got there,' he said.

I placed the backpack against the kitchen table as he walked towards the fireplace.

'Well, well, well,' he said, his back to me, fumbling in the fire pail, 'would ya look at the cut of ya.'

'You're looking well yourself.'

'Cut your hair.'

'I did.'

'Lost the earring as well,' he said.

'Ah yeah, got rid of that a long time ago.'

'You're home for a while?'

'I am.' I picked up a spoon from the table, twirled it in my fingers. 'For a week. Is that all right?'

'If ya can tolerate an old man.'

'If you can tolerate me.'

'On holidays?' he asked.

'Sort of, yeah. Back to pick up the green card. Have to go up to the embassy in Dublin one of these days.'

'Thought you were in London?' he said.

'Well, I was, yeah. I'm in the States now.'

'I see. What ya doin' there?'

'Bits and pieces. Nothing much.'

He scratched at his head and let out a bit of a belch: 'Nothing much happening here these days, either.'

'Looks the same, except for the river.'

The fluorescent kitchen light fizzled. 'I'm fishing every day.'

'Every day?'

'On the quest for a giant pink salmon down beyond the bend. I'd swear the fucken thing's taunting me. Up it rears every now and then and looks like it's waving.' He stretched out his arms. 'This bloody big.'

'A salmon?'

'That's right.'

'In the river?'

'Why not?'

'What happened to it?'

'What?'

'The water.'

'Oh, they put in a few more gates by the meat factory.'

'Why?'

'Don't know. For cleaning the carcasses or something.'

'It looks slow.'

'But chock-full with that big one.'

'Yeah.'

'I'm telling ya, this bloody big.'

He stretched out his arms again, a three-foot expanse between liver spots. But I was sure that the only thing more than three feet long in that river was the rod that he threw in, in a fit of anger, one time long ago. I had come home from secondary school wearing a gold hoop in my ear, and he flung the rod by the cork handle all the way to the footbridge and told me that if I didn't take the piece of shite out of my ear he'd give me what-for and no doubt about it. Which he never did, and never would.

'No kidding,' he said to me, 'ya should see it.'

'Where?'

'By the bend, I told ya.'

'Really?'

'Yeah. Running around like a fart in a bottle.'

I laughed as he bent down, rubbing his knee.

'An absolute bloody giant,' he said.

But giant salmon or not, it looked to me that he shouldn't be going down to the river too much anymore. Might catch himself a bad cold. Or tumble in. Get blown away in the breeze. With his shirt open to the third button he turned around from the fireplace. His chest was a xylophone of bones sticking out against his skin. His face and arms still held some tan, but the vale at his throat was lost to whiteness and the remaining chest hairs curled, acolytes of grey. His neck was a sack of sag and his trousers were huge on him. Not too healthy for him to be out in the cold, although it would be lovely if I could see him cast in the way he used to – even when I detested him there were times I was astounded just to watch him cast. Back when the river was alive, those flicks of the wrist like so many fireflies on the bank, the hooks glinting in the lapel of his overcoat, that huge sadness of his disappearing as the rod whipped away, him counting under his breath, one-two-three-here-we-go, lassoing it to the wind, brisk upward motion of the tip of the glass rod, sometimes drying off the flies by false casting, finally watching them curl out over the water and plonk, reeling the surface into soft circles, stamping his feet on the bank, spitting out over the water, all sorts of hidden violence in the motion.

He coughed again, fumbled in his pocket for a handkerchief, pulled it out, and some coins fell to the floor. I stooped down to get them. I stood there looking at the new tenpenny coins.

'When did they change the coins?' I said.

'Oh, a year or so ago.'

'I see.' I looked at the harp. It was finely etched.

'It's nice to have ya back, Conor,' he said finally.

His lip quivered as he moved towards the fireplace with the poker, knelt down, prodded softly. A few large chunks fell out on to the cement slab and he mashed them down with his thumb, licked at it to soothe the burn, spat a few pieces of ash from the end of his tongue. He struggled to get up from his knees and I put my arm under his right shoulder.

'Right,' he said with a sudden whiparound. 'I'm not a bloody invalid, ya know.'

'I know.'

'So I can get up on my own.'

'Fair enough.'

'Without a lick of help.'

'Okay, okay.'

He placed his hand on the concrete and raised himself, using the mantelpiece as a fulcrum. One of Mam's pictures

– she is standing by a fencepost in Mexico – was still leaning against the mantel. He didn't look at it. Just stood up, wheezing, straightened himself in the air and yawned, made a helicopter of his arms as if to expand the universe of himself.

'Ya see?' he said. 'Fit as a bloody fiddle.'

He ambled his way into the kitchen and came out with a bottle of whiskey and two glasses, one of which chipped when his trembling hand cracked the bottle against the rim. Poured himself a big glass, handed me the bottle. 'Take it from the neck,' he said to me, 'all the other glasses are dirty.' I think it's the first time in my life that the old man has seen me drinking – although when I was younger and Mam was gone, he would tell me his stories, and afterwards I would steal pound notes from his pockets. I would go downtown to buy flagons of hard cider, then return along the riverbank to clear the names of the two Protestant ladies underneath their explosion of cerise wildflowers.

He was almost twenty-one when he stood in a Fascist camp and watched great white loaves of bread showering down on Madrid, the strangest rain the city had ever seen. The bread zipped through the winter air, over the clifftops of the Manzanares River, parachutes of it moving like snow, bombarding the city. It fell on the streets, a miracle of propaganda, beautifully arced from hidden airplanes by pilots who played at being a 1939 Jesus in the clouds.

Reports came back to the Fascist front that the bread had descended from such a height that windows had been broken in the Royal Palace. Craters had been made in the snow. Birds and starving men were in an uproar upon it. Slates had been knocked off the roofs of houses. Books, used as sandbags, had been shaken from windowsills. Little boys in the city had stopped collecting shrapnel and were being won over by the bread. A Communist had been squashed to death by a flying bale. A priest on the Fascist front was heartened by the news of this angelic death – if only they could shower Madrid with holy wine they could have a mass for all the godless dying. Bread, said the priest, was even better than bombs.

But within a few days the bombs started again. Fires raged in Madrid. The joke was that the Communists could make toast.

My father stood in the camp, a holy medal at his throat, and watched as the bread and bombs zipped in towards his friend Manley, who was in the city somewhere. He envisioned Manley tracing the pattern of the strange parcels with a Lewis gun held at his shoulder, blowing a bale of loaves to bits, crumbs of it floating down around him. Maybe Manley would hallucinate and think it was a flock of birds, with the trajectory of doves. Or maybe he would be given a loaf by a *novia* who loved him. Or maybe Manley was dead – it was the end of the war and there weren't many Communists left.

The siege of Madrid wore its way through winter, and my father watched it through the eye of a camera, knocking frost off the soles of his boots, flecks of snow melting into the uniform of Franco.

Manley had left Ireland long before my old man. The vulgar suits were left hanging in a cupboard and, drunk on Marx, he had sauntered away, leaving my father alone in the town. There was a narcosis to Manley's going, but it was two years before my father followed. He left on his twentieth birthday, no politics in the leaving, simply bored. He sold the house, paid the grave of the Protestant ladies a final visit, gave Loyola to a young boy in town. He pinned most of his inheritance into the rear waistband of his trousers. A few strange stares followed his going – the dickybird camera had become something of a fixture around the town, and perhaps people would miss it. He packed a rucksack and moved out, brutal with innocence. Two new Leica cameras strung across his breast. A huge skip in his stride. He didn't stop to get blessed by the priest who hailed the virtues of Francisco Franco and General O'Duffy.

The old man hitch-hiked and walked his way through storms along the seaboard towards Cork. A wiry unshaven man in a brown hat, wandering through fields, splashes of blood-red poppies like a premonition in the ground, his last look at Ireland for almost three decades.

The only ship going out was full of Irish Fascists in blue shirts. Songs were summoned up about good ways to die in vineyards. Beards grew thick as the waves knocked the boat around off the coast of France. They landed in a blue and delicate Spanish bay, where a melancholy guitar was drowned out by the shouts of the men. They punched the air and grabbed at their crotches as girls at windowsills blew them kisses. But the songs were muted when one of the soldiers was kissed by a teenager, a Communist sympathiser, who bit his tongue out and spat it in his face. The girl was shot to death, running away through a field of hay, a silence descending on the regiment as they stared. By the roadside a priest incanted prayers and doled out holy water to the soldiers. They moved on, the stub of a tongue flickering uselessly in one man's mouth. Suddenly there were olive trees, bloated bodies, lemon groves, *butifarra* sausage, stretchers, mangled faces. My father sent photos of severed limbs and discarded bullet shells to newspaper editors. They chucked most of them in the bin, but every now and then one was found tucked in the bottom corners of an English newspaper, beside the colourful reports of some daring young journalists. The photos were dark and brooding – a chaplain in a field, stepping over the dead, a woman picking shrapnel from her thigh as if bored by the enormity of her wound, an obese surgeon smoking over a

19

stretcher, the sucked-in bones of a village after an aerial bombardment.

The old man bribed ambulance drivers to let him take his shots, bellowed in cafés, slept in the open under stunted trees, made his way towards Madrid where Manley and other Republicans were being besieged. He had no politics, my father, he was only a photographer, shooting visions, but he placed the holy medal at his neck for safety. On one of the Leicas he pasted a portrait of Franco. He didn't care about the man – it was just a convenient blur to him, a safe passport, a foxhole. Nor did he care for Manley's hero, Stalin. He might have looked vaguely comic out there, riding along on the backs of vans, handkerchief tied on his head, four-knot style, under the hat, men with guns in a circle around him. His rucksack, with two Foxford blankets tied on the bottom, was his only link to home.

He wore a pair of big black boots that he had taken off the feet of a dead Welsh Republican. The body was found, fragrant with death, in a clump of bushes. There was a letter in the inside pocket of the man's uniform, telling his mother, back on the banks of the Teifi River, how much he missed her cooking. 'Mum, that stuff would . . .' and the letter finished there. The old man undid the laces, pulled the boots off – he needed new ones, his own had begun to flap. Some newspaper was stuffed into the toes, and he wrote a note to the family, saying that one day he'd return them. On the bottom of one sole was a carving of a sickle, so that every time his right foot landed it left an impression of the sickle in wet ground. He left sickles behind him for miles, until a soldier in the regiment, walking directly behind him, levelled a rifle and forced him to remove the boots – 'Communist boots make a Communist man.' He left them on the ground where the soldier riddled them with bullets. Bits of leather splayed around and the laces lay in some sort of mourning. Maybe there was a family on the banks of the

Teifi who waited for years for a large brown package to arrive, waited for some totem of a dead son, waited for a story of some heroic death, waited and waited, among mounds of food and mouldy leftovers.

The dead soldier's name was Wilfred Owen, an echo of the World War One poet. Years later my father's life might invoke a line of the poet's for me: 'Foreheads of men have bled where no wounds were.'

He bartered his way into another pair of shoes – rope-soled *alpargatas*, and as the weather got colder, snow in countryside drifts, he bought new boots. The holy medal still shone at his throat and, by the time he reached Madrid, he was well able to sing the praises of nationalism.

He waited outside the city among the gum trees and watched the bread being loaded onto airplanes to swell the nostrils of a pilot. Thousands of loaves. Some of the dough still rising. He stood in the camps as the planes flew off and wondered what it was that had brought him here, took shots of the nationalists as they waited for the planes to return, drilling their way through time and howitzers and dark-haired whores. There were as many pictures of prostitutes as there were of bread. The prostitutes held a peculiar fascination for him, girls who rolled their skirts up on the rubble of their thighs. It was fashionable to be a little plump, so the girls sometimes wore four or five skirts over one another to give breadth to their hips. The men around them were articulate with their penises, a natural extension from the barrel of a rifle to the absurd freckle sitting on any man's undershaft. One of the shots shows a line of men in a tent, Germans, Spaniards and Moroccans, impatient with sweat, waiting in queue for a thin pockmarked whore in baggy underwear, panties around one ankle. She is kneeling down in front of an equally thin soldier with her mouth at his crotch. At the back of the queue another soldier raises an air-punch in anticipation of the soldier's climax. His fly is already open and his scrotum leaks out like an underwater polyp.

In makeshift hospital tents there was as much syphilis as shrapnel. Years later, when I went through boxes in our attic, there were shots of women naked in lamplight, women parading in front of his camera, women with sheets pulled coyly around them, women with their heads tilted sideways and an eye in half a wink. I was a teenager when I discovered them. I'd sit, perched on a slat of wood in the attic, thumping away at my body, in the beginning of its own articulation. I became the camera, became the camera-man, and all the time hated my father for being privy to these visions. I walked into the photos, parted the canvas doors of the tents, stood, bemused at first, talked to the women. The women smiled at my curious appearance, beckoned me backwards to the 1930s, asked me sly questions. I hung in behind the camera as outside the planes droned in the clouds with their bounty. The women would move around in the photographs for me, come behind the camera, take me by the hand and lead me somewhere no lens could watch, let me touch them, open my shirt buttons with a flick of their fingers, let me wander, sleep beside them. Sometimes I swore that I could hear the bread falling outside.

When Madrid surrendered, the graveyards of Spain were full of men the world could not do without – other wars would need them.

Manley was found in the charnel of the city, minus one leg in a bombed-out house, babbling, a row of stale loaves around him. The doors and windowframes had been torn off and used for firewood. Manley was strewn out on a mattress that smelled of urine. Unshaven. Huge boils on his neck. He spat in my father's face when he saw the holy medal, but the old man wandered around the city that day and bought some forged papers for his friend. They were in the name of Gordon Peters. Manley became a man who crawled around on crutches and invented a new past for himself. He and a few other stray Republicans hid in the city with their new identities. My father still had his inheritance, pinned away in plastic at the back of his trousers. He and Manley made arrangements to leave the city together, but Manley disappeared one morning while out buying provisions. My father sat in the shell of the house and waited, days giving way to weeks, cameras gathering dust, the mattress beginning to fester. He searched for his friend, walked around in a stupefied ache, couldn't find him.

One afternoon he found Manley's crutch along the banks of the Manzanares – it had been carved with the initials G. P. – and he felt sure his friend was dead, although the body couldn't be found.

The photos that they had taken years before in Mayo, with Manley in his outrageous suits, became my father's most vibrant memory of his friend. When the old man talked of Manley he remembered him as a sixteen-year-old with a lustful glint in his eye, rather than a legless soldier who reeked of piss at night. It was something the old man often did – if a moment existed in a photograph, it was held in that particular stasis for ever. It was as if by taking a photo he could, at any moment, reinhabit an older life – one where a body didn't droop, or hair didn't fall out, or a future didn't have to exist. Time was held in the centre of his fist. He either crumpled it or let it fly off. It was as if he believed that something that *was* has the power to be what *is*. It was his own particular ordering of the universe, a pattern that moved from past to present, with the ease of a sheet dropped into a chemical bath. Manley was sixteen once and, because of that, Manley was sixteen forever.

Even today I suppose he might still believe that there's a loaf of bread in flight above Madrid, a single one, or a parachute-load of it, making its way gracefully through the air from the belly of a high-flying bomber, preparing itself to fall.

After the whiskey he fell asleep in the chair. He woke when I knocked over the kettle in the kitchen by mistake. Pulled the blanket from around himself, clacked his lips together, reached into his shirt pocket, took out a box of Major. After a few minutes he fell asleep again with a cigarette burning down in the ashtray. I stubbed it out, went upstairs and took a hot bath in the iron-coloured water. A bit of a waft from my clothes, though not as bad as him. He's fairly pungent. The smell was hanging all around the house. A deep unwashed odour, the disappearance of himself, the sort that smells like old campfire. When Mam was around all those years ago, she would wash our clothes in the sink – exiled in a farmhouse kitchen, watching the vagaries of Irish weather, black crows defiling low over a brown bog, telling stories of the colour that once used to exist in her life. She would lift me up and sit me on the sink, gaze out at the columns of crows, talk of other birds – vultures, grackles, red-winged hawks – in other places. She had a couple of sarapes and sometimes they would animate themselves on the washing line, fluttering out over the land, reds and yellows and greens. Mexico existed on the washing line for her, hung out to dry, the woollen ponchos full of life beside the ordinary clothes of our days, my father's vests, his trousers, his underwear, the banality of them held tight with wooden pegs.

These days, without Mam around, the old man has let the rings of dirt settle down around him – eleven years of it on his shirt collars.

In the bathroom, clumps of hair sat in the sinkhole, under the waterlines. A tiny sliver of soap in the dish. I got some shampoo out of my backpack, sank down into the bath. It was nice, that black silence outside the bathroom window, no mosquitoes or dune bugs battering against the air. Only a couple of harmless moths throwing themselves stupidly against the window. I lay in the bathtub until the water grew cold. At midnight I woke the old man to see if he wanted to go upstairs to his bed, but he grunted sleepily: 'I'm grand here, it's comfortable, I sleep here all the time.'

The edge of the chair made a red line on his face, which ran down to the sparse grey beard. His beard may have its own entropy, so that instead of growing outwards it is shrinking inwards to his skin. It looked like a stubble of only one or two weeks, but it has probably been there for months. Two large patches on his cheeks, where the hair doesn't grow anymore, adding symmetry to his bald pate. I watched him as he woke. He rubbed the red line away from his cheek, coughed, reached for the stubbed butt in the ashtray, smelled it, flicked it towards the fireplace, lit a new one. 'They taste bloody awful when they've been stubbed out,' he said. He held the new smoke between his teeth, looked around the room. 'Jesus, it's chilly enough though, isn't it?'

I went to the cupboard underneath the stairs to get the blue beach blanket. It smelled a little musty. Waited for him to finish smoking, handed it to him. He pulled it around himself, tucked it up to his chin, gave me a wink. He brushed my hand away, though, when I offered him a cushion to put behind his head.

'Conor,' he said, 'I thought you were dead, for crissake.'

He's the same crotchety old bastard that he was when I left five years ago. Bit stupid for me to come home and think that it might be any different, I suppose. But a week is a week and we can probably tolerate each other that long – besides, I'll have to make arrangements to get up to Dublin for a few days, get everything sorted out for my visa. But I wonder what he'd say if I told him that these days I'm living in a cabin in Wyoming, working jobs that hardly pay the rent, just drifting along. Probably wouldn't give a damn, though, wouldn't faze him one bit. Living his days now with those slow castings.

I sat up in the bedroom tonight and looked out the window to the bible-dark of the Mayo night, the stars rioting away. In a strange way it's nice to be back – it's always nice to be back anywhere, anywhere at all, safe in the knowledge that you're getting away again. The law of the river, like he used to say. Bound to move things on. When I left home I promised myself I'd never return – at the train station he shoved a ten-pound note in my hand and I threw it right back at him as the train pulled away. But enough of this. Enough whining. I am home now, and a million possibilities may still lie outside my window, curlews resurrected to the night if I want them to be.

# WEDNESDAY

## *grand morning for the dogs*

Cooked breakfast for him this morning, but he didn't want any. He said that 'sunnyside up' is an American notion and that I've developed a bit of an accent to go along with my cooking.

He just sat with that lazy inertia in his eyes and peddled the eggs around on the plate with his fork, leaving a trail of grease. Every now and then he touched the fork against his teeth. His lips moved as if chewing something, the lower one reaching out over the top. They made a dry sort of smacking sound, settled down to nothing again. He steered his finger through the grease and wiped it on the sleeve of his blue workshirt, stared at me for no particular reason. Told me that half the town have their green cards or their English dole numbers by now. Nothing but old men left. All the sons and daughters coming home for Christmas, elongating their words and dropping haitches all over the place. He said he was surprised there wasn't a row of haitches and 'gee-whizzes' between here and Shannon Airport.

We were silent for a long time until two stray dogs came barking through the outside yard. A black and white collie and a golden labrador with a red collar. They wheeled around down by the barn, chasing each other in tight circles, tails wagging. The old man rose up and shuffled over to the window, clacked his lips again, leaned against the frame, rolled the curtain between his thumb and forefinger, watched them. The collie cornered the labrador over by where the darkroom used to be – a burnt-out shell now – and danced ritually around her for a while, climbed up.

The old man chuckled, rubbed his hands along the curtains, and turned away from the window while they continued their bout.

'Grand morning for the dogs anyway,' he said.

We laughed, but his was a strange laugh that didn't last very long. He sort of threw the chuckle out into the air and immediately swallowed it back down his saggy throat. He ambled into the pantry and got all his equipment together while the yelping rose up from outside, chopping through the dawn. Asked him did he want some company for the day but he shook his head, no. He said it's much better fishing when things are quiet, it doesn't disturb the big fish, they have acute hearing, they can sense a person for miles, it all has to do with wave vibrations and the motion of sound, salmon are particularly sensitive. I knew he was bullshitting, but I decided to leave him be. Down he went to the river, shouting at the dogs to clear off as he walked.

He gave a slow push to the green gate with his foot, climbed over the stile with difficulty. He has worn a path through the fuchsia bushes to the bank. The path was muddy in the middle from last night's drizzle, and he had to straddle it at first, one foot at either side of the puddle. Then he just gave up and slopped his way drowsily through the muck, wiped his boots on the long grass. He set up his equipment and started casting away, settled himself down into the grey caisson of his loneliness. The dogs went off down the lane, stopping for another yelp of lust down by the bend, where the big potholes are.

The old man hung around Madrid in confusion until, in the summer of 1939, a soldier from Mexico – a Communist with only two fingers left on his right hand – beckoned him to another continent. Other wars had erupted all over Europe and the soldier said he knew of a place in the Chihuahuan desert where a man could get away from it all, sit and get drunk and lay a hat over his face and dream and run a full set of fingers over a bottle or a guitar or a horse or a beautiful woman.

My father wasn't interested in horses or guitars, but the soldier carried a picture of his sister on the inside of his uniform. He held it delicately between his two fingers like a cherished cigarette, a photo of a young woman, no more than seventeen years old, in a billowy white linen skirt, flour on her hands. The photo was a good and sufficient reason for my father to latch on an impulse and go. And there'd been enough dying. He wanted to forget about Manley. Leave Europe to its bags of butchery and bones, to its internecine slaughter. He filled his rucksack with film, swapped his cameras for another Leica, a newer model, and offered the soldier a large amount of money for the shot of his sister. The photo had already grown yellow around the edges, but the soldier wouldn't part with it. Instead, my father took a picture of the Mexican holding the picture. They were in a market area on the southern Spanish coast, vegetables arrayed about them, the soldier standing, small and wiry, with a wrinkled face that was not unlike an old vegetable patch itself. When he smiled, he showed very bad gums and the darkest of teeth.

The Mexican and my father took a ship that was

returning to the green neck of the world with a cargo of rotten bananas. The shipment had been refused at the Spanish port, owing to a vendetta. The captain dumped the bananas not far out to sea – my father said that they fell like absurd black fish into the clear water. On deck, he and the soldier played poker and dreamed bilious dreams, fought with other passengers, threw cigarette butts into the wake behind them, watched them fizzle out in the air, charged the sailors for portraits taken down in the engine room, making a little bit of money together. The Mexican walked around on deck, staring at the photo of his sister, promising my father great things: a house on the edge of the Rio Grande, a grove of tamarisk trees, twelve very healthy chickens, a motorbike that wouldn't sputter.

He lost the soldier in a dockside crowd in Veracruz when the boat pulled into the Gulf of Mexico.

A Friday afternoon, the day of some festival, and people shoved gigantic bottles into my father's hands as he roared out for his friend over the heads of the crowd. Fish were being cooked over fires, women in shawls guided donkeys, a fashionable car beeped its way through the market, where parrots and snakes were on sale. Fights and songs were full of mescal. He searched for two days but there was no sign of the soldier. So he walked through the town and out along the coastline paths. Walking was holy – it cleared the mind. He wandered northwards, through small towns full of fishing boats and people bent over nets. They took him into their homes, bedded him down for the night, fed him frijole beans, woke him with coffee, ground corn on *metate* stones for the going. At other times men spat at his feet – to some of them he was nothing more than a gringo fool, a *fuereño* in a derisory hat. But I can imagine him sauntering through the sun-yellow streets, wiry and broad-stepped, stains on the underside of his shirt, his money still pinned into his waistband, the brim of the hat casting a multitude of shadows on his face, thin red streaks of tiredness in the whites of his eyes, chatting to women in his broken Spanish, gesturing to men, drinking, cavorting, constantly struck by the rivers of moments that were carrying him along, slamming him from one bank to the other, ferrying his way ferociously to no particular place.

He took photos as he moved his way up and down the country, along the eastern coast – a prostitute in a blond wig, leaning out of a window; a boy playing soccer alone in a laneway; a man on a boat dumping a dead child, covered in lime, into the sea; men in cotton trousers; boys in the rain flinging stones up at birds; political slogans on the walls; a pig slaughtered at the rear of a church; a woman in an adelita dress moving very precisely under a parasol. Colour seemed to exist in his black and white shots, as if it had somehow seeped itself into the shade and the shadows of his work, so that years later – when I sat in the attic – I could almost tell that the parasol was yellow, it had that feel about it to me. His photos spoke to me that way. Many other things were yellow in my ideas of Mexico at the time – the leaves of plants, the leftovers of malaria, the sun pouring down jonquil over the land.

He spent a couple of seasons with fishermen close to Tampico, living in a palm-fronted hut down near the water. One of the men, Gabriel, inhabited his photographs. On the far side of his sixties, with a patch of hair on the front of his forehead, Gabriel tucked bait in his mouth to keep it warm. Worms, or sometimes even maggots, were held between his gum and lip, causing the lower lip to bulge out. It was as if he carried an extra tongue with him, jutting out over a cleft in his chin. Even when he was fishing with nets or lobster pots Gabriel kept the bait in his mouth. It was a trick he had learned as a child – warm bait, he claimed, made for a better catch. He would lean over the side of his boat and let some foul-looking spit volley out over the water.

31

He taught my father about nets and reels, hooks and flies, carried a note in his pocket that read, in Spanish: 'If you want to be happy for an hour, get drunk; if you want to be happy for a day, kill a pig; if you want to be happy for a week, get married; if you want to be happy for a lifetime, go fishing.'

Gabriel had developed an aversion to land. His legs wobbled when he walked on dry soil, so he stayed in his boat most of the time, feet propped over the edge of the deck, taking his worms from an old tobacco can, shoving them down in the pouch of his mouth. He visited his wife in town occasionally, preferring to sleep with her in a hammock because of its rocking motion. Gabriel and his wife had eight children together. Gabriel had called his youngest son 'Jesus' with the idea that he would one day walk on water. But Jesus had walked elsewhere, along with other sons and daughters, leaving Gabriel with nobody to take to sea – his wife got seasick in the bath.

Every Sunday, Gabriel brought my father out on the boat instead of going to mass. While church bells rang, my father left his hut and went down to the dock and out to sea. The old Mexican would kneel in between two small shrines he had erected on either side of the rowlocks. Wooden saints were nailed into the boards. They hovered above the blue, pellucid sea. Gabriel said prayers while the boat bobbed out on the ocean, maintaining that on Sundays his shrimp nets were fuller than ever. My father saw him every day, but there weren't as many photos of Gabriel as he would have liked – film was becoming scarce. Gabriel was almost like a father to him. They filled a void in one another. Gabriel wanted to teach my father ballads, but he soon found out that he had a voice not unlike the ravens that came down to feed on discarded fish heads. So the old Mexican insisted that he just listen, not sing. Raucous tunes rolled from Gabriel, songs that he made up as he went along, eyes cast to the sea. He sang of other days when he was able to dive to great depths and take up precious things from the ocean floor, of traditions, of curious motions that arose from waves. The two of them rowed together through bays and inlets, season piling into season, my father's face reddening at first, then darkening in the reflected sun- light, his accent improving as he learned Spanish from Gabriel, who rolled his vowels around the parasites in his mouth.

Gabriel's wife came down to dockside with plates of food, the plates covered with an old cloth to keep them warm. She brought only enough for her husband to eat and seldom even gave a nod to the gringo with the cameras. Sometimes she hung around to listen to the mournful sound of her husband's four-stringed guitar.

My father knew then that it was time to head on but before he did, a strange thing happened. A group of landcrabs made their way up from the shore to invade the shacks of the seafront. They scuttled in unison, a barrage of them, almost in formation, clambering over stones, a wash of movable eyes. Gabriel was on land at the time, the bait between his gum and lip. The sea had threatened storms, and he was out mending nets on a pier and securing his boat when the invasion happened. He ran home, towards his wife, but found himself surrounded by the creatures. In the photograph Gabriel is perched on a fencepost, much like a bird, scared, looking down, staring at the crabs as they go past, his lip jutting out, letting gobs of maggoty brown spit down upon them. His shabby jacket hangs around him. An old black glazed sombrero with a large brim and steeple crown sits precariously on his head. A perplexed look on his face. The crabs look bizarre and out of place, a bit like my old man, moving crabways through people's lives, bound to incongruity.

When he got back to his hut, my father found that the

place had been ransacked. He suspected Gabriel's wife, but couldn't prove a thing. The rucksack, a few clothes, and the Foxford blankets were all missing. He felt it lucky that he always kept his cameras and money with him – but there was a portent in the robbery. Gabriel walked out of town with him, and a few miles beyond – a big sacrifice for a man with an epileptic tenor in his legs – offering my father the shell of a landcrab as a memento. The crab had slithered up and died on Gabriel's porch. My father hung the shell from his new rucksack and continued north, along the seaboard, towns thinning out, the Sierra Madres looming.

At night the old man slept with his equipment in much the same way that he might have slept with a woman, coveting his cameras, everything curled in around him, the film in a special bag, even the tripod ensconced at his feet, a little piece of string tied around it and hooked to a big toe. He still had enough money left to go where he wanted, but he kept it tucked in his waistband in case of emergency. He moved inland, took a job painting fences for a rich rancher in the grasslands, sleeping in a horse barn with ten vaqueros. The other men played poker at night. Eight long months, keeping to himself, sulking around the corral, making enough to move along once more. Working on the fences, hammering a tamping bar into the ground, he often thought of the Mexican soldier's sister. The photo had burned itself like magnesium into his mind. Every now and then he woke up and saw two dreamlike fingers beckoning him. He would go and find the girl. He wandered all the way north, towards the Texas border, hitching occasional lifts across the mountains from small grey trucks. Sometimes men told him about a massive war that had erupted on the other side of the world, rumours of skinny women walking barefoot into gas chambers, rows and rows of them pale as Easter lilies, small mines bobbing on the Pacific, an eruption of barbed wire in a halo around Europe

– but all of that was an eternity away, he couldn't fathom how men could continue their lust for dying after the agonies of Spain. He was treading the middle line between drifter and coward, I suppose. He could have gone to Europe to photograph or fight, but instead he continued his peregrinations, heading westward, away from the smell of the sea, wind in the vast emptiness, all the way through the mountains, across Coahuila, to the eastern side of the Chihuahuan desert.

He improvised a white shirt hung on a branch to keep the heat from beating down on him, looking as if he were surrendering to the land, white sleeves fluttering amid lecheguilla plants and sagebrush and miles of mesquite, kicking his way along endless arroyos, saluting the footprints of grasshopper rats and desert foxes. Nobody lived in that vast red country. Sunsets fell through the western sky, the colour of blood through a fistful of water. Grass grew through the skulls of dead animals, rattlesnakes lay coiled under rocks. He taught himself survival on those long walks – learned to listen for the rumble in the mountains that suggested a flash flood, figured out how to set a trap for a small animal for dinner, caught lizards between his fingers, built teepee fires with dead mesquite. In the morning he rose early and sucked on pebbles to extract whatever dew or moisture had come down the night before. Sometimes he could whisk the dew off blades of long desert grass with his fingers. If things got bad he sliced open a cactus with his knife and tried to suck out its residual moisture. During the hottest time of the day he rested and made water for himself. He would dig a small hole in the ground, piss into it, place a can in the hole and cover it with a piece of plastic. He weighted the plastic in the middle with a small stone, and left it for the sun to evaporate the moisture, which would gather, then drop down, slowly, drip by drip, into the can.

35

He was intoxicated by it all, this drinking of himself, this wandering, the beard that began to crawl on his cheeks. At night in the desert it got viciously cold, and he hid himself behind rocks or in natural shelters, lit small fires, sometimes walked a little in the night, watching Polaris, the polestar, and flapping his arms to stave off the cold. He spent a week near a streambed, straining water through his handkerchief, watching the rhythms of the country around him, rimrock, valleys, fossils. Once a wolf padded across his path, stopped and stared at him, cocked its head and trotted away.

In the high desert country he eventually found himself in a town three days walk from the border. Low houses were caressed by big swells of dust that billowed through narrow twisting streets. Cottonwoods and tamarisks ranged along the riverfront, a feeder off the Rio Grande. Up from the trees the town gathered along dry brown roads, into a plaza, then out again. A couple of large houses lined the outer streets, but the rest were mostly adobe shacks, interrupted by a Catholic church, shops, a couple of bars, and a town hall. At the edge of the town barefoot kids threw pebbles around him, in a large circle. He ended up resting against a low fence, smoking a cigarette, hat down over his eyes, the sun sluicing its way through the sky, when he saw a young girl gandering around at the back of an old house, followed by a bouquet of older boys. She looked nothing like the soldier's sister. Her hair was cropped short and a small scar lay under her eye from a fight. She had bruises and cuts on her legs, a linen skirt that was hitched up high above her knees, a length of horse halter used as a belt, tied with an expert sailor's knot.

She pursed her lips provocatively for his camera, her blouse open flirtatiously, her head thrown sideways like a film actress. Her mother screamed at him from the porch of her house, where she stood in the shadows, skinning a rabbit.

'Don't you ever set your eyes on my daughter again, understand?' she said in Spanish.

The knife went skillfully from the neck of the rabbit all the way down to the crotch, and she hung the carcass upside-down on a clothesline. He nodded, stuck his hat on his head and walked on, having a shave in a silty irrigation ditch. Next morning, he beckoned the girl as she came outside. She moved for his camera and put her arms behind her head, unashamed by the beginnings of armpit hair.

My father pitched camp near the irrigation ditch. Later that week the young girl invented some fabulous lie about how my father was related to John Riley, an Irishman who had commanded the San Patricio Battalion in the Mexican War. My father was hailed as an incarnate revolutionary, though he had never heard of Riley before. He put a red necktie over a white t-shirt to go to the house. The girl's mother wore a fresh apron and greeted him at the door, wiping flour off her hands, covering her chest with a forearm, waving him in with a sweep of the other hand. My old man was allowed to sit near the head of the table, a newly embroidered serviette folded at his place setting. Laughter rang out around the small adobe house when a cooked rabbit was laid in the centre of the table and the mother stuck a knife into its belly, where it vibrated for a moment. Fresh maize tortillas were laid out in front of him, with large amounts of beans. Drink was slurped from the necks of dark earthenware jars. Songs were swapped and more lies told. My father assured the mother, in his broken Spanish, that Riley had been born in his own household in Ireland, generations ago, the birth enabled by some enigmatic great-grandmother who plucked magic potions from flowers, the birth made fluid by pulp from dandelions.

He was allowed to stay in a small shed near the house,

watching the stars through a hole the shape of an upside-down apple in the roof. He always remembered that the light from the rising moon first appeared in the bottom stem, then gradually filled the rest out, as if the hole were being peeled as it gathered light. He had a single wooden desk and a mattress stuffed with rabbit skins. But he still went walking in the desert. One week he wandered north and across the river to Texas to search for film – a long journey to Fort Stockton, walking again, hitching lifts. When he got back, the young girl stood flagrantly in front of his camera, thick red lips, jutting cheekbones, small snub of a nose, an array of colourful clothes drawn around her.

She wasn't performing for the camera – she was performing for him. She never asked to see the prints. There wasn't an ounce of vanity in her poses.

Early in the morning she would stand outside her house and hug herself into the weather, the peculiar patterns of clouds that scurried over the Mexican sky, winds that blew from a million different directions, carrying strange scents, sounds, squalls of rain, bits of dust. The wind had peculiarities that she made her own. When she was eleven years old she had given the wind different colours. A red wind carried desert dust, a brown one came riverwise, a grey one brought the scent of mesquite, a curious green one came one summer carrying swarms of locusts. Her favourite at the time was a black wind – a wind that did nothing at all, that didn't exist, when the town turned black and torpid with its static heat. She always thought the wind would gather in a man for her – maybe that was why she fell in love with my father, I don't know. She called him 'mi cielo,' my sky, and a lazy black wind blew through.

Perhaps she visited my father's shack late at night, the weather temporarily forgotten, her blouse fully opened, her head cocked back under candlelight, the scar under her

38

eye muted, the hole peeling with moonlight, I don't know, I have never found out, but they were married a year later. She was eighteen, he was twenty-seven. It was the year that the war ended, puff-faced leaders leaning over a table to sign an uneasy peace, a plane drifting off from the western edge of Japan in the shadow of a mushroom cloud – but they had little idea what was happening in the world and were slightly aghast when they found out, months later, that their wedding was held on the exact same day that Buddhist monks were burning alive in orange robes and rope sandals in a city called Nagasaki.

On the morning of the wedding, two dozen rabbits were strung out on the washing line, like a row of very dark red lungs, penned up with giant clothes pegs, ready to be eaten at the feast. The photograph at the church shows them smiling. His hair is slicked back but a cowlick negotiates his eyebrows. Her feet point in opposite directions from under the hem of her white linen gown, crocheted flowers at the edges, her hair threaded and ribboned where it had begun to grow out, the dress tight to the forearm and puffy at the shoulders, her hands in fingerless lace gloves, resting on her hips as if she were already waiting for something wondrous to happen, another strange wind to blow in. A crowd of men hang around them uneasy in suits, jackets shiny at the elbows, one woman reaching up to the side of her husband's face, maybe taking shaving soap from his ear, maybe brushing back a hair. They moved in a long procession from the church down to the house, my mother and father in front, an accordion ringing out, a trumpet, a guitar, children picking up coins that were flung behind the cavalcade, a particular burro leaving a healthy trail of manure along the way, small girls beside them, swinging the hems of their dresses, someone belting out a song from a window. A red breeze blew for my mother on her wedding day, tiny amounts of desert dust stinging her bare ankles. And they claimed that they heard a coyote singing in the distance, a magnificent howl that broke its way through the air. Endless dancing and fighting and loving and drinking were surely done that night, people in sweaty white open-necked shirts, kicking against the dry soil and brown skin of a land that, years later, swamped its heat over me.

He came back from the river for lunch and didn't eat a single thing, again. Told him that he's just going to fade away.

'Jaysus, now there's an idea,' he said.

He walked out to the grey-stone firepit to burn the rubbish, carrying one Spar bag, full to the brim with bread crusts and tea bags and hardly anything else. He says it's two weeks' worth of rubbish. He has this curious bend to him as he walks, looks hugely lopsided. The wind was raving and he had his collar pulled up around his neck. I went outside to help him, but he was already at the pit, dumping the bags out, the crusts falling, thick brown shafts into the ash. I came up behind him.

'Can I give ya a hand?'

He turned to me: 'What are ya doing out without a coat on, for fucksake? You'll catch your bloody death.'

I reached down to pick up the red petrol can at the side of the firepit and unscrewed the top, but he took it from me. 'Right now, I can do it on my own.' He sprinkled petrol over the rubbish, took out an old army Zippo from his pocket, hunkered down, lit the top of a long piece of straw, held it out. The fire whooshed up momentarily, a sucking updraft, died down.

'Go on so, I'm grand,' he said, looking down at the flames as if he might stand there for days, incalculably patient.

No point in pissing him off, so I ambled back to the

house, put the kettle on, and watched from the living room, where he had another fire lit. His photos of Mam in Mexico are still around, although they look tired now, a binge of them around the room. The painting job that we once did has faded.

I dragged a chair to the window, propped my elbows on the big high armrests, watching him in the farmyard. When he was done with the burning he turned to come back from the pit, and still the whole of his body was leaning over, walking at an angle, paying some sort of homage to the ground. He shuffled back along the little muddy trail, stopped and scratched at his head, then moved his fingers curiously along his right cheek as if trying to ruddy it, walked over to the wheelbarrow. For a moment he took hold of the handles and lifted it. He shoved the wheel-barrow forward a couple of feet as if it were an empty flying seat at some carnival, but it ground itself down into a hole in the middle of the yard, let out a few sparks, stopped. Scrunched up his lips and let out a glob of spit from the side of his mouth. Took his glasses off, had a look at his watch, wound it, glanced back at the house. I gave him a wave but he didn't respond, even with the glasses back on. Perhaps the light was glinting on the window, but I was sure he couldn't see me – most likely his eyes are on their way, too. Bodies fall like rain at that age – drops collide into one another.

His mouth was drawn downwards across the falling. He looks closer to his nineties than he does to his seventies.

He stopped for a moment and lit up – it's not me who'll catch my death at all. In the living room, even with the waft of peat, it smelled musty and dank, the tobacco having sunk into the wood. I took all the ashtrays out to the bin and dumped them, cleaned them with a rag. Got them shiny and black. Maybe this way he'll see how much he smokes – used to be he only took a few drags from each one, put it out, but now they're all smoked down to the quick, dark around the filters. They'll whisk him away before he knows it, sucked up on the ember updraft of himself. I've heard it's more difficult than going cold turkey. Not long after leaving Ireland, I met an Algerian in one of the cheap hotels on Bedford Street in London. He was trying to kick cocaine. He had set up a dartboard in his next-door room to occupy himself. But one afternoon he sold the dartboard for a line of coke that he did in the public toilets in Victoria Station. Even paid his tenpence to get in and snort it. Afterwards he had nothing left and he locked himself away in the room, where I could hear him scratching at the walls, shouting for another line of coke and a cigarette.

Those days of mine in London were long and grey. Eighteen years old, having just left home. In a train station, in black drainpipe trousers and a shirt of tentative blue, I pondered my dual heritage, the Irish in me, the Mexican. An explosion of blood made the shape of a flower around my nose, where I had failed to make a place for a small silver stud. I had wanted to announce my manhood with a nose-ring. An old landlady brought me to a bathroom to put Dettol on the side of my face where the blood had strayed, saying: 'You hacked your bloody face, son, what in the world are ya doing?' And me thinking it could have been my own mother tentatively dabbing a cotton ball against my nose. I moved through London as if wounded, working on building sites where they changed my name to Paddy. A plethora of paddies in knitted hats and construction belts moving their way around scaffolding. I checked in and out of small rooms all over the city. Walked around with a skin of doubt – dark, but with a field of freckles across the cheekbones. A childish voice inside me asking: 'Who the hell are you anyway?' In bookshops on Charing Cross Road I looked at guidebooks to Mexico, wondering if my mother might step out from the pages and appear to me, maybe a sarape around her, maybe standing under a clothesline, fluttering her thinness out towards the Chihuahuan desert. In those bookshops – with the smell of words, the promise of existing in another place, the feet moving by me as I sat lotus-legged on the floor, the clerks staring me down from the register – I decided that I would make my trip to my mother's country, find her, make her exist for me again.

And now I wonder what the old man remembers about her these days. Maybe nothing. Maybe silence has cured him of memory. Maybe there's an absolute vacuum in the anathema of age.

The kettle gave out a high whistle from the kitchen. When I went outside to tell him that the tea was ready he had his back to me – 'tea's growing cold!' – but he didn't hear me at all, his shadow sliding away from the wheelbarrow, lengthening across the yard, folding against the aluminum siding of the barn. He looked fairly content as he shuffled over to the side door and bent down, started feeding something to the cat. The cat was running around and around his feet like something possessed. He reached out every now and then and grabbed it by the tail, lit himself a cigarette which chugged away from his mouth. A drizzle came down upon him from some rat-grey clouds.

I went up behind him and touched him on the shoulder and he whipped around, startled. It was as if he had forgotten I was there. The cigarette dropped from his mouth.

'Tea's ready,' I said.

'Ya put me heart in me mouth.'

'I looked for some biscuits but I couldn't find any.'

'Haven't had a biscuit in a while.'

'I'll go shopping tomorrow.'

'Fair enough,' he said. 'Sounds like a bargain to me.'

He bent down to try to pick the cigarette up from the

ground but his fingers couldn't quite get it. I reached for it, but his boot crunched it first, ploughed it into the ground.

'I need some smokes too, Conor.'

'No you don't.'

'Come off it, now. Don't be doing that to me.'

'What?'

'I love the odd smoke,' he said.

We were quiet for a while, then he rubbed his hands together: 'You're getting like Mrs McCarthy for crissake.'

I reached my hands down into my pockets, felt the breeze lisp its way into me: 'Well, come on so, the tea'll be fit to dance on.'

'Just a minute,' he said, catching the cat's tail. 'This little bastard's hungrier than any I've seen before.'

The town was thin. Dogs and cats were bony. Burros exposed brown racks of ribs as they nudged in along ancient paths. On dusty streets clothes were hung from windows, taking siestas in the sun – the clothes were sparse and worn, bits at the elbows rubbed away, knees vanished or threadbare. Even the vultures that rode the thermals above were lean. They made spirals in the air, their wings beating sparsely against the heat, looking down on the gauntness beneath them, comic black kites with red-raw beaks. Boys aimed up at the vultures with slingshots, tried to keep them in the air, exhaust them. But they flew on, generation giving way to generation, leanness to leanness.

A priest, a mestizo with a face like a poppyseed roll, came once a week, late on Sundays, to celebrate mass. He moved his way through the town on a bicycle, from one church to the other, all sorts of confessions ringing in his ears. Hungover men in shirtsleeves pulled back as the bicycle moved along. Music spilling out from old jukeboxes in the bars died down in reverence. My father took a photo of the priest once, his black cassock raised high in the air as he

44

negotiated an open sewer behind one of the bars, exposing some very dark legs and thin ankles, moving delicately over the river of urine, lips pursed, nose scrunched. Something about the clergy always moved him to expose the pathetic. He delighted in the shot of altar boys getting drunk on mass wine, hair upshooting on their heads, red dribbles down the front of their vestments. But he got in a fierce amount of trouble one morning, just after dawn, when he snapped my grandmother as she prepared to go to church. She was wearing only her undergarments, a corset that could have come from another century, lace zigzagging across it, breasts stuffed into it like a sausage roll, a patina of age upon it. She was stealing out on to the porch to get her Sunday dress, which was drying in the sun. 'Pig!' she shouted at him, 'Go back to your pigpen!' She was a tiny woman, four feet tall, with a voice that could raise generations of the dead. It boomed from deep inside her bosom-burdened body. 'Go back and eat slop!' She threw a bottle at him, narrowly missing his camera. Later, as she moved her way down the road to mass, he tried to apologise, pulling off his hat as he ran beside her, but she spat on the ground in front of him and tilted her own hat on her head. 'Pig!'

Four weeks later she agreed to talk to him again – but only after he swore that he would go to mass for the rest of his life, every Sunday, without a shadow of a doubt. She lived a life sustained by faith and rosary beads. My mother stood in the corner of the kitchen and giggled when she heard the promise. She was nineteen years old at the time and still given to giggles. She called him '*Obispo* Michael' – Bishop Michael – after that and gave him a scapular to remind him of his words. He wore it irreverently, walking around with his shirt off in the house, the scapular moving back and forth over turrets of dark chest hair. But he was forced to go to mass every Sunday, up along the street, past the poolhall, and over the small aqueduct that conveyed water from the river. He couldn't slouch at the back of the church, he was dragged to the front pew with my grandmother, who was so delighted by the outcome that she gave him her favourite set of rosary beads, a black pair that he was embarrassed by when he fished in pockets to look for change. They were made of obsidian and caught the light in a peculiar way.

My grandmother lived with them in the adobe house on the outskirts of town. Her own husband had died ten years before, left dumped in an old oil barrel, his throat cut after a vicious fight. She took up his pastime of skinning rabbits – using the knife as if avenging the death. Every time a baby was born in town she presented the parents with a rabbit's foot preserved in a jar. The charm was supposed to be especially good in staving off cholera. Only one boy hadn't been given a rabbit's foot – his father was suspected of the murder, though nothing could be proved – and my grandmother was looked upon with a mixture of awe and suspicion when the boy died of diarrhoea and muscle cramps in the middle of his second summer. After that, when a woman in town got pregnant, they hurried over to see her, bearing gifts and making oblique references to good-luck charms.

When no rabbits were available for butchering, my grandmother sat on the front porch and simply swiped a knife through the air, back and forth, endlessly, her body swaying with her. The buzzards moved above in their scavenging circles.

One morning, when she was out walking, she flung a stone at a passing cottontail, near a mesquite tree, caught it in the head, stunned it temporarily, hobbled over on a walking stick to finish it off, but tripped in a pothole and broke her leg. 'I wish I'd gotten that creature,' she told the doctor, 'I'd have died happy then.' What disturbed her the most was that the cottontail had been left to the black birds, the carcass swooped down upon quickly – there wasn't even a skin to be found. The doctor laid her up in bed for months but others brought her rabbits to skin. Propped up by pillows, she laid old grain sacks around her to contain the blood and hides. The Virgin of Guadalupe stared from the bedside table. When my grandmother was finished she laid her head back on the pillow and muttered a melody of strange prayers to the small white statue. She insisted on wearing a big straw hat, even in bed.

My grandmother tried to get Mam to learn how to skin rabbits, learn the skill, preserve the tradition, but my mother wasn't interested.

Geraniums grew up from old paint pots that were hung from the porch of the house. A cow skull, decorated merrily with colours, was hung near the front door in front of the rusty fly screen. On top of the roof was a weather-vane that never moved anymore, simply pointed east, even in the strongest of winds. My father climbed on the roof and tried to get it to move – Mam had asked him to fix it so she could watch the direction of her winds – but it wouldn't budge. During the wedding a drunk had climbed up on the roof and played the guitar for them, but he fell and landed sideways on the vertical spindle, cutting himself and leaving a nasty scar on his ribcage. His wife said that the cut never healed, that he still felt the breeze roll through the wound and that my father – by virtue of being a gringo – should pay him some compensation. Seeing the man outside the town bar, my mother pointed to his ribcage: 'Which way's the wind blowing today, Benito?' The man reared up his leg and let out a giant fart, to the delight of some men squatting on the ground. 'I think it's heading south,' she simply said, as she turned and walked away. That night she left a plate of beans outside the man's house – it was fair compensation, she said, and the only compensation he would get.

When she walked around the town the local boys still flung big glances at her. Maybe they thought that the man in the big brown hat was some sort of wicked apparition, that one morning they'd all wake up and he'd be gone as easily and as mysteriously as he had come.

But they saw her settling into her new life, bit by bit. Her hair grew out. She began growing vegetables near the porch – tying herself to the soil. It was rough and bitter work, kneeling down in patterned dresses, mangy dogs scrabbling around the fence, dirt so hard that it ripped out the underneath of her fingernails. She gave the job a tolerable accent with a little tequila, sipped from large bottles as she worked on her hands and knees. When dust was kicked up in her face she spat it out on the ground. Still, she was raven-haired and beautiful. Men still found profligacy rising up in their groins. They sat on porches opposite the house, waiting for her to stand up from her work so the sunlight could filter through the thin dress, give an outline of a round breast, a long leg, a back arched with her hands on the lower buttocks to loosen and stretch herself. Somebody took to dropping off chocolate on the doorstep late at night, wrapped in big cubes of ice to keep it from melting. Dishes of *pollo en mole* and flowers appeared with oblique handwritten notes. She ate the chocolate and the chicken dish and shoved the flowers in vases, didn't search the admirer out, she wasn't bothered, she was happy. Secretly she wondered if it was my father who was leaving the presents on the doorstep.

Another sign to the local men that she was no longer available came when she bought the chickens. They arrived one day in wooden crates, eight hens and a rooster. A chicken pen was put together from scrap wood. She named the chickens after people in town. The mayor was the fattest, with a huge fleshy chin wattle. It laid very few eggs. Many of the birds were named after men who went across

48

the border to work on vast oil derricks and ranches in Texas, coming home with fistfuls of money. The part-time barber was a strange chicken, without a head comb, bald as could be. And the barber's wife was a wild one who flew up in the air at the slightest of sounds.

There was also an odd rooster that never crowed in the morning. She called him José after a local character whose lips had been sewn together when he lost a bet in a bar. Even after the stitches were taken out José never said a word. He walked around silently with his ebony hair slicked back with cooking grease, his mouth in a sneer, the bottom lip peppered with scarholes. When he passed my parents' house José stared at his namesake rooster with a great brown bitterness. One morning they found the bird strangled on the front doorstep with a note in Spanish that read: 'Now we speak.'

My mother grew to adore the chickens in the same way that my grandmother adored rabbits. Two groups of them – one raised for eggs, the others for sale – and every now and then some were butchered and cooked. My grandmother did the butchering, deftly pressing her fingers on the point of a neck, cracking it. Mam watched the weather and tied the best times for egg-laying in with its vicissitudes. The colours of the wind had a lot to do with it. Her lazy black wind was a fitful time. The brown one, riverwise, carried nothing but problems, the river coming from somewhere foreign and unfathomable.

My grandmother laughed at her daughter's curious superstition, wondered why she didn't attribute the brown wind to Benito and his beans. 'Are you my daughter at all?' They sat out on the porch and talked to the chickens as they pecked at the ground, some strange sort of soap opera developing amongst them, particularly when breeding was going on. The new rooster was named '*Obispo* Michael' after my father, who sometimes came out from his darkroom to watch the spectacle of breeding, tucking his hands into his waistcoat and rocking back and forth in pleasure. 'That's a fine method I have there, I must say,' he said. My grandmother eyed him suspiciously and said something about Riley and the dry bullets of new revolutionaries – she was expecting a grandchild any day, but the only grandchild would be years coming, in another country, almost another universe.

While my mother tended to the animals the old man worked on his photographs. He borrowed a truck, used most of the remaining money on another week-long journey to buy supplies in San Antonio. At the back of the house he built a darkroom – he always claimed it was the finest of its kind in the northern hemisphere. In a place of great light – light that swept its way in a hard yellowness over the land – not a chink got through. He put double doors in. The second door bolted from the inside so that when he was developing the photos wouldn't get ruined. He saturated himself in red light. Only my mother was allowed in. For a joke he hung above the door a chastity belt he had found in a rubbish dump. A sign in Spanish read: 'No Entry Beyond This Point.'

Sometimes drunks came hammering at his door. They were fond of reaching up and tucking their empty bottles into the belt. The bottles clanged together like an odd doorbell, but he seldom answered. The coterie of drunks would hang around outside, mouths flapping away under thick black moustaches. They were often looking for money – any man who could afford to take photographs had to be rich. He didn't have much to give, but he set up a row of hammocks for them outside the door of the darkroom. The men lounged there and shared precious cigarettes, speculated on the nature of his photos. They listened to the floating voices of my mother and grandmother as the chicken opera developed in the yard, *Obispo*

Michael going hell for leather whenever he got the chance, a couple of delighted screams rising up when he went after the barber's wife who, in real life, had a cleft palate and a tendency towards body odour.

One of the drunks, Rolando, used to stand by the front fence in his huarache sandals and roar them on, leaning over to clandestinely spit on the one named after the mayor. But when my father came out to watch the episodes, Rolando moved away, sneaked up behind him and either flicked my father's ear or tweaked his nose, particularly if *Obispo* Michael was having a hectic day. After the first flicking, Rolando would stare into my father's face, reach up and pull or flick again. But the tweaking stopped one afternoon when Rolando got drunker than ever before and touched a lit cigarette against a mole on my father's forearm. My father recoiled, and with his elbow – he said it was accidental – caught Rolando in the mouth. The blow could have been harmless; only, Rolando had rotten gums. Teeth were spat out on the ground. Guilty, my father picked Rolando up from the ground while my grandmother went crazy on the front porch: 'Animal!' 'Pig!' 'Leave Rolando alone!' Rolando settled down in the dust, fingering his mouth. My father shooed my grandmother away, went walking to clear his head, bought a bottle of tequila for Rolando. They searched together on the ground for the teeth, one of which was never found. While they were searching, Rolando burnt my father's mole with another three cigarettes and let gulps of laughter roll down into the neck of the bottle.

Still, slow times lay in that dry soil for the old man – dust billowed in the air when the rare car or pick-up truck went past on the potholed road on its way down to the petrol station, where gas was pumped by hand from an ancient American pump. When he was finished work he sometimes sat with Mam on the front steps, slurping bottles with the men, swatting mosquitoes, and staring at the vehicles, wondered where they were off to, dust settling back down around them. They put their arms around one another, and he told her of other places. They watched the sun sink its way southward on the horizon, month giving way to month, season giving way to season. It was strange for my father to stay so long in one place, and he wondered where the two of them should go next. Once or twice planes were seen in the sky over the Chihuahuan desert and the whole town stood, mesmerised. But still the dust settled on the ordinary. Night rose up on the banal. The days often merged into lethargy as they sat with one another, holding hands. Even the sight of a burro or a cart gave him the want for movement. It thumped within him, haunted him, as it always haunted him – and maybe still does.

Down beyond the barn a bored raven landed on the telegraph wire, and the old man watched it for the longest time as he stroked the cat. I thought about that wire and how a billion unknown voices might be running under the raven's feet, moving through the long black body, through the shaggy throat feathers, scuttling along through hollow bones and stringy ligaments, all the way to the wedge-shaped tail sheening with black and purple, voices all the way to the core, to the heart. Those townspeople in Mexico could be voiced here in seconds, talking of its new cafés with their giant wine racks, Miguel's chandeliers, its tarmacadamed streets, the screeching grackles, the lottery-ticket sellers, the abandoned cinema, the low adobe bars, the malicious heat. I can still feel it. All that heat. As I walked along those roads. In that colonial hotel room with the dancing ceiling fan other voices talked to me. When I went looking for their house there wasn't a weather vane in sight. And Mam wasn't there, not her, not her ghost, nor her image, hardly even her memory. And he was summoned up from only a couple of throats. The streets at dawn had a retinue of red, a typhoid rash over the morning. I walked along, under a grove of trees, under the sun, under a universe of curiosity and doubt, a telephone wire within myself, gurgling.

A boy in the town, Miguel, Rolando's son, was fond of drawing maps, and the old man bought them from him, hung them on the walls of the house. They were copied from a school atlas, but his versions were full of fabulous and unusual colours. Miguel drew magenta oceans, white mountains, green rivers, purple roads, a red tongue of river, and sometimes he rubbed a little soil on the maps to give the countryside a brown tint. If you put your nose to the maps, you could smell the soil. The cities were shown with little pieces of metal that could rip the tips of your fingers if you ran your hands along them. My father moved the maps from wall to wall, switching them from the kitchen to the living room and back again so that he felt as if he were going somewhere. The year was 1949, and he was over the cusp of his thirties – if he couldn't go in reality he would go in his imagination. At times he took my mother's hand and led her all the way around the world within that small house, teaching her English as they went, so that she quickly acquired an Irish accent, the sound of it merging with her own native euphony. She would write new words down in a spiral-edged book, wondering when she might get a chance to use them. In truth she was a little frightened by it all, this possibility of going. Still in her twenties – the difference of nine years sometimes a ravine between them – she had never set foot outside her town. Even if she wanted to, there would be no moving anywhere for a while – my grandmother made sure of that.

'You can leave when the sun comes up in the west,' she

said, heaving around under her chest. 'And maybe even a few days after that.'

Miguel's maps were a sign that my father's feet were itching again. He even invited the young genius over to draw a few maps on the wall of his darkroom, but Rolando refused to let his son go. A chicken had been named after Rolando – he had been delighted at first, came over to the house every day, leaned over the fence, a grey crooked eyebrow dipping down, talked about how much uglier the mayor was. But then the rooster had seemed to take an overwhelming fondness for mounting and treading Rolando's namesake, and Rolando was the butt of feral jokes, especially among the other drunks. 'You're walking funny today, Rolando.' 'Watch those feathers fly!' 'Have you room for another egg?' He never came over to the house anymore, even after the hen was renamed. Young Miguel sneaked over to the darkroom after school, sat in and talked with my father, but he never managed to get the maps finished. He was trying to figure out a way to get a particular mound of soil to suspend itself in the air – it kept dropping down near the vats of chemicals, even when he made a shelf for the soil from tiny pieces of wood. One day when he came over he found a note tucked into the chastity belt above the door, 'Sorry, Miguel, closed for a while.'

The old man took a job in a small copper mine far south of the town. Wanting to take photos of the mines, he left town with a truckload of men on Sunday mornings, wearing his dirty vest and his hat. With the help of a few men he smuggled cameras into the mines. At the end of the week he came home coughing up red spit, his vest showered with dirt. Copper coloured his skin. He and Mam locked themselves in the darkroom, working together, and sometimes they fell asleep, waking up the following day with a plate of my grandmother's stew grown cold outside the door. The work consumed them both. Agonised faces came to life in the chemical baths, the whites of eyes appearing like coronas, dirt smeared on chins. Backbent by the work they had done and backbent into the future, the men leaned on picks as they sucked copper dust into their lungs. They stared with an anger of dispossession, their cheeks gaunt, a fury of poverty in discoloured lips. But he also captured them in the bars and the whorehouses, sometimes even at home with their children, happily kicking a soccer ball outside a shack. The miners took to him, hailed him when he came down the shafts, all of them helping carry the hidden equipment. But he came home bloodied one afternoon. He had lost a fight with a foreman after taking a photo of a dead boy being carried from the mines. The boy was no more than ten years old, the same age as Miguel. My father was hit with the long barrel of a gun. It left a small scar in the shape of a gondala on the right side of his temple. He tried a few times to go back, but the trigger of the same gun was cocked.

He went back to the house and the chickens, walked around the yard, muttering, scattering spit like seed. 'Fuck this for a game of soldiers.' Mam came out and ran her fingers over the scar, maybe kissed him there. They retreated to the darkroom to work on his photos. More plates of stew piled up outside the door.

After a time they sold two cameras and three dozen chickens in order to buy a clapped-out car so they could bring the eggs to neighbouring towns. My old man drummed his fist on the dashboard as the engine rattled, the panels held together with wire, the roof covered in birdshit from grackles. The car – a 1928 Model A – would fling him outwards once again. They began to save money, and the circle of their wandering moved gradually outwards. At first it was no further than a few miles, then it grew and grew, ripples reaching out, towards Jiménez, Delicias, Chihuahua and even south to Torreón. Once or twice they went all the way to Mexico City, a three-day drive, where they bought supplies of film, paper, trays, chemical fixer. I can imagine those shop clerks, with thin moustaches sliming on their lips, hair cut short, in very well ironed shirts, garters on their sleeves, giving the once-over to my father as he leaned over the counter, in clothes sometimes still faint with the smell of chickenshit.

On those nights in the city they went celebrating together – my mother told me that they were crazed and lovely evenings in the cafés and the bars, with the accordions and the guitars and the wine and the white tablecloths and the waiters and all the things that a fistful of money could bring. Those few evenings in Mexico City were pure colour to her memory – the way it rose out of its crater, the thick traffic, the rows of red-clay flowerpots, the grey sprawl, the streaked darkness of poverty, the men in blue coming out from the factories, the brown naked children outside shacks, the soldiers and police with giant loping strides underneath their hats, the lines of whores in flimsy clothes on narrow streets with eyes turned to dusklight, the hustling boys, the double-breasted suits, the smell of rotting fruit, the belch of steel – the jazz of it all – the vivid oppressive redness of a southern sky, the houses of the rich with pale blue swimming pools, the grasshoppers fried by an old woman in a market. My father took photos of Mam under bright streetlamps and flitting clouds, her eyes looking cocksure into the lens, hair thrown back like a horse's tail. In one of the shots, down by the Palace of Fine Arts, I noticed that she carried flowers, white dog roses clutched between her fingers. On the long drive home she stayed awake in the passenger seat, passing bottles of Coke to the old man, a mesquite wind blowing through the open windows.

My grandmother had swapped some rabbits for a few bottles of wine, and she gave them to my parents in the hope that the drink would somehow spur on a grandchild. Ancient as the notion of love, my grandmother went to bed early, whispering fertility prayers. My parents drank. Mam had her own special mug – a clay one which she had cast herself years before, but the old man broke it one night in an argument, smashing it against the bathroom door when she said that he'd had too much to drink. For a while he slept outside and my grandmother was hysterical at his disappearance. It was viciously cold at night, with no clouds in the sky to hold the heat, and sometimes my father might have thought about walking forever, skimming over the arroyos and the cacti and the flowers that held water with a startling parsimony. There were plants that would bloom only once every hundred years. He went searching, but never found one of them in bloom. One evening he went wandering too far and got lost, found himself a small cave and lit a fire in it. The heat expanded the rock. A piece of it unlodged from the roof of the cave and fell down, hitting him on the shoulder. He improvised a sling with his shirt, wandered, lost. A local policeman found him – a search party had been sent out because of some bad news in town.

My grandmother had passed away. She had been sitting on the porch, waiting for his return, when her hat lifted off in a strong breeze, and she had fallen to the ground. The end of her cane had lodged itself in a gap in the porch steps, and she tripped face forward on to a sharp rock, slicing her forehead wide open, a gash the length of her eyes. It was said that a strange wind blew across her dead body, a circular whirl that carted the rabbit-foot hat around and around and around her corpse, as if in prayer, a rosary of upkicked dust.

My father found Mam at the edge of town, hysterical, with fists flailing at the sky – she thought that she had lost him too. At home, she tended to his arm and then sank into a deep long-skirted mourning for her mother. Nestling herself under the limbs of the house, she listened for church bells, watched the paint peel on green wooden chairs, remembered things. Rabbits and the way they were skinned. Curious poultices for cut knees when she was a child. The way a pudding was stirred. Blue azaleas embroidered around a pillow. In her family there was a tradition of a year's grief after a loss, and Mam carried it to full term. My father was different – he had loved the old woman and her eccentricities, but she had been an anchor to the land, to stasis, to the unmoving moments. They were alone now, with no duty to my mother's family left, so he suggested trips all over the world, strange exotic places the names of which she had only heard whispered in the movie theatre. My mother wouldn't listen, pulling sable-dark clothes higher on her shoulders, refusing to move around Miguel's maps until the mourning was finished.

It wasn't until eighteen months later that she shed them in favour of some muted skirts, which led to colour once more, and then she began to listen to the whispers.

In early 1956 a special letter was delivered – half the town was gathered down by the post office while my father opened it. His shoulder still hadn't recovered fully and he opened the envelope with one hand, using the nail of his little finger to reach in under the flap. It was from a magazine in San Francisco, courting him with the offer of a huge sum of money, or at least what seemed like a huge sum of money then. A weekly salary. Bylines. An explosion of his own name. It had come as a result of photos he had sent of the copper mines – he assured the townspeople that they too would be famous, their faces and thick arms would appear on news-stands in California. A party was held in his honour that night. Backs were slapped. Jugs were passed. Music coughed out around the town, and my father played the spoons – coins were dropped in his big brown hat for the going. Rolando stood up and sang '*Las*

*Golondrinas*,' a song of leaving, offering lodging to a lost swallow. My mother stood at the edge of that crowd with other women, watching, listening to the song. She might have wondered about the paucity of grief that my father showed for the departure, reeling his way around, singing. A wind without any definite colour must have gathered her in as she shoved her hands down deep into dress pockets.

Rolando brimmed with a toothless grin – he saw the gaps as some sort of autograph now and he chugged his way beside my father. A picture was taken of Rolando, his finger pointing at his mouth in pride, the other hand clenched in a fist, a hat askew on his head, his face a field of stubble.

But the greatest pictures were not the ones of the copper mines, or of the people in the town. They were the ones of Mam's body. My father had taken them in their bedroom. She was nude, not flagrantly so, but her stomach was smooth and dark, it held no creases, her legs curved softly, white sheets exposed small tufts of hair. Some of the shots were hazy beneath mosquito nets, so they took on a Victorian attitude of lounge and lust, as if being peeped at through a curtain, black and white photos that never even suggested colour, a cheek propped up on a hand, the body a streambed running down from it, cavorting through bedsheets and a canyon of desire, once or twice a suggestion of quiet lechery, a tongue held out against a lip, fingers in a V around a dark nipple, a sideways shot of her by the washbasin with her hand bellied on brown, fingers spread out; a hazy portrait of her wearing panties and stepping into a long white dress, hitching up her chest into it, the eyebrows raised in an attitude of impishness. When I first saw them – years ago now – they made me sick to the stomach. I hardly even realised it was her at first, and unlike the ones of the women in Spain, I never again looked at them in the attic, never found myself part of them. I knew what they had done to her and I couldn't understand why she had let them be taken.

She almost seemed to leaf her way into the lens, a brooding silence of body, an acceptance of danger, an ability to become anything that he wanted her to become – and never once the feeling that she didn't want to do it. The photos revealed a peculiar fascination with a beauty mark on her lower right hip. Even now I shudder to imagine her with her head thrown back in laughter, in some dark room sealed to mosquitoes and Peeping Toms, light reflected off a cheap umbrella, licking her lips at the camera, her dress in a formless puddle at her feet, while outside white hydrangeas closed their petals in a row underneath a woodwormed window.

Just before they left town, José with the Sewn Lip broke into my father's darkroom and found some of the prints, somewhat underexposed. He ran around screaming – he finally got his voice back, the people said – flinging the photos of my mother around the town courtyard like so many pieces of confetti. A picture of her was found – impaled on a hitching post – down by the courthouse steps, and the joke was that there was a new candidate around for mayor. But the poppyseed priest wasn't happy, and the women in town weren't happy, and although the drunks and the men in the poolhall were delighted, they all pretended that they weren't happy either, so my parents left next morning, very early, before the café was open, before truculent rumours jumped out from the white-shuttered windows and the thick walls. They didn't have a lot to leave behind – a few wooden chairs, a couple of hair clips, the red geraniums, vats of photographic chemicals, a few chickens pecking at the ground as they cranked the front of their car, poultry feathers flying up from the back seat, dirt filtering off the wired-up runningboard as they drove, birdshit still patterned on the roof.

★

He dribbled egg down the front of his chin this evening at dinner. I made sure they weren't 'sunnyside up', cooked them on both sides so he'd eat them. The yoke was still soft inside, and it streamed down amongst the stubble. Wiped it off with the edge of his sleeve. He says the tops of his fingers are a little bit numb. Every now and then he pinched his thumb against his forefinger to bring them back to life. The fork slid through them anyway, and it took him an age to push back his chair and pick it up from the floor. A clump of dust and hair stuck to it. 'Not too hungry,' he said to me, putting the fork back on the plate beside the eggs. He looked down at the slick of yellow drying on his sleeve. 'I'll suck it out later.' Then he cracked the edge of his lips in a smile. At least his mind is still there, churning away in the skinhouse. He sat back in the chair and lit a cigarette, smoke rising up to the ceiling. But his fingers were jittery around his mouth, all sorts of liver spots moving in a blur. He sat in silence and gave me one of his old winks. Left his cigarette in the ashtray to burn all the way down to the filter again.

The kitchen seemed to have been sunk in formaldehyde, laid down in some vast tub of years. The black and white linoleum was as cold as ever, the copper pots hung on the same nails, and even the wall was still streaked above the stove from the time Mam set the pan on fire. A jamjar – one from the sixties with a picture of a golliwog on the front and mould flowering on the inside – sat in the cupboard above the sink. 'How about we open a museum?' He nodded and smiled, although I'm not even sure he heard what I said. I walked around the kitchen. The black skillet all sloppy with grease. The jar of flour. Mam's woollen cosy with embroidered trees all out of proportion, the upper limbs fatter than the trunk, a sewn picture maybe reminiscent of her world, always about to topple. The teacups with all sorts of stains near the rims. One or two tins of cat food. A slab of bread and a box of tea in the pantry. A couple of slices of Michelstown in the fridge. I moved them around on the shelves to make the pantry look fuller, but it didn't matter. It's no wonder he is so thin. I suppose he just eats bits and pieces, although he told me that Mrs McCarthy brings him dinner some days.

I set about cleaning the place when he went down to hunt out his big salmon. 'Going to catch that bastard, tonight,' he said. Off he went with the rods on his shoulder after he fluffed out his flies in a stream of steam from the kettle, rejuvenating the hair and feather dressings.

Some spiders were living in the mop when I got it from the cupboard. Took it outside and ran it under the spigot. They scuttled away. Strange to feel the drizzle settle on my hair. The wind blew it in from the bog as I rinsed out the bucket. That's a smell that has always lived inside me – the pungent black earth all slashed through with turf-cutters, although I could smell the factory belching out its slaughter, too. It left a scent of offal in the air, fanning out over the land.

It was when the factory came that the old man and I stopped our swimming in the river, our dawn race against the current. One morning we were out there shivering on the bank – I was eleven years old – when bits of offal from slaughtered cows starting floating down past us, blotches of blood in the water, stringy ligaments and guts spinning away on the surface. They came in spurts, a punctured vein on the river. The old man stared at it and ran his fingers along his body, walked away from the river, disgusted. Mam collected some pieces in a bucket and went up to the factory and dumped them on the factory floor. We never went swimming anymore after that. Mam got up in the early mornings and walked down to the water's edge by herself, sat and watched the pieces flow by. She was silver-haired by then and I suppose much of the bitterness had settled in.

But they've cleaned up their act these days, and I don't see any scum on the river, although the gates have slowed the water down to its pathetic trickle.

I saw a few men in their blue uniforms moving down past the end of the laneway on their bicycles, back from the meat factory. I went and got one of the old man's cameras with a zoom lens to get a closer look, couldn't make out any of the faces. They were trudging along. A few kids were out playing, too. Every now and then their heads bobbed up above the hedge. Four boys came down along our laneway and stopped to pick up conkers from under the chestnut tree. They were all fighting with each other, fooling around, throwing big punches that missed. From the distance one of them looked like Miguel's son – hair in a black ramble on his head. I moved away from the window into the kitchen, put some washing-up liquid in the bucket, swirled it around with the handle of a wooden spoon, started cleaning the floor while the evening rolled on. Otherwise this place'll be swimming in filth and he'll just wade through it for the rest of his days. Swirl the mop in a circular motion. Let it glide through your hands.

That was a hot summer morning, four years ago, walking with Miguel through the town, looking for their old house. I was nineteen years old, just arrived from London, stupid with hope.

Miguel's son – another Rolando, named after his late grandfather – held on to Miguel's hand like it was glued there. Little Rolando wore a sailor's suit and scoured his finger up his nose. He was scared of all the strange words coming from us. I had only a smattering of Spanish, picked up from a phrase book I'd bought in London, and Miguel's English was useless. We walked slowly down the street, in the gathering heat; through the market, where the ribs of pigs dangled in the air on hooks and men in overalls with

63

splatters of blood cried out as if they themselves had just been butchered; past women with sun-dried faces as they sold bananas and apples and reams of boxed vegetables, impervious to the flies that were buzzing around them; out to the street where a lorry coughed fumes; beyond a giant white adobe house with roses growing in the courtyard, a hipheavy woman out watering red and white geraniums; past a café advertising tamales; alongside some slum houses, a dog slinking through dustbins; the sun flailing down as we skirted the edges of a dry-soiled park where two old men played chess. Children were out on bicycles – they were raggedy but there were no open sewers for them to negotiate. The town had changed from the one Mam and my father told me about. Underneath the Mexican flag in the plaza the Star-Spangled Banner fluttered. A boulevard in town had been renamed to welcome American business.

Miguel had a puffy face that pillowed itself into silence. He must have known all along – it was as if he was trying to stall me – but the house had been replaced by a clinic that was run by a young man from Italy, a rainbow of freckles across his cheeks, his hair shiny and black around his ears. He had knocked the house down, darkroom and all, and built the clinic, a low white affair, where he gave his services free of charge. I looked through the gate and foot-scuffled at stones. Miguel ran a hand across the top of his brow, where beads of sweat had settled.

A row of scraggly kids waited with their mothers outside the house, where the chickens used to peck. The Italian was wrapping a white bandage around a teenage girl's leg and he was humming some tune, maybe something about his own mountains far away. He saw me, with the backpack huge on my shoulders, and beckoned me over with a tug of his head. 'Come,' said Miguel, taking my arm, 'meet Antonio.' But I didn't want to meet Antonio. I didn't want to meet anyone. Little Rolando was screaming at the top of his voice.

64

Miguel slapped him on the bare legs and he stopped. We went back along the road, great silence between us.

'Did she ever come back?' I asked later, in his house.

'She no return,' said Miguel emphatically.

'Are you sure?'

'You ask many questions,' he said.

'I'm sorry.'

'It's okay. You will have *una cabita*? She come again no.'

His wife, Paloma, prepared glasses of rum and Coca-Cola for us. Maps hung on the walls. They dotted the hallway, light coming on them from a fancy glass chandelier. Miguel had grown artistically. Now he made faces from contour maps – geological and ordinance surveys with eyes from history staring out of them. All sorts of Mexican revolutionaries were drawn within the valleys and the troughs, the towns sometimes used for eyes, hills for hair, the rivers for arms. He located Riley for me, a tiny figure drawn from the contours of a hanging valley. His head was leaning against the knee of Santa Anna who was slumped beneath the shoulders of Emiliano Zapata. The strange thing was that Miguel didn't have to distort the lines – he had stayed true to the contours and the faces were fluid within them. He made a good living from it, sold them to galleries all over the country. Someone had commissioned a portrait of Salinas. Miguel was working on it. He said his art had nothing to do with his politics, but the face of Salinas looked chubby and wobbly, and it seemed as if there was an American eagle on his shoulder with television sets for eyes.

The drink was served in cut glasses with gold around the rims. I sat and sipped. The day's heat pushed us down. Paloma held her glass with her little finger extended daintily. An emerald ring bobbed on it. Her fingers caressed the air as she spoke. She sounded as if she'd been sucking on helium.

'You stay?'

They offered me a bed on their porch, mosquito screen all around so that it made something of an outdoor room, an old army cot with the cleanest of sheets standing in the corner, a Bible on a bedside table, candles in silver holders beside it.

But I moved on – wanted to be on my own – and booked myself into a hotel down near the courthouse, in the old part of town.

The hotel stonework was arthritic. Bits of it crumpled down into the street. The hallway carpet had cigarette marks on it. Soap operas rang out from neighbouring rooms. In the back of the hotel there was a pool of water in a blue tarp that hung above the patio. The mosquitoes gathered in the tarp as if in communion. At dusk they would enter my room, even through the smoke of a mosquito coil. I swatted them with a towel, leaving marks on the wall, along with thousands of others from previous tenants. Even the ceiling was splattered, a collage of red spots. A cleaning lady came in early one morning, when I was sleeping late. Hipheavy in her uniform. She looked up at the wall, counting the fresh stains. *'Te la pasaste matando moscos anoche, verdad?'* she said to me. You spent the whole night killing mosquitoes, true? A fat brown finger wagged in the air and she laughed. She came over to my bed and ruffled my hair, ran her fingers along my cheek, and for a moment I thought she was going to climb in beside me. Instead she dipped her cloth in a bucket and wiped a few of the marks on the wall away, said she'd be back later to make the bed. I went down the corridor to the broken urinal down the hall, where the water was constantly flushing, wet my bandana in the sink and came back to the room to wipe the spots off, but fell asleep in the heat instead.

Graffiti rolled in red on the courthouse walls. Policemen, chameleons in the shadows, flicked in and out between the scrawls. Old men sat outside the cantinas, gesturing. A labyrinth of laneways ran outwards towards a brand-new shopping centre. I pulled back the curtains and stuck my head out, felt a slight breeze. A young man sat on the hotel steps, a ghetto-blaster perched on his knees, heavy-metal music pumping out. Within the music, grackles in the trees exclaimed in high pitches, let their droppings down on to the streets. I kept a large knife handy in the side of my backpack, just in case. I had heard things about Mexico – foreigners robbed, dumped in prison, bellies stuffed with a steel blade, people fucked over into a roadside ditch, left to the turkey vultures who made those great hungry spirals above the world. I fingered the steel blade, put it in my waistband, decided against it, walked out into my parents' old town.

Nobody disturbed me. Maybe it was my dark skin and hair, inherited from Mam, but I don't think so. The town was quiet among strangers and sunsets, and settlings of dust.

A boy with a violin busked in a plaza full of red flowerpots and a bordello-sweep of litter. The song was raucous and stripped bare, a sound that could have belonged to a forest animal. An elderly woman and her husband – he was wasting away handsomely in a collarless shirt – came and stood beside me on the curb as I listened. The man took his wife's arm in the crook of his and danced. She kept her hands tentative at the sleeve of his shirt, but they laughed as they went down off the curb and in between two parked pick-up trucks. His feet were slow, his body creaking. Holes opened and closed in the toes of his shoes, two brown sieves showing calloused toes. He put his head near his wife's shoulder, smiled, moved his dentures up and down in his mouth. She reached up and touched her lips against the stubble on his cheek, kissed his ear, danced on. I tried to imagine my parents once doing the same dance, couldn't.

The boy with the violin extended the song for us, played it with a huge lustful energy, nodded slightly when I dropped a bill in his musical case. The elderly man saluted me with a bow as I went away, swooping his hat across his knees, and his wife smiled.

The town was bigger than I had imagined. I wandered for days, through bars and cafés, bills coming crisply from my pockets, ordered up shots of tequila, tried to picture myself here forty years before, in a stetson and boots. But the simple truth of it was that I was leaning drunkenly against a bar counter, wearing a gold earring, red Doc Martens and a baseball hat turned backwards, in a town where I could hardly even understand what people were saying. It was only with enough tequila in my system that I could make sense of the stories my parents had told me, their endless incantation of memories. I sat in a bar chair, looked at a photo album I had brought with me, let my mind wander. Somewhere 'Las Golondrinas' had been sung. Outside was the hitching post where her image had been impaled – but there were no posts along by the courthouse any more. Earlier I had seen a row of grasshoppers impaled by shrikes on a length of barbed wire. The butcher-birds had been neat in their execution, the grasshoppers equidistant on the barbs, a strange wind blowing over them, one of Mam's coloured gales. I stood and saluted the desert. Further out were the places where the coyotes had perhaps sung.

I ambled with my head down, a foreign language swirling in calypsos all around me. Would she suddenly appear? Would she come down the street? Would someone recognise her in me? A smell of food hung on the air. I breathed it down, took it to my lungs. *Salsa*. A thick *salsa* smell. She had made that when she exiled herself in our Mayo kitchen, hunched over the stove.

Breezing into the poolhall, I heard the clinking of ivory balls fade as if the last few notes of a seedy hymn were sounding out. An ancient man with very strange lips stood in the corner of the hall, drinking a Coca-Cola. I wondered if it was José with the Sewn Lips. I tried to say something in Spanish, but he just guffawed loudly, propped his underarm on his pool cue, using it as a crutch, whistled to his friends, pointed at me. Blue smoke was making spiral galaxies over the pool tables. Someone spat. I turned and walked out, while a man in a red baseball hat came towards me, proffering an empty pool tray, as if I might leave my eyeballs there for them to shoot around. On the street a boy was selling bits of useless copper and strange-shaped rocks. He weighed them on a brass balance. I bought some obsidian, left it in the ashtray in my hotel room, lay on my bed, drew the curtains, put my hands behind my head, watched the fan as it whirled, fell asleep.

I woke up, hungover, mosquitoes delighted around me.

My shoes developed a tiny tear in the rim near my little toe. In my hotel room I glued them together. I took a long sniff at the tube of glue, brought it down deep into my chest, tried to get high – felt stupid and juvenile – threw the tube away, took a very cold shower, squatted down, let the water wail on my back, thought of fire trucks along the roads of another town a long way away.

In the town library, records were stacked in boxes. I couldn't understand them – the young woman behind the counter didn't have time to help. She was handsome in an academic way, cropped hair, her blouse too big, small gold-rimmed spectacles. I wanted to ask her out, but swallowed my words. I saw her a few days later in the foyer of the hotel. She was sitting in an armchair, sipping on a drink, a large stick of celery mashing against her upper lip. She gave me a curt wave, turned away. I passed through the foyer, my daypack swinging off my shoulder. The warmth outside came in a blast. It was another man's ordinary question that assaulted me: What am I doing here?

I walked on, chatting to myself.

Back in the park the two men were still playing chess. They remembered my parents. 'He was crazy,' they said to me in Spanish, 'big and crazy, always with cameras. She was crazy, too, not as crazy as him.' They said the house had lain empty for years after Mam and my father left. Nobody lived there until the Italian moved in with his clinic. The men stuffed the chess pieces in their pockets, walked with me to a graveyard. They pointed towards a wooden cross at the southern edge of the cemetery. I thanked them, and one of the men took my cheek between his thumb and forefinger and twisted until it almost hurt. 'You are young,' he said, 'very young.' He winked at me and opened a pouch that hung around his neck, took out a tooth. He said something about carrying the mouths of the dead around on his chest. I asked him to explain, but he just shook his head. I watched the men as they disappeared down the road, bent into their days, their games, their repetitions.

My grandmother's cross was white and simple. It stood to the side of a thousand others. The black lettering of her name had faded. I got on my knees and introduced myself to her.

'Hi, I'm Conor. The sun came up in the west.'

There were bedbugs in the hotel, and a string of bites, like red pearls, ran down my legs. For days and days I trudged around, the glue holding strong on my shoes. I hung out for an afternoon at an abandoned cinema, sat against the wall under a faded Kung Fu poster, under a black arch. I imagined films coming in tin cans, off the back of a filthy truck, boys in shorts waiting around, glorious under a hot sun, slicing the thick air with kicks and sideways arm-chops. A woman came and gave me a bottle of water. She had long skeletal hands: *'Has de tener sed; toma.'* Here, you look thirsty. Her eyes were incandescent – did she know something? I tried to talk to her but she simply shrugged, a little perplexed, a little amused at my attempts at the language.

A bell sounded on the hour. A man in an ice-cream van was singing. It was time to go. That's what he was singing: It is time to go. I heard it clearly: It is time for you to go, there's nothing here.

In the room I tried to sleep after lighting a mosquito coil. The smoke drifted up to the fan, the ash in a gyre to the centre of the coil. Music vaulted up from the street. It was the ice-cream man singing again: It is way past the time for you to go.

I took one last look, waited for a face to appear around a corner, grey hair, arched eyebrows, flecked eyes. All I found was the boy with the violin, but he sounded strangely strangled that day and hardly sang at all. Only a few pesos in his violin case. He shrugged his shoulders when I dropped some more money in and hurried away. Miguel came with me to the bus station on a Friday morning when thermometers in gardens were edging their way dangerously upwards.

'Good luck,' he said.

He shook my hand lightly. Great damp ovals rolled from the underarm of his shirt. When the bus left, the driver whistled a tune, the same tune, all the way to Monterrey, as if a gramophone needle was stuck in his lavish Adam's apple. We changed drivers and plunged south towards Mexico City. After a while I sat in the middle of the bus, where the impact from the ruts in the road was gentler. The windows were fully open, a yawn that let the created wind through. We rattled along in darkness, through the desert, and small towns on the edge of spectacular canyons, and into vast city suburbs. I caught a glimpse of a circus setting up its tents, a girl riding around on a unicycle, feathers leaping from her hair, her breasts spilling out from a tank top. I wanted to reach for her, touch her, see if she was real, but the bus hammered on.

At the station in Mexico City I walked with my head down – the floor was spidered with moving sandals. I had noticed them before, young foreigners in plastic Teva sandals, their Lonely Planets hugged to their chests, enviously eyeing the size of backpacks that others were carrying. I walked out into the city, a leapfrog of sky-scrapers, smog, granite-grey sky, white pigeons pecking under archways. I wandered in a daze, still waiting for Mam to pop her head around some corner, hail me with a wave. My flight to San Francisco wouldn't leave until the next day, but I knew it was a brutishly stupid notion anyway, this searching for her. On a crowded street I saw a newspaper being trampled underfoot, and I suddenly remembered it was my birthday, my twentieth. I bought a bottle of tequila and sat in the corner of the airport, sipping furtively. Sounds rang out. Buzzers, intercoms, machines. It struck me then that I knew the sound of airport metal detectors better than the shrill call of coyotes I had heard so much about from my parents.

Years later, in America, I was told that Navajo Indians believed coyotes ushered in the Big Bang of the world with their song, stood on the rim of nothingness, before time, shoved their pointed muzzles in the air, and howled the world into existence at their feet. The Indians called them songdogs. The universe was etched with their howls, sound merging into sound, the beginning of all other songs. Long ago, when they told me their stories about Mexico, Mam and Dad, I believed they were true. And I suppose I still do. They were my songdogs – my mother by the washing line, my father flailing his way against the current. They tried very hard to tell me how much they had been in love with one another, how good life had been, that coyotes really did exist and sing in the universe of themselves on their wedding day. And maybe they did. Maybe there was a tremendous howl that reached its way all across the desert. But the past is a place that is full of energy and imagination. In remembering, we can distil the memory down. We can manage our universe by stuffing it into the original quark, the point of burstingness.

It's the lethargy of the present that terrifies us all. The slowness, the mundanity, the sheer plod of each day. Like my endless hours spent strolling through Mexico. And my father's constant casting these days. His own little songdog noise of a fishing line whisking its way through the air.

When the old man came back to the house he surprised me. 'Sorry,' I said, leaning the mop up against the door, 'I was miles away.' He nodded, rubbed his fingers along his scalp. He was amazed at the floor. It didn't shine, but if he drops the fork again, it won't get quite so dirty. 'Not a peep from the big one today,' he said, as he hung up his coat on the peg inside the door, a blade of grass stuck to the side of the sleeve. He opened his lunchbox with a dramatic gesture of the hand, a sweep to the ceiling. I was gobsmacked to see a small trout in the box, maybe a one-pounder. Some fish in the river, after all. I told him that it mightn't be too healthy, all that fertiliser and shit dumped by the farmers and the meat factory, but he raised his eyes to the ceiling.

'Get a grip,' he said to me, 'you and all the other greenies. The river's clean as a fucken whistle.'

He gutted the fish with the long kitchen knife, hooked his finger in to pull out the guts, ran it under the tapwater, made himself a nice fillet. I told him I wasn't eating any but he said he didn't give a damn, he'd cook it anyway. He prepared it in the skillet and took his place at the table, ate quickly, lit himself a cigarette.

'So what did ya do all day?'

'I told you, I cleaned the floor.'

'Oh.' He rose up to flip on the radio, decided against it, leaned against the sink, put out the smoke on the wall of his teacup: 'I mean, after that, what did you do after that?'

'It took all day.'

'It's nice and skiddy anyway,' he said, taking one stockinged foot out of his slippers and gliding it along the tiles. 'I hope I don't fall and break me neck.'

From the kitchen window I watched the wind roll through the long grasses at the edge of the laneway, the blades bent, supplicants to the river.

The marmalade cat seems awful fond of him – she was rubbing her spine against the back of his calves after he fed her the fish head. She's a stray, he said, wandered in a month ago after another one died, came up to him and started purring. He doesn't seem to have a name for her, just calls her Cat. Picked her up from the floor and started stroking her with a long, hard, heavy roll of his hand, as if that might stop the trembling of his own fingers. She was looking for more food, meowing away. 'Aren't ya full yet, Cat?' All of a sudden he looked up from her, eyes reduced to dark wrinkled slivers, and said: 'They come and go these days like you wouldn't believe.'

I followed him as he lumbered up the stairs, the floorboards creaking away. 'Goodnight so. Ya did a grand job on the floor.'

'Thanks.'

'Tomorrow'll be a fine one.'

'Why's that?'

'Red sky at night.'

'It wasn't too red.'

74

'Ah, it was a bit red anyway,' he said, scrubbing his glasses on his shirt.

'I'll get some more cleaning done tomorrow.'

'Don't be doing that, for crissake.'

'What?'

'You're like an oul' woman, cleaning. A bit of dust never did anyone any harm.'

'I suppose.'

'It'll be a perfect day for fishing,' he said.

'Perfect.'

'Conor?' he said, on the landing. 'When are ya off up to Dublin?'

'Next week. Getting rid of me already?'

'Just asking,' he said angrily. 'Listen up a second.'

'Yeah?'

'I want to know something.'

'Fire away.'

'Why didn't ya write?'

'Ah, ya know me and letters.'

'No, that's the thing, I don't know you and letters.'

'Ah, I'm just not very good at it.'

He nodded and used a hand against the wall to guide himself along the landing: 'I thought you'd have written.'

'Sorry.'

'Yeah,' he said.

'Well, I am.'

'I believe ya,' he grunted, his back to me.

I found a mosquito coil tonight, shattered into little green bits at the bottom of my backpack. Those mosquitoes in Mexico were always ecstatic in the hot, hot air. Waiting. Hovering. Moving away from the smoke under the ceiling fan. It was truly vicious, that heat, but in an odd way I liked it. When I arrived in San Francisco it was the coolness of it all that assaulted me. The immigration officer in the airport looked at the Mexican stamp in my passport. 'Hope you didn't catch the clap,' he said with a grin, waving me through with a sweep of the hand after stamping a six-month stay in my passport.

# THURSDAY

## *a deep need for miracles*

Brutally romantic, of course, but he has kept every single one of Mam's dresses. They hang in a riot of colours amongst a dozen mothball bags. The cupboard was open in his room this morning when I looked in before going downstairs. Hems spilled on the floor, edges that were unsewn over the years, continually dropped another inch, always lengthening, until even her skirts covered her calves. The sleeve of an old adelita dress stuck out. Some blouses. A dressing gown hung with one shoulder on a hanger. Her sarapes neatly folded on the shelf beside some coiled belts. I stared at the old man asleep in the bed, the marmalade cat on the pillow beside him. His hat was perched on the bedside table, beside a full bottle of Bushmills. There was a bit of a smell in the room – he has bad gas these days. Finds it hard to control. Let one go at the kitchen table last night.

'Oops!' he said. 'Barking spider around here somewhere!'

But I could tell he was embarrassed by the smell – even

77

got a bit of a flush in his cheeks as he walked upstairs to his bed. But at least he sleeps. When Mam was here there were nights she would get out of bed – she was sleeping in the room at the end of the landing at that stage – and sometimes she would go down to work on her stone walls, those black bags collecting under her eyes.

It was the first time Mam had seen the northwestern part of Mexico, and the Model A negotiated narrow roads that often ended in dry floodbeds. They drove over cracked platelets of mud, past weedgrown churches, through long sweeps of prairie where whitewashed haciendas rose up and flared out against the grasses. In the mornings the towns were alive under spectacular red reefs of cloud, migrating flocks moving through them, and once a single white crane seemed to follow them for miles, noisily flapping in the air, until the bird veered off and joined a mate. Mam looked backwards over the car-seat – she wanted to feel the rhythms of her land before they went to *El Norte*.

It was a quiet trip, except for the crunch of three jackrabbits under the wheels of the car along a dirt road in Sonora. Mam wanted to chop off the paws of the rabbits at the side of the road – some tribute to her mother – but the old man drove biliously on, disturbed by the rattling gearwhine of the car. Besides, Mam already had a jar full of rabbit's feet with her, and as they moved westward she affixed a half-dozen of them around the rim of his hat. It looked ridiculous – the way they pattered around his head – but my father bent to Mam's superstition, put the hat on while he drove. In the vast expanses they haggled with gaunt garage owners over petrol prices. Children in ragged shirts stared as the car threw out smoke. Riders pulled their horses over into ditches. The horsemen sometimes carried rifles, and my father slowed as he went past,

78

guffaws rising at the sight of his hat. He drove with fingers drumming heavily on the wheel, impatient with places, little traces of sweat beginning in the furrows of his brow.

Years later, in our Vauxhall Viva, which we drove around Mayo, an old Mexican paw and a St Christopher medal hung from the stem of the mirror. At times the paw would swing, animated, bashing itself against the windscreen, and Mam watched it as if it might break its way through the glass for her, bring her back to those moments in her country. When we were left alone in the car together, Mam and I, she would hug herself into heavy sweaters, tell me bits and pieces about that trip to America in 1956, how they abandoned the car and never saw it again.

They made it all the way to a coastline dock near Tijuana when steam suddenly flocked up from the engine. They must have looked a sight, the old man waving his hat over the open bonnet, my mother blowing her breath from her lip up to the fringe of her hair, trying to figure out what weather might be blowing in, what colours she might create. As the dockside darkened, my father wanted to tape the hosepipe together, but they had no tape. He crawled in underneath the engine, pounding the underside of the Model A with his fist. Mam began tearing a strip from the bottom of her dress to see if that might work. It was a white hem, she later told me, a single inch of cotton. She recalled it so vividly that it must have haunted her – it was one of the last things she remembered doing in Mexico, her foot propped on the bumper, knee bent, ripping her dress to try to fix the car that was taking her from her homeland.

As she was tearing the dress, a stranger with raven-coloured hair wandered up – the captain of a cruise ship that had docked nearby for emergency repairs. The captain offered them free passage to San Francisco. Some of his crew had disappeared into drunkenness in the tight alleyways of Tijuana, swallowed down into bottles of mescal. In return, he said, my father could bartend and my mother could waitress. The old man crawled out from underneath the car, shook the captain's hand, flung the car keys away along the dock.

They sailed the rest of the way to America. Umbrella drinks were served by waiters in white shirts. Jazz notes copulated madly in the air, bits of Al Jolson songs mashing against Billie Holiday numbers. The yawning head of a pig was laid out for supper the first night, a red apple in its mouth. My father stood behind the bar in a black bowtie, hair slicked back, revealing the beginning of two small indentations of baldness on his crown. He invented cocktails, shook them with drama. Mam was unable to work, sick the whole time, retching over the side of the boat. She stayed in her cabin while dinner was served. A grey wind blew off the sea for her, the boat combing its way over the waves for a day and a half. Occasionally there was sunshine, but most of the time dolorous clouds drifted with them. When they got near the port in San Francisco, Mam brushed her hair with an old comb and decked herself out in a strawberry dress and a wide-brimmed hat. As she leaned against the railing, the ship jolted against the pier, rocked her sideways, and she lost her stomach again.

My father lumbered heavy suitcases down the gangway. 'Great day for a wander,' he told Mam, people flowing past them, 'great day for a wander.'

That afternoon they went to an old tumbledown building near the Mission, to the offices of the magazine company which had written to my father. The old man had a meeting, and Mam disappeared to the bathroom. Combing her hair in a broken mirror, she must have been amazed at what the cracks did to her face, fracturing her eyes down to her nose, sending cheekbones into a land-slide, displacing one ear upwards so that it almost floated above her head. Maybe she ran her brown fingers over the broken sections, reached to take the ear, watched it float away again, her body not belonging to her anymore, the rhythms of the boat journey still moving within it. Maybe she could smell her eyebrows giving off salt and her teeth full of gulls flickering away into flight from a pink deck. I can picture her mouth moving into a small black O, falling out again into lips drained of colour, the heaves of the imaginary waves carrying her face into further fractures as if it were a kaleidoscope, or a million people lending her a piece of their faces, meshing and unmeshing until it wasn't her there at all, staring at herself. Perhaps one green eye, one brown, one azure, one red. Water splashed up and formed beads within the cracks, beads that held the same broken images, mirrors within mirrors. Reaching for the sink – propping herself up against it, the strawberry dress against the porcelain, her chest heaving – she felt a pair of arms wrap around her.

'You okay?'

Mam's face flicked up in the mirror again, meshed with the face of the woman behind her, so that it was all at once brown and white, smooth and pockmarked, full and emaciated.

Cici Henckle had a cigarette dangling from her lips, which the shattered mirror razored into five different parts. She bent my mother over the sink, a liquid sickness splattering her fingers. 'You go ahead and get it all on up,' said Cici, smoke billowing from her mouth. She was dressed completely in black, a turtleneck, an obsidian necklace, long skirt with tassels. Her hair was dark, too, lopsided and limp around her shoulders. Long hands held Mam up over the sink for half an hour. 'You're whiter'n a sheet,' said Cici as she washed her hands and rubbed some rouge into Mam's cheeks.

Mam said nothing. She was propped against the sink, accepting the rouge, watching the mirror settle itself down. Calcium marks ran like musical notes on Cici's fingernails, moving around Mam's cheeks. 'Who're you with?' said Cici. Mam flicked her head towards the door of the bathroom.

Outside, my father was slumped in a chair, hat on. The magazine had told him that there'd been a mistake, they needed him in New York, they'd written to him in Mexico, the letter mustn't have arrived. They gave him cash for the shots of the copper mines, told him to get on a bus across country.

'Your girl here's sick as a dog,' said Cici, when they came out of the bathroom.

'Come on, love,' the old man said, ignoring Cici. 'We have to go.'

Cici, nonplussed, guided Mam to the chair. She kept one arm wrapped around my mother's waist, and with the other took out another cigarette, lit it, kicked my father's outstretched feet as if it were all just one natural motion. 'Say, lover boy, I said your girlfriend here is throwing up God knows how many years of food. And you're sitting here doing sweet nothing. What sort of goddamn man are you anyway?'

'We have to be somewhere,' he said.

'Where?'

'New York.' He said the words breathlessly, as if there were all sorts of camera bulbs erupting from his throat.

'She's about as fit for New York as that goddamn hat of yours. She needs to see herself a doctor or something. Get some rest.'

My father nodded, lit a cigarette. 'She's just a little seasick.'

'Seasick my ass – this floor isn't rolling, is it?' Cici sat down, leaned towards Mam. 'You can come to my place if you like. Nothing special, but I got an extra bed. Lover boy here's welcome, too. Long as he doesn't make you carry the suitcases.'

Cici's apartment was in an old house on Dolores Street, not far from the Mission. Sickly white azaleas ranged along the wrought-iron railings, and scraps of graffiti welcomed them along the stairwell. The apartment was filthy. Suitcases were stuffed with clothes, and around them lay papers, ashtrays, bottles, half-eaten biscuits, lamps shorn of their shades. A newspaper photo of James Dean, a voluminous quiff of hair on his head, was propped against a wall, three candles beside it. Cici threw the picture a kiss. Mam's head still spun as they laid her down in bed.

Cici didn't have any clean towels available so she dipped a white sock in the sink and mopped Mam's brow. Cici stayed there for almost two days, sitting by the bed in her black turtleneck, cigarettes tight between her teeth as if she was afraid that they might jump from her mouth and leave her. She was thin as a rib, older than Mam, about thirty. She talked to stay awake, wandered around the room, parted the curtain, pointed out trees, named cloud formations, chatted to Mam as evening stole shapes. A poet, Cici had gone to the magazine offices that afternoon to try to sell some work. She had written one book, which had sold one hundred copies, a small beige edition, the spine of which crackled and tore when opened. It was about a summer spent in a fire lookout in Wyoming. She had typed it on a ream of butcher's paper while ensconced in the tower, waiting for fires. The paper had rolled incessantly through her typewriter, collecting in giant curls on the floor while a radio bucked behind her. When the book was printed she stayed in Wyoming for two years, trying to sell it, but only a ranger named Delhart paid attention, touting copies around under the seat of his green pick-up truck, amongst empty coffee cups. She had fallen for Delhart, lived with him in a cabin near the edge of the forest, but left him to come to San Francisco with a suitcase full of the beige books. She read the poems in jazz clubs. Men were strung out on Zen and amphetamines, small dharma dolls hanging from the buttons of their lumber shirts. They clapped their hands together at the feet of trumpeters whose bog-black skin glistened with sweat. Shrines of cigarette smoke rose around the bar. Cici's only payment was a slurp from a jug of red wine, so she had taken a job as a singing waitress in a burlesque club for Asian men. Delhart wrote to her. His letters were full of bottlecaps which she kept in a row under the James Dean picture. Delhart also sent a blade of grass and told her to use it for a ring, quoting Whitman, 'I believe a blade of grass is no less than the journey-work of the stars.'

Mam looked down, through her fever, saw the blade of grass on Cici's finger, encased with tape now, the journey work towards humus.

'You know,' Cici told her, 'you two should come with me back to Wyoming. Not much of a detour.'

She wandered out to the living room where my father was sprawled on the couch. He had a tendency to smack his lips together while he slept. 'Looks like he's eating his dreams,' Cici laughed when she came back in, hovering over Mam: 'So, how about it? Wyoming?'

'I would like,' said Mam.

But later the old man shook his head, looked out the window of the apartment, said they were in a vicious hurry.

'Why you don't wait, Michael?' Mam asked. 'Why don't you wait for a day and we will go then? I need some time to get feeling better.'

I can imagine him nodding, pulling his overcoat around

him, going out to find a phone, calling the magazine in New York and telling them he was unavoidably delayed. For the next two days he stayed out of the apartment during afternoons, while Mam and Cici talked. Walked down by the water and threw smoke rings out over the bay, the collar of his coat turned up even though it was the beginning of summer. Foghorns keened in. Hell-divers swooped down from loaded clouds above the Golden Gate. He swung off the edges of cable cars, camera poised. When he got back to the apartment the two women were there, in yellow rubber gloves, laughing, the apartment clean, the suitcases packed, and a stack of forgotten books in the corner.

They took a bus across a huge slice of America, where interstates weren't even built yet. The roads were long and black and shimmery, sometimes interrupted by wandering cows, or herds of antelope kicking across the tarmac, bounding fences. On the journey Mam was sick again. The bus was stopped every fifty miles, and Cici held my mother as she vomited behind the wheel well. She put her coat around my mother's shoulders, took dry bread out of her rucksack, fed it to her, mopped her brow when Mam began to suffer from another fever. The bus travelled slowly. California stretched itself into a dry desolation; Nevada reared up with sagebrush and juniper; a few wild horses moved in unison through the high desert. Before they got to the Idaho border, the bus almost hit a boy with a dirty white bandage on his thumb. The boy had fallen asleep at the side of the road while hitch-hiking.

'Goddamn it, son,' said the bus driver, who stopped and woke him.

The boy had short yellow hair up in wheatfield rows on his head. It turned out that he was on his way to San Francisco, and Cici gave him a crisp new five-dollar bill and two addresses that he wrote in ink on the side of his burlap sack. Some years later, in the sixties – or so Cici told me – she met the boy again at a party, when they were both strung out on LSD. The yellow hair was longer by then, and the boy gave her back the five-dollar bill – he had soaked it in lysergic acid. They ate the bill together over the course of the next three days. Two months later his body was found washed up on the southern end of Half Moon Bay Beach in California. Cici saw it as a peculiarity of her life that faces and moments kept coming back to haunt her – when I met her she told me that she was amazed at how much that bus journey still moved within her, all the people she met, the things she saw, she could recall it all, the bandages on the boy's thumb, the rattle of the bus engine, the white cloth in her fingers, rubbing its way delicately over Mam's brow.

The old man sat in the seat behind them, amazed by America moving past. He kept his face glued to the window, fingered his cameras.

By the time they hit Boise, my mother was so dehydrated that not even Cici's rouge could help her. They booked into a hotel room, stayed for thirty-six hours while Mam recovered. Cici hovered by the bed and talked about Delhart. He was a brown-bearded brute of a man with pellucid eyes. In particular she remembered his hands – huge boats with dirt under his fingernails. She had thought of those hands often after she went west to see the Pacific – they sometimes caressed her at night in her imagination. She had met him after a fire; he had come up to her lookout one evening and ended up spending the night, loving her, afterwards coughing up reams of smoky phlegm into the pillow.

From Boise they hitched a lift on the back of a pick-up truck and my mother began to feel better, the open air rushing over her, the fevers cooling down, a world settling itself in her stomach. Cici, sitting beside her, feet over the tailgate, stared out at the passing of Idaho: 'Why don't you guys come stay with me for a day or two? I'm not up in my tower until next week.' During the night the pick-up sidled its way to the edge of the Tetons, up narrow switchbacked roads, through forests of fir trees, over huge passes where red-tailed hawks were gliding. They huddled together in the freezing cold, under blankets. Cici lit up a cigarette, twisted at the blade of grass on her finger.

Delhart met them in the morning outside a café in Jackson Hole. The ranger had a scar on his face the shape of a horse's hoof. He kicked at imaginary pebbles. 'I've something to tell you, Cici.' He waved my parents off, took Cici's hand and guided her towards a café with elk antlers on the wall, ordered coffee. Delhart told her that he'd met a Ute Indian woman, he'd been afraid to tell her in any letters. The woman was pregnant. He said they could adopt the child, raise it themselves. Cici leaned back in her chair, watched the sweat that came from Delhart's brow, slowly, in drips down to his chin. 'What is she? A goddamn postman or something? Pony goddamn Express?' 'What d'ya mean?' said Delhart. The coffee landed very neatly on his green shirt. 'You're an asshole,' Cici said, 'don't come near me.' She stirred her coffee as Delhart left, looked at her hands as if they didn't belong to her anymore.

That afternoon Cici, deciding that she wanted to visit her tower in the mountains, borrowed a truck and some keys from another ranger. While my father slept in a hotel at the outskirts of town, Cici and Mam drove down long, winding dirt roads together. Mam sat in beside her, leaning over, comforting her. 'I'm all right,' said Cici. 'It don't bother me none.' The wind rushed through open windows, already threatening fire with its dryness.

Cici carried a jug of wine as they hiked up the five miles

to the lookout tower, said nothing as she climbed, a long green stare from her. My mother trudged behind in a pale yellow dress, up the mountain, around frost-veined boulders, along dirt trails making narrow canyons in the light-shafting trees. They moved up towards the treeline, passed a few remaining snowbanks, stopped together to catch their breath as Cici burst into laughter. 'I don't give a shit about him, he's an asshole.' Cici was whistling to scare any bears that they might stumble upon. She stopped whistling when they hit the edge of some scree, no longer threatened, and slowly negotiated the boulders towards the summit.

It was an astounding place for Mam to see – snow on the northern faces of the mountains, the sweep of green underneath, eagles on the thermals, no dust for miles.

The tower, a small grey building, was perched on the top of the mountain like a bird ready to explode into flight. A lightning rod stuck up, an obscenity in the air. The rotten carcass of a baby deer lay not too far from a rusting water trough. The door of the tower creaked when they entered, and the air was heavy with must. They sat together, lotus-legged on the floor, wrapped in old mangy blankets, wine passing between them. No clouds in the sky to hold the heat in, they shivered in the cold. 'I don't give a shit,' said Cici again. 'I don't give a shit about him, sometimes people just ain't what they seem, you dream them up for yourself, then – shit, I don't care.'

She was plucking at the long strands of hair that fell down over her face, rocking back and forth, her knees to her chest. Her eyes fixed on a spider web, insects caught within it. It moved slightly in the cold breeze that came through the open door. Cici rose and closed it, flicked at the web with her fingers. 'I never gave a shit about him.' The wine went down and later on, while Mam was sleeping, Cici's body was a rhyme, a singular rhyme that slipped its way out of the tower, walked across some scattered rocks, down to the water trough, tripped her way to the edge, drunk, stumbling against the metal sides. She stared down into the water and, reeling with alcohol, chuckled.

She swept insect larvae from the surface of the water, kicked her shoes off, placed her socks neatly in them, laid her hands on either side of the trough, swung her body across and climbed in, felt the coldness through her legs, her spine, her hands, the water sloshing around the edges, some drops jumping out to the ground. She moved in the water, watched the creation of ripples, and then propped her feet and elbows on the edge, lay there, chuckled again – 'I don't give a shit' – watched the night, the stars rioting away, the moon a heap in the west moving towards morning, felt the water weigh her clothes down, the larvae fondling her hair, some fireflies flicking luminescence from their bellies around her, and she laughed as she sat in the tub of rainwater, waiting to freeze to death.

Dawn had left some freckles in the sky and it could have been the most peaceful morning in the world when Mam woke up, indolent birds on the thermals and the insects busy at the ends of long grass stalks and the sun moving itself into yellowness beyond the edge of the lookout. She came out of the tower to yawn off a hangover and saw Cici's body, arms and legs draped over the water trough, blue. '¡Carajo!' Cici's face looked like it might have been prepared for a mass card. Her lips were set into something approximating a smile. The black hair flared out from the whiteness of the skin. The insect larvae had settled now and they clung to her legs, to her thighs. Mam reached in. The water was oily as it lapped up against the trough.

In Mexico she had once picked up the body of a dead bird, amazed at how light the bones were. She reached under Cici's languid back. You are so light, she thought.

Mam propped her hands under the shoulders and began to lift Cici out, the feet languishing behind in the trough, propped up on the edge. Mam tugged again. The feet fell, hard and lifeless, against the ground. She dragged Cici back to the tower. A small cut opened between the toes. Mam looked around the tower, frantic. No radio. She laid Cici down on the floor, took off the wet cothes, wrapped blankets around her cold cold body, put her fingers in under the blankets and rubbed her heart, where there was still a faint slow thumping. Her hands moved furiously, penitently. Mam took off her own clothes and covered Cici with them, put some socks on Cici's feet. 'Michael!' The shout to my father echoed around the mountains. Nothing stirred. '¡Por Dios!' The carcass of the deer rolled up in her mind. She took Cici's hands and placed her fingers in her mouth. For a long time she sucked on the fingers, until she saw the first stir, the head moving sideways a little. Come on. She fitted as many fingers as possible in her mouth, let the warm saliva roll over them, the nails with the calcium marks – when she was a child she had been told that calcium marks, when they rose to the top of the nails, were a sign that she would get a gift. With Mam's tongue down by the lifeline of the hand, Cici moved again.

Mam scoured her hand over Cici's ribcage – my father had told her of the famine in Ireland where once a man and his wife had been found frozen to death by the hearth of an empty fire. The woman's feet were frozen to the man's breastbone where he had tucked them under his shirt to warm them. It was as if they had been nailed there. Mam, her mouth dry, rose up, took the blankets and rubbed them over Cici's body. 'Michael!' Cici's fingers were moving now, slowly against each other, as if counting money. Mam leaned up and whispered things in her ear. She suddenly noticed how grey and bare the tower was, but it was still too cold to drag Cici outside. The sun wasn't high enough. 'Come on!' She took Cici's head in her hands and the head lolled as if broken. There were acne marks on Cici's chin and tiny hairs that stuck out like the needles of conifers. The mouth moved within the pock-marks and Mam went furious again with the blankets. Cici mumbled something and my mother leaned down and left a dry kiss on her forehead.

'You will be all right.'

Keep her warm. Talk to her until the sun rears up further. Try to find some food. 'Michael!' Cici began to move a little more, to almost laugh, tiny exhausted gollops.

From somewhere very far away, down the mountain, came a faint shout. Mam clasped Cici's stockinged feet, rubbed warmth into them. A curious thing occurred as Cici's eyes opened wider – a swarm of giant brown butterflies flocked out from the trees below them, all of them in unison, one giant dun sheet that ran its way through the forest, thousands of them at once, barrelling out, into the trees and upwards again, their wings pound-ing their slender bodies. My mother attributed it to some sort of miracle – there was always a deep need for miracles, she thought. Cici later put it down to the simple vagaries of nature – the butterflies had obviously been flushed from their habitat by an animal in the trees, a threat of some sort, a natural phenomenon.

When my father came up the path with Delhart, half an hour later, he carried a jug of wine. He was amazed to see Mam naked, rocking back and forth in the sunlight, with Cici beside her, under the blankets, dressed in Mam's clothes. A washing line was strung up between pine poles, and Cici's garments flapped, animated in the breeze. 'What happened?' said Delhart to my mother. My mother gave him a vicious look, turned and stared at my father. 'An accident happened, Michael.' Her voice quivering.

Cici looked up from the bed of blankets. 'Oh, it's the lover boys.'

The old man sat down on the ground and took his hat off, left it beside Cici. Delhart went away, down the mountain, without a word, carrying the wine. Mam went over to the washing line and put on Cici's dress.

'I am staying,' she said to my father. 'I am staying here until she's better. And don't ask me for changing my mind.'

Old Father Herlihy didn't recognise me in the Spar. He was in buying a packet of cigarettes, flirting with the girl behind the counter. 'And how's the studying coming along?' he was saying, a glint in his eye. She looked like one of the O'Meara girls, dollops of freckles on her cheeks. Father Herlihy has put on a bit in the girth, it was propped out over his trousers, mashing against the buttons of his thin black shirt. He was shaking absent-mindedly in his black jacket pocket for some matches. The counter-girl gave him a smile and took out a box from the side of the register: 'Don't worry about it, Father, they're on the house.' Out he walked, smiling, straight past me without a second glance. He left fifty pence on the counter and she was in a right tizzy for a moment. She shoved it in her pocket and started looking at her nails, bits of red polish on them. Turned up the radio and smiled at me: 'I love this song,' she said. I must admit it wasn't too bad – felt like slamdancing through the washing powder myself. Filled up five bags of groceries, put three of them in the front basket, hung one on either side of the handlebars.

The black Raleigh was none too comfortable, the springs gone in the seat, and there was a big fat skip in the pedals, a hiccup. It wasn't easy to balance with all the heavy bags, and I had to retrieve a packet of biscuits that skipped out when I grazed against a lamppost. Goldgrain, his favourite. I think they've changed the packet though, and I almost overlooked them in the shop. Got him a pack of Major too, but that's the last one of those I'm going to buy, he'll be hanging his lungs out on the clothesline to dry, like grandmother's rabbits, fluttering away in the wind.

Down along main street, some of the old farmers, fresh from the pubs, were leaning across the doors of their cars. Fine Gael posters from the election strewn out around their wellington boots. One of the farmers was crunching his boot through a politician's face. All the Fianna Fáil signs were still up on the lampposts, looking out over the town, but someone had ripped the others down. The town's not much different, little has changed, a bit like the kitchen. A tawny labrador scrounged around the back of the video shop, nosing his way through the boxes. Inside, two young girls, swamped in bright colours, were staring upwards at the television screens, entranced. Onwards and away, I said to myself. The red tiles on the town lavatory walls hadn't faded a bit. The smell hit me when I went past – a curious cocktail together with the distant sea.

A couple of drowsy gulls moved up from the sea and over the roofs of the houses.

I rode down along the river, chocolate wrappers floating on the surface, past the old house of the Protestant ladies – I've no idea who's living there now, but it looked a bit tumbledown, a rotting hulk of a car in the gateway. A couple of schoolboys hung around in the entrance, throwing pebbles. They gathered together and started elbowing one another. One of them gave me the middle finger – a new gesture in these parts. Heard a truck rumble behind me, beeping madly, and suddenly the created draft sucked me outwards, almost smacking me into the truck.

93

But it felt nice to be out and rolling, that song from the shop jumping around in my throat, all the three miles home, the sea getting closer and closer, me never quite reaching it.

A bird had made a nest in the back of an old discarded fridge near the grotto where we used to scrawl our graffiti. Nothing written on the good Virgin these days, although years ago someone scrawled *Man United Rules* across her chest in vibrant red ink, and there were always great jokes going around about Norman Whiteside knocking in a header from Mary Magdalene, and Bryan Robson putting one over on poor Saint Joseph, and nutmegging the good Lord himself. We would sit with our backs against the gate and slurp our bottles, smoke cigarettes in the cups of our hands so the red glow couldn't be seen from the road. Sometimes there'd be fights in the woods and we'd gather in circles, chant them on. But it seems quiet and litter-free these days, apart from the fridge. I stopped and peered in the big white carcass – thrush eggs sitting on one of the metal racks, down near the vegetable drawer. Twigs wrapped in near the back coil. Some birdshit on the electrical cord. I sat for a while, but a few people stared at me from their cars and I felt a bit strange, got on the bike again. Curious how different the sense of space is here. In Wyoming I can take off and go walking for miles on end without seeing a soul, only a few cattle scrubbing away on the lands, every now and then a horse breaking the hills. Land like that seeps its way into you, you grow to love it, it begins to thump in your blood. But it's confined here, the land, the space. Doesn't feel much like mine anymore – it's like when I'm with the old man, floating around him, not really touching him.

I got used to the skip in the bicycle pedals – a bit like learning to dance with a limp – and I began counting the number of rotations my feet made. Still, it was an effort getting up the hill by O'Leary's pub. Stopped in to see Mrs O'Leary, but there was only a young boy behind the counter, sipping a glass of red lemonade behind the brand-new mahogany bar, lots of plush red seats roaming around the room, not at all like it used to be when Mam came here in the afternoons and chatted with her about chickens and the like. The bartender told me that Mrs O'Leary had passed away three years before, went in her sleep. Felt my stomach sink, had a quick pint of watery Harp, toasted her vast memory, pedalled on.

I came back to the house, a vision of Mrs O'Leary rolling in my head. I had once seen her dance across her bar-room floor with a chair clutched lovingly to her breast, feet sliding in beerstains and her hair thrown back in red ribbons – she was one of the few people around who made Mam laugh.

All of them going, I thought, all of that wild and leaping world on its way out.

The old man still had that Victrola of Mam's in the living room, but it must have conked out years ago. I tried to crank it up and play some mariachi music of hers in honour of Mrs O'Leary, but he just laid his head back in the armchair and shook his head, no. He rose up and went to the kitchen, all lopsided with the pain again. He didn't notice the bags of groceries at the front door. He was going to make himself a cup of instant soup, but, when he lifted the pan off the stove, the boiling water slipped a little. The pan fell down into the sink, toppled over. I heard it gurgling down the drain. He looked at the pan for the longest time, spat down on to it, turned around, saw me.

'I'll put on some soup,' I said.

He ran a hand across his mouth: 'I can put on the fucken water myself, all right?' But he didn't. He brushed past me, back to his armchair. He smelled terrible. This body of his is an effigy, he carts it around on the stick of himself.

I put on the pan – had to wash the spit from the bottom – and made the soup, along with a slice of bread and some butter. He nodded his head, slurped, coughed: 'I could have done it myself, you know.' He finished off his soup, left the mug on the floor, and went to wipe his lips with his hanky – it was caked in snot, with a little bit of blood speckled in it. He tucked the hanky away in his trousers pocket and washed his dish.

I took out the packet of Major and threw it on his lap.

'That's the last of those,' I said.

'Ah, you're a star, Conor, thanks a million.'

'I heard Mrs O'Leary's not around anymore.'

'Oh, she kicked the bucket a long time ago. Chock-full of whiskey, of course.'

'Of course.'

'A grand way to go, I suppose,' he said.

'I suppose.'

'Took four bottles down with her.'

'Took what?'

'Took four bottles down into the ground with her.'

'You're kidding.'

'Bushmills.' He smacked his lips together. 'Someone went along to the graveyard one night and dug up the fucken coffin.'

'You're not serious.'

'Some thirsty bastard,' he said.

He ran his fist across his mouth. 'Talking of – is that tea ready yet?'

He sat back and slowly, ritually, banged the bottom end of the packet against his palm, took the plastic wrapper off, turned one of the cigarettes upside-down. 'For good luck,' he said. I went upstairs and took a shower, got dressed. Came down and asked him if he was interested in going for a pint in O'Leary's, but he just sort of laughed at me.

'What would ya want to hang out with an old fella for?'

I wasn't about to start arguing. Enough of his self-pity. Before I left I went over to the fire, put on some peat, and ruffled it with the poker. He had some of his fishing flies placed on the stonework, to dry them out. He sat up and said that fishing flies were like good women – they should never be stored away while moist – and laughed away as if it was the funniest thing in the world.

I left him sitting in the chair and went back out on the bike again into the boneblack night.

When I came back from O'Leary's, he'd collapsed in the chair. His fly was open like a wound and his hands were down by his crotch. His handkerchief was tucked into the nape of his neck. It was as if he'd been about to serve himself, then forgot. In the kitchen I could tell that he'd been pissing in the sink – he hadn't rinsed it out and there were still two saucers there, one of them with little splotches of yellow on the side. Disgusting. The least he could have done was take out the saucers.

Watched him as he dozed. He raised a hand to wipe something from his eye, maybe some sort of vision, a dream, an absurdity. But I can't imagine him having dreams anymore. What would he summon up? Maybe something slow and soporific, moving itself into blackness, a slow waltz towards oblivion. Or might it be some secret of technicolour? Who knows? Perhaps life goes out as it once came in – down to the secular brilliance of a single hydrogen atom, imploding back on to itself, the emergence of a songdog on the rim of nothing. A fatuous idea really. Too many pints of Harp in me. Didn't recognise anyone in O'Leary's pub, not a single soul, maybe everyone has emigrated. Sat in the corner and flipped a few bar coasters up and down on the table. Plenty of old men in there though, moving their dentures up and down in their mouths, the oval dawns of yellow nicotine stains on their hands.

# FRIDAY

## *god, i was good*

Woke up late, feeling a bit nasty. All that Harp. Nectar of the dogs. He gave a laugh when he saw me, went to the cupboard and got out the whiskey.

'For what ails ya,' he said.

I took a quick shot and drank a few glasses of water. He upped himself from the table, said he was going to go down to catch his fish. But he must have run out of good flies, because he got out some bait from the very back of the freezer shelf – old shrimp of some sort in a plastic container. Boiled water in a saucepan and placed the tub in the hot water, stood over it, inhaling some of the steam, said it was good for cleaning out his head, that I should try it myself. Every now and then he pushed the container down in the water with his fingers, submerging it, licked at his fingers. They must have been burnt from the hot water, but it didn't seem to faze him any. He plucked the plastic tub out, said he didn't have time to wait for the shrimp to thaw, put some of it in his overcoat pocket. Stale shrimp won't help the smell of him any, I thought, once it unfreezes in his pocket it'll really stink him to high heaven. Illegal bait, too, but he said he didn't care, a fish is a fish is a fish, especially if he catches that giant salmon of his.

Took myself off into town on the bike for a bit of breakfast in Gaffney's hotel. Same old place, yellowing table doilies, ducks in flight on the wall, carpet curling up at the edges, the waft of brewing tea, farmers smoking cigarettes in the corners. Sat at the table nearest the door and read the back page of the *Connaught Telegraph*. Ordered up a big feed with extra sausages. The waitress knew me. Took me a while to remember, but I finally did – Maria from the convent school, cheekbones you could abseil, hair to the waist. I used to blow kisses at her when she walked past the handball alley.

She kept coming over to my table with bits and pieces – butter, marmalade, an extra spoon – until she finally asked me. I wasn't in the mood for talking, pretended it wasn't me, put on my best-dressed Wyoming drawl.

Still, nothing better than a few sausages and rashers for a hangover, and I felt like ninety afterwards. Left a pound coin for a tip and she came out running after me, hair flying, said we don't accept tips in this part of the world. She said she knew it was me all along – the dark skin, I suppose – and smiled.

'How long are you back for?' she asked.

Told her about the visa and she said I was lucky, she'd give an arm and a leg to take off herself, she has a brother in Louisiana who shucks oysters, a sister in Washington State doing nursing in a home for geriatrics. I shifted my weight from one foot to the other and fooled around with the buttons on my denim jacket. She asked about the old man, said he used to come in for breakfast every Saturday, she hasn't seen him in a while.

'Oh, he's in flying form.'

'That's great news altogether.'

She was jangling coins in her apron pocket.

'Well, I'll be off,' I said.

'Fair enough so. Come in for breakfast on Monday before ya leave.'

'I will.'

'It's on me.'

I walked back home by the riverbank, wheeling the bicycle. Had to detour by the factory, where they've raised the barbed wire another few feet in the air, the shouts of men amongst the squeals and the shit and the slurry. Sat down a couple of hundred yards from the factory, in the long grass. Had an urge to just get in and swim, even if the water was disgusting, black as berries, the slow roll of it through the rushes. Took off my t-shirt and trousers, hung them on the brambles of a bush, sat in my underwear, feet dangling in the water. A life of half-emergence. A consistency of acceptance. Enough of the old man's disease, I thought. This contagion of days, teacups and nods. A vision of Maria rose up in me, a vertigo of lust and genuine longing. Should go back and sweep her off her feet, roll the coins from her apron in my fingers, do something ridiculously romantic for once, carry her off to the beach, ride palominos along the water's edge, shove ogham stones in our pockets, ride out to sea.

Kowtowed over the riverbank, I decided that I would swim, went into it up to my knees, balanced myself on a few underwater stones, rocked back and forth, and was just about to dive in when I heard a rustle in the bushes near my clothes, maybe a rat or a bird. I got up on to the bank and shook the water from my toes, pulled on my things, walked along towards home, a factory horn ringing out behind me. The old man was there with the familiar routine, and a bitterness sped its way through me as I watched him casting. Something nestled in my stomach and gnawed at me. He lives his life now in the grip of some comfortable anaesthetic.

If I were to choose an anaesthetic myself, I'd probably do what Cici did – have some visions while I'm at it. When I met her, she looked like she could have been grandmother to a hill, but there was a lustful energy in her and the things she remembered. She was living near Castro Street, where all the finest dying in America was done – but Cici wasn't dying, Cici was her own songdog, Cici was still howling in the creation of other days and places.

A summer of fires, that summer of 1956. They licked their way salaciously through the trees. Ran like lizards along-side ridges. Leaped their way over brown streambeds, languished for a while by new ditches and blackened the yellow hardhats that were left hanging on the branches of trees, tongued their way out towards the northern corners of the forest, were beaten back by Delhart and his rows of men, all of whose teeth became the shade of smoke. The fires settled down for a day, then whipped up again with a single cinder carried on the wind. At night the sky was lit up. The east was dappled with orange and the smoke took on different shades, pink and yellow and red, like so many different slices of skin, as if an aurora borealis had decided to stay for a while, to hang on that part of the world, propped up by the mountains, the low rivers, the generous orange violence.

In the forests frightened animals broke for cover. The carcass of a Rocky Mountain elk was found near a fire break, its burnt jaw opened in blackness. An escaping grizzly was shot on the main street of a northern town, lumbering madly on the footpath when it was circled down into the sight of a rifle. After a dozen bullets it fell, letting out a huge desultory cry that was imitated by a madwoman who stood on the corner by a feed store. She screamed so loud that it was said that she tore her larynx to bits. My father was hanging around down by the café and his photo shows her with her arms upstretched towards heaven. Her cry must have echoed its way around the town's Sunday-morning church services, as 'Amen!' after 'Amen!' rang around the pews and preachers searched in the Book of Revelations for words about fires and the blue-hot end of the world. Mouths opened up in hymn as army helicopters flew overhead with bags of water meant to douse distant flames.

Boys made hatbands from the dehydrated snakes – timber rattlers and hog-noses – found at the side of forbidden forest roads. They sliced the snakes open long-ways with their fathers' penknives, skinned them, wore them around their heads as a ritual that signified their stance at the cusp of manhood – another fire about to break. Rocks cracked open in the extraordinary heat. Firs brittled down to stumps. A box of lost bullets exploded near the edge of the forest, the echoed thump of them flushing men from their houses. At night, prayers were remembered by bedsides, and wives tenderly kissed their husbands' fore-heads as they went out the door, yellow jackets hung in the crook of their hands, leather belts carved with their initials around their waists, husband and wife stretching out from one another on an expanding waistline.

An old rancher down by the creekbed refused to leave his stockman's cabin and went up like a Buddhist – the body was taken out on a makeshift stretcher, the flesh of the hands melted into the stomach where he had folded them in anticipation. His grey hair had vanished. The burnt man's funeral was postponed for two mornings as sirens sounded out, summoning men to other fires. When it eventually took place, tired men leaned their heads forward on pews and wept secretly into Sunday handkerchiefs. For the wake, jugs of lemonade were laid on white picnic tables in the brown grass outside the church, and children played with buckets of water, splashed each other. A pall hung over the town. Women leaned against wireless radios to see if the fires had made national news. Buzzards rose and wandered in the alpine air, flapping continuously – sometimes the sky was black with them, descending like so many priests to a Eucharist below.

My father hung around with Delhart and the firefighters. He told them that he was on commission from a New York magazine – in fact, he'd been fired before he had a chance to begin. On the phone they said that they had hired another man. 'Right-y-o,' he said, his throat dry. He got drunk in a town bar that day, drowning both sorrow and a slight elation at the freedom of it all. The young barman, with lemon-coloured hair, had made a special drink for the firefighters, The Bloody Blazer, with a touch of tabasco in it. I can imagine the old man, sitting at the bar counter, taking it down in big gulps, bitter at the thought of losing his chance because his wife happened to like this place, wanted to stay. The drinks, I'm sure, stung the back of his throat, rocked through his belly. He sat with the other men around the bar as they coughed up into bandanas, ditch diggers on an afternoon off, fingers blistered from shovels. Hard men, they were democratically diligent at the buying of rounds. They must have regarded the old man as a foreigner at first – the early photos of them have a comical rigidity, you can almost feel the teeth clenching as they stare into the lens, their features just about recognisable in the windowlight from the bar, smudges of black obscuring their cheekbones.

Every morning the old man descended the mountain to where he kept a bicycle propped up against a fir tree, rode the seven miles to town with cameras strapped around him. The young boys in their snakeskin hats sometimes followed him and stuck out their bony chests when his lens moved towards them. After a while, the rangers and firefighters relaxed for his camera, regarded it with a mixture of off-handedness and anticipation. In solitary shots, he laid a white sheet at their feet, bounced the light up to give them harsh shadows on their faces, while they pretended they weren't interested, hung their heads and rubbed ash-black hands together. They called him 'Irish' because that was what he still exuded – the retreating curls, the green eyes, the big shoulders moving under white shirts. He began to give himself over to that summer, my father, raging along with it all, catching the fires in their magnificence and brutality, even thanking Mam for her foresight in wanting to stay there – these were his best pictures, he was sure of it, they'd make him famous, he had no doubt.

Delhart was the only one who never wanted a photo taken. His face was not unlike the shovels of the ditch diggers – long and brown and weathered and too well used. Delhart hated cameras, had hated them ever since the Depression, when a photographer had gone through his town. He had been very young, and the photographer had gotten him to take off his shirt and show his distended belly. Delhart's mother had ripped the photo to bits when it came out in a book years later, bought up all the copies she could find, burned them in a wood stove.

'You can see around ya with your eyes, can't ya?' said Delhart. 'No sense in using that thing.'

My father simply nodded, said nothing.

Delhart moved like a war general around the fires – the movement may have kept his mind off his problems. Whisperings abounded that he had gotten the Indian girl pregnant. Someone had seen him digging a fire ditch at the back of her house to protect her, but nobody brought it up, it was a sensitive issue, a ranger with a native American girl. Little was known about her because she never spoke to anybody, but there were rumours, and the rumours grew with her silence. Her speechlessness was attributed to having had her tongue cut out at a reservation in Utah, in punishment for her doing the same to a dozen magpies. Or her father had been a medicine man who had mistakenly caused her voicebox to burst with a potion. Or she had eaten the bones of squirrels and they had stuck in her throat. It was said that her name was Eliza. Her eyes were dark and hollowed, like someone who had suffered, but there was a beautifully fluid quality to her movements, as she hoed the soil in the back of her cabin. Some said she was a prostitute, but when men went to pay her a visit, she took a shotgun from behind the door and silently threatened them with it.

Delhart said nothing about either Cici or the Indian girl, but the old man had seen a copy of Cici's book under the driver's seat of Delhart's truck, the beige-coloured spine cracked, all sorts of recent sootprints on the pages. He figured that Delhart was still in love with Cici and that things would eventually work out, but kept his musings to himself.

Cici brushed the thought of Delhart aside, and developed a vague and manic sparkle in her eyes. She and Mam leaned into the radio, pinpointing co-ordinates on giant brown maps, looked out over the fires, reported them to rangers below. 'Shit, girls, you're lucky, it's a madhouse down here.' The lookout and the mountain stayed intact. Smoky skies drifted by. The heavy wooden door creaked and groaned. Boiling water on their small stove, my mother swore that she could hear the bubbles bouncing off one another. It took ages to boil at that high altitude. Her own breathing came back to her in soft, regular patterns. While Cici wrote her poems, Mam went walking outside. The days stretched out on elastic, time passing with the rhythm of silence. And the silence collapsed into itself – a falling pebble on the scree, a cicada beating the plates of its abdomen, a call on the radio, a deer nudging up to the salt block down near the treeline, an insect moving in the outhouse, all of it became part of the quietness. Even the pine needles down in the forest broke with a brittle roar when she stepped upon them. The outhouse rustled with spiders, and when lime or ashes were thrown down to stifle the smell, flies rose up from the bottom.

In the tower an immaculately clean horse's skull was nailed on the wall, looking down over an iron cooking stove, one chair, a table, a bed, a few cupboards, a rucksack frame. Other lookouts from previous years had scrawled graffiti on the walls. For a joke a spiralling staircase was nicknamed 'Yeats' after the gyre of his poems. Cici wrote a letter of his name on every second step. She laughed that she climbed Yeats every morning, rattled him, swept him clean, descended him with her binoculars in hand, perched on him and read, ran her hand along his banisters, stood in the middle of the 'A' and made her pronouncements to the world.

Cici and Mam took in the relative humidity of the world, the maximum and minimum temperatures, the quickness of the wind, the speed of the clouds, the upkick of dust, the possibility of more blazes, radioed them back to the headquarters. The distance of a storm was measured by counting the seconds between lightning and the receipt of the thunder blast. And it was up those stairs, surrounded by reams of graffiti, that Cici wrote her poems, reading them from the staircase when she was finished. Mam enjoyed her friend's wild rantings, the sounds thrown out around the tower, laid her head on Cici's shoulder, listened.

At first all three of them slept on the same floor, like a row of coloured biscuits in their sleeping bags. But Cici went crazy over her writing one night – she hadn't put a word down in three days and she stalked around the tower, ripping up pieces of paper and throwing them around. 'What the hell are you guys here for, anyway? Get away!

Get out of here!' My parents took their sleeping bags outside and heard the faint echo of high-pitched rants from within the tower. Every now and then Mam went up to make sure there wasn't another episode like the water trough. She still half-expected to see Cici dangling from a rope above a kicked chair, the manic sparkle having its own darkness.

Cici apologised the next day, but my parents grew to enjoy those cold nights outside, where swarms of insects sang. The old man set up a small camp for them down near the treeline, fashioned an elevated platform from some pine poles, frapped it with red twine. Only when the lightning was bad did they stay in the tower. A small stepladder led up to a five-foot-high platform that creaked when they walked upon it. Mam climbed down in the mornings, isolated the sounds, gulped them down, let the air rush over her body. Some photos were taken when the sun came up, my mother unclothed once more, but more subtle, more precise around the edges than the ones from Mexico. There was one of her simply lying in a rope hammock, her body meshed into a series of diamonds where the ropes were tied, one knee raised slightly in the air to cover herself, a bandana tied around her hair; another of her pulling on a pair of forest-ranger trousers which my father had borrowed from Delhart, with her surprised by the camera, breasts exposed, mouth in the shape of a lemon; and one sitting in a blouse and underwear, propped up against a tree, eating a sand-wich, watching the weather, gazing around as if there wasn't a fire for miles.

Cici told me that, from a distance, she watched some of those photos being taken, and she envied my mother the use of her love. At times, despite herself, Cici still thought of Delhart and his boat-hands, let them row her through blackened trees and things that roared up from the pieces of fizzling sap.

\*

Got to thinking about Cici again today while the old man was chasing his fish down there.

In San Francisco she was ensconced in a flat near Castro Street, on the third floor. I walked up the stairs, nervous, the backpack pulling against my shoulders. The walls of the apartment building were freshly painted, and a kid in short pants was sniffing at them. The sound of a distant piano rolled through the apartments. A cactus plant had been overturned in the hallway, bits of rock strewn around it. I sidestepped the pebbles, knocked on her door, introduced myself. She let me in, past a mountain of junk letters at her feet, as if she had known me all her life.

'How did you find me?'

'Dialed information,' I said.

'Why didn't you call?'

'I didn't know if you'd want to see me.'

'Oh, God, of course I would,' she laughed, ushering me in further, silver bracelets jangling on her wrist.

I looked around. A mirror on the wall wasn't generous to her. Her hair was quartzite-grey, flecks in it, her face the same colour. I dropped my backpack on the floor. Doodles ran along the margins of a newspaper, happy faces in a row down the page, in red ink. Some macaroni was caked on the inside of a saucepan left lying on the floor.

'I brought you some flowers.'

'Aren't you just lovely?'

'Do you have a vase?'

She didn't reply. She looked at the ceiling: 'How's your mother?'

'She's fine.'

'Oh lovely, lovely, lovely.'

'Have you heard from her?' I asked.

She looked at me curiously. 'No.' She closed her eyes. 'Say, that's a heavy bag you've got there.'

'Been travelling a while.'

'Hey, why don't you just stay here with me forever?'

'Pardon me?'

'Forever and an extra day.'

'Yeah, okay.' I nodded. 'She never writes to you, no?'

'Never. Haven't seen a Christmas card in – oh . . .' Her voice fell away. 'I really don't know how long.'

'I see.'

'Say, what's your name again?'

'Conor.'

'Ah, yes, how could I forget that? You look just like her, you know.'

The television set was covered with a sheet of white crêpe paper – Cici liked watching it with the sound turned down, a magical box producing a weird flare-out of colour. You could see the fibres in the paper and the fuzzy static lifting it away from the screen. She had taped the crêpe paper to the top of the television set so that if she wanted to watch something on television she could just lift the paper up.

She moved over to the sofa, stretched out, lay back and laughed, a loud cackle that rang its way around the apartment, the shelves lined with amulets, a strange foot-long marijuana bong on the coffee table, the mantelpiece full of candles, a few paintings on the wall, some O'Keefe prints, a Warhol imitation. She wore a white nightdress, hair tumbling down to her shoulders. She might as well have stepped off the stage of a Tennessee Williams play. It seemed that she had scattered herself all over the country for years, came back to Castro Street, where people flowed in and out of her apartment. She entertained them with syllogisms. Women swanned in, and she chattered with them about how to keep your gums, your fingernails, your virginity – maybe all three at once. She told stories of beat writers who had taken all three from her. Hollow-faced men knocked on the door, looking to talk about how their body cells were being destroyed, beaten down. They brought her flowers – her place was a riot of flowers. Cici rattled on about movement and politics, about stasis and love, about the romantic muckheap of the sixties, about men who'd gone down in Vietnam – 'occidental death,' she called it. She was a shaman of sorts, a holy rage lived in her. And she always prefaced her stories with a single phrase, 'Lord, I remember.'

That first night, when her apartment was quiet, Cici's face dropped when I told her what had actually happened with Mam.

'Jesus,' she said, 'I had no idea.'

She rolled her eyes sadly and jabbed in under her fingernails with a toothpick when I asked her again: 'No, no, I haven't heard a single thing, imagine that. She just left?'

'Upped and left,' I said. 'Without so much as a note.'

'Where did she go?'

I shook my head.

'Did you try Mexico?'

'Of course.'

'Nothing?'

'Nothing.'

She went to the kitchen and came back with a bottle of vodka and some ice cubes, poured two glasses, stared at the wall.

'Tell me about the fires, Cici.'

'Why's that?'

'I just want to know.'

'Why?'

'She used to talk about them. My old man, too.'

'Ah yes, your father. How is your father?'

'Haven't seen him in a while. He's home in Mayo.'

She pursed her lips and shrugged.

I sipped at the vodka. 'So tell me about the fires.'

'Oh, everyone around here talks about old times,' she

said. 'Day in, day out, I talk about old times.'

I nodded.

'I mean, that's all anybody ever talks about. What it was like back twenty, thirty, a million years ago.' She moved a little on the sofa. 'You know what I think?' she said. 'I think memory is three-quarters imagination.'

I sat back.

'And all the rest is pure lies,' she said.

'Yes, yeah, I know what you mean.' I mashed my hands together.

I knew what she meant, yet she sang to me like a wren, on and on, memories of startling lucidity, incidents pouring from her, a threnody of nostalgia, nightdress billowing in the breeze from a fan. And Cici remembered that look on my mother's face, in the broken mirror – 'Lord, I remember' – as if it had happened just yesterday.

A smile hung permanently at the edge of her mouth. At any moment I expected some sort of clap to sound out around the theatre of herself, and she'd draw her hand to her lips and cock her head sideways and say, chuckling, to an enraptured audience: 'God, I was good.' Then she might look up again from the rim of her nightdress, questioning: 'Wasn't I?'

I saw her late that first evening, moving a needle around her legs. The tracks stood out on the inside of her thighs, which I suppose were one of the few hidden places left she could inject. I stirred in my bed, on the floor. She caught my eye. The needle flickered momentarily.

'Oh God,' she said. 'Did we put sugar in the flower water?'

The needle sunk in.

'I always forget about the sugar in the water,' she said.

She pushed the top of the needle.

'Are you all right, dear?' she said to me.

'Yeah, I'm fine.' I sat on the floor, curled my feet into my stomach. 'Why do you do that?'

'Makes the flowers last longer.'

'No,' I said. 'That.'

'Oh.' She looked at the needle, twirled it in her fingers. 'It's just a little something.' The sofa gathered her in and she sat back, eyes closed, sat up suddenly, looked at me: 'Did you know that Morpheus was the god of dreams?'

She had finagled a permanent supply from a local doctor in return for four first-edition books by minor beat poets. She wasn't addicted, she said, just an occasional habit that she'd developed recently. She sat on the side of the sofa, leaned across to me. 'No more stupid poems,' she said, 'I don't do stupid poems anymore, poetry isn't worth a damn. I'd much rather sit here and talk. There's a grace in doing nothing, don't you think?'

There was a roll of butcher's paper in the corner of her flat, but no typewriter around. At times she picked up the bong from the table and twirled it in her fingers. It was draped with a bear's claw. Somehow Cici ended up with it after it had been confiscated from another tower by a forest ranger in the sixties. She had given up dope, stuck entirely to morphine, but she had a few dime bags hidden in the bottom of her underwear drawer. The grass was old and dried-out, but I smoked some of it anyway, letting the bear's claw scratch my lips, letting her world drip around me.

I stayed with Cici for three weeks. She took to calling me 'babe.' At times she was frantic with energy, moving up and down the apartment, opening the door, letting people in. Sometimes she moved to the balcony and conducted conversations with people down on the street, dropping words from on high. The traffic roared and men linked hands, waved up at her, wrapped into each other. A woman was pulled along by a wolfhound, her anaemic overcoat flapping behind her. Sirens rang out, the street in full throat. The barbershop pole swirled in red and white and blue – a sign outside mentioned clean razors for a shave. A man with a sandwich board advertised the street as Sodom and Gomorrah – he was like Moses out there, a sea of people parting around him, a pillar of salt.

One evening, when Cici was sleeping, I stepped out on to the fire escape. A man on the opposite side of the street was standing on his balcony, gyrating his heavy hips, singing malevolently into a hairbrush. He saw me, but he didn't flinch, kept on singing. He was middle-aged and wore a necktie, but no shirt. A few words from old Cole Porter songs filtered across, over the traffic. He sang with an ineffable longing, the hairbrush moving like a swinging trapeze around his lips. Sometimes he twirled the brush around in his fingers, picked clumps of hair from around the teeth. Cici stepped out on the fire escape with me, put her hand on my shoulder.

'Babe,' she said.

She stood beside me and sang 'You're the Top' with the man, a doppelgänger of voices, out of synch with each other, drifting over the traffic. She winked at the man, who tucked the hairbrush in his back pocket and smiled, put her arm around my waist, guided me back inside, put some hot milk on the stove to help us sleep. In the morning a skin had developed over the milk, which hadn't been touched. Cici scooped it off with a spoon. 'You're the top,' she said, laughing, as the skin of the milk was thrown down into the drain.

It was a vibrant and eclectic place, and Cici fitted in perfectly, a living cornice, among the bits of white bricks, pieces of old wood, crumbling cement around her. In the afternoons she was thankful to have someone who would cook. I made a stir-fry and concocted a chocolate dessert which she left sitting on her plate. 'It just looks too nice to eat,' she said, 'don't you think so, babe?' With her fork she made another happy face in the chocolate pudding. Behind her the crêpe paper was swimming in colour. She tried desperately to remember my name every day, but couldn't, yet she recalled things that had happened years ago as if they had just occurred, an irrepressible want to live them again, a misery that she never would, a pilgrimage into desire. Cici no longer saw me as a visitor. She left the door of the bathroom open when she went to the toilet. The nightdress hitched up on her legs when she sat on the sofa. I turned my back when she got out her needles, filled the bowl of the bear's-claw pipe, floated away.

The Haight, she said, had been momentary, sexual, magical to her. The mid-sixties – a decade after the Wyoming fires – had seen her swinging her hair around, strung out on LSD, bracelets around her neck, hard skin on the bottoms of her bare feet. I went down there to check it out, stood on the corner of Haight and Ashbury, found myself swamped in old bearded men begging for money, and a fresh sourdough smell hovering through the air. Its re-creation was its sadness – ponytails, nose-rings, compact discs, expensive beads, a shirt with a peace sign drawn into the badge of a Mercedes-Benz.

In the park a juggler threw oranges. She was wearing a short tank top, and every now and then would push her hand across her breast, to wipe away sweat. She noticed the small tricolour I had sewn on the outside pocket of my daypack. 'Advertising,' she joked, 'everyone loves the Irish.' She was from Galway, but not a trace of accent was left. We walked to City Lights bookstore and I looked for Cici's poems among the rows of beat poets, but they weren't there, and we went on to a bar, played pool – she juggled Guinness bottles in the air. 'I'm a tosser,' she said, and all of a sudden the Irish accent was back. 'Ah go on, give us a goozer.' She leaned into me, kissed me, and I put my arms around her, but then she whispered that I looked like someone she'd once known. I left, hailed a cab.

I sat back and watched San Francisco move by. The whole world was looking for someone who was gone.

Night birds flew over Castro and, down the sidestreet, Cici was awake under them.

'I like Frisco,' I said to her, still a bit drunk.

'Oh, don't call it Frisco, babe, only tourists call it Frisco, call it, let me see, call it the whitewhite city.'

'Okay.'

'I met someone tonight.'

'That's nice, just don't fall in love.'

'I won't.'

'Oh go ahead, for crying out loud.'

'Go ahead what?'

'Fall in love, lose your heels, fall in love with a million of them.' She rubbed her eyeballs. 'And let me tell you something – all at once is best.'

'Fair enough.'

All at once in love with a million women from the whitewhite city – it could have been Cici's epitaph.

A man came and collected two months of bills. He shoved his foot in the door to keep it open, waving the bills in our faces, threatening court action. I paid the bills for Cici. She was astounded: 'Don't do that, babe, oh God, you don't have to do that.' It wasn't charity, I just wanted to lose something of myself in that room. It was pathetic, but money was all I could think of. Guilt assailed me – Cici was exhausted, I had dredged up things in her that maybe would have been better forgotten. In the deli I stocked up on food and wine. I cooked up a meal of beans and tacos, and we drank a little white wine, toasted my mother. Cici said, simply: 'To Juanita.'

A taxi beeped for me underneath the apartment next morning. I could just about hear it above the noise.

'You really can stay if you want to.'

'I'm on my way to fall in love with a million women.'

'What a great idea, take me with you.'

'Okay, come on.'

She laughed and shook her head.

'See you,' I said.

I kissed her on the cheek.

She drew herself back, pouted comically, wrinkles puckering into her cheeks, pointed at her lips, pursed them again. We laughed. She held the back of my hair, and ran one hand along my back as our lips touched. I wanted to kiss her again, but didn't.

'Where to now?' she asked, letting go of my hair.

'I have a bus ticket to Wyoming.'

'Say hello to it for me.'

'Can I call it Wyoming?'

'You can call it whatever you like, babe.'

'Okay.'

'And say hello to Juanita when you see her. Tell her she owes me a letter.'

The taxi took me past the whiteness of San Francisco. Cici's face came with me, all cratered. She had promised me that she would give up the morphine but just before I left I saw her, ferreting down her thighs with another small needle, looking for a place without a bruise. 'Just one more,' she said, chuckling, the euphoria already washing its way over her. 'You know, babe, you have to go slow with these things.'

One morning, when dawn had finished its rumour, and the old man was gone for the day, she and Mam were languishing together down near the camp.

Mam wore a magenta dress that buttoned at the front. The row of white buttons ran all the way to the hem. Her brown legs emerged, twigs. She was lying back in the grass, shielding her eyes from the sun. Cici was beside her, her head propped on her hand. 'It'll rain one of these days,' said Cici. She moved slightly, in a disguise of nonchalance. The shadow over my mother's eyes lengthened infinitesimally. Cici held a blade of grass between the gap in her front teeth. An insect landed on Mam's stomach, and Cici moved to brush it away. Her hand hovered over Mam's body for a moment, fell slowly and laid itself on her belly. Nothing was said. The insect flew off. The shadow was held. Cici's fingers made little circles around one of the buttons. Traced the outlines. Only the very tip of her fingers touched their way inside the gap between the buttons, moved against Mam's skin. It was a tiny demesne of stomach that Cici wandered over with her fingertips, and maybe my mother moved her head in some sort of ecstasy, maybe her black hair scrunched itself into the ground, maybe her back arched itself up to make a bridge of air beneath her, maybe she waited for the fingers to explore further, maybe she thought there would never be any rain, but Cici pulled her hand away and began to laugh.

She rose and went bounding away to the tower. Mam found her later, enmeshed in maps, talking on the radio to one of the rangers. The two of them held hands for a moment as a voice hacked through the radio: 'Have you two gone barmy up there yet?'

They went back down to the water trough, and Mam slipped in, wearing the magenta dress, to see how it felt. The water wasn't cold anymore. They had swept the larvae from the surface. She slapped the water out around her with her hands, put her head fully under, came up with her hair tangled. Cici sat down beside her at the edge of the trough and scribbled in a notebook – doodles and squiggles that later formed a lyric. It was a fabulous moment, Mam and Cici together – or so Cici told me – letting the sky drift past, saying nothing. Later the dress was hung out on the line to billow. My mother went back down to the camp and made some sandwiches for my father's dinner.

When the old man came back that night, I'm sure they climbed the stepladder and lay down to sleep, as usual, arms reaching around one another. An owl maybe hooting in the trees, dropping balls of hairy scat on to the world, like a gift.

Delhart's baby came the next week.

The ranger and my father had been sitting in the bar, their clothes smothered with the smell of smoke, when Eliza came in. She was in her early twenties, but strands of white already flicked through her hair, falling out of its braids. She had a face that looked like it had been fashioned from some brown bank of soil. Her dress was wet where the water had broken, but she carried herself well. The barman moved from behind the counter to swat her away as if she were a fly, but Delhart rose and moved to Eliza. She clenched her teeth, all wild arms and acrimony: 'I want you to see what it's like,' she said. Eliza folded over and clutched at her stomach. They were the first words that anyone had ever heard from her. Delhart pushed the bartender aside and took her into a backroom, hitched her dress around her waist.

The old man ran out to find the doctor, but he was off on another call – a boy had burnt the palm of his hand in a smouldering field while searching for snakes.

When my father returned, Eliza's teeth crunched down on a very thick piece of cardboard. Beads of sweat were erupting from her brow. A smudge of blood stained Delhart's arm, the baby already halfway into the world, guided now by four old women, who fretted and coaxed. 'You men know nothing!' My father went outside to wait, where the bartender smiled deliriously – news of the birth had spread and dozens of people had gathered in the bar, watching the grey snow on a television screen. A hum drifted around the bar, speculation about whether Delhart was the father at all. Some women were hoping the baby would look like him – they muttered that there were too many brown-skinned people in the town already.

When the baby boy was born he was dark under the blood, dark as Eliza's neck, coal-coloured hair scattered on his head. One of the women asked Eliza what she would call him. 'Kutch,' she said, almost spitting the word out. It meant 'dark one' in her own language. Delhart carried the baby out into the bar, wrapped in towels, as if he were some sort of godsend, but Eliza called the ranger back, said she wanted him to have nothing to do with the baby, she would raise him on her own – if Delhart ever came to her cabin he would end up like the grizzly that had stumbled into town at the beginning of summer. In the background, word filtered from a radio that lightning had hit one of the northern ridges and that there might be new, even more ferocious fires the next day. There weren't any more fires. Clouds came, and for the next week rain teased intermittently, the clouds sat above the mountains like strange horses. But they were spooked by the need and they shrugged and meandered on north towards Canada. From their lookout, Cici and Mam watched insects flicker around rocks, birds gather on trees, their southern flight imminent. Animals howled from a distance and at times Cici yammered back at them.

She had heard about Delhart's baby and shrugged as if tossing off a blanket. 'I still don't give a shit.' But her poetry was full of births – seeds bursting from pods, scattering on a Wyoming wind, a black bear in the forest, hysterical for her cubs, two golden eagles spiralling downwards while mating on the air. Rolls of paper gathered on the lookout floor. Mam made her cups of tea and sometimes they went walking, put their arms around one another's waists, sang to keep the bears away. Cici taught her what she knew of weather patterns in the area, the names of certain clouds in English, the white filmy cirrus, stratus, the flat-based cumulus, the cumulonimbus which would, one day soon, pile precipitation down on them and finish their summer. Mam learned how to gauge the relative humidity. She sometimes chatted on the radio with the other operators.

'This is gonna be my last summer here,' said Cici, on one of their walks.

'What are you going to do?'

'I don't know, maybe go back to San Fran.'

My father came up the mountain, drunk, breathless. He'd decided he would publish a book of that summer's photos, and said maybe he'd include a poem of Cici's. Cici said nothing. That night he drank a jug of wine on his own, and in his imagination he was in New York City, where he wore a big black overcoat and a lopsided beret to a publishing party where the only fires were the ones under trays of hors-d'œuvres, keeping them warm. He got drunk late into the night, and read, for the first time, Cici's poems. The old man never said a word about her poetry again – they were worlds apart, he and Cici. He razored the beard off his cheeks, ran a comb through his hair, looked down the mountain, wondered where he and Mam would go.

Young Miguel's maps might have flashed through his mind. The smell of clay. All those jagged edges for cities.

They ended up waiting for the rain, all three of them together. In the evening they watched the fires flickering in the east, and in the morning they stood rooted to their shadows and watched the play of dark clouds across the valleys. From the top of the mountain, they could see all the way across to Idaho. My father took pictures of the tower, the radio, the cobweb in the corner, the aggregation of daddy longlegs that throbbed on the eastern side of the building, curious rhythmic pulsations that made them look like a single giant organism, as if they were warding off some predator. There were pictures of the water trough, the trees, their camp, his bicycle leaning against a tree. My mother packed their bags. They had no real idea where they might end up next, but they had to go somewhere, in a few months the whole of their summer would be covered in snow. They gazed at the clouds fattening in the sky, puffed up like so many swollen chests. Outrider billows blew across, promising squalls and cataracts and downpours. When the rain eventually came it was the hardest, purest, greyest, most beautiful rain any of them had ever felt in their lives. It whipped in massive sheets across the world that leaned towards autumn and caused the fires to smoulder and collected in rivulets and slammed against berries and dripped from trees and caused seeds to burst and melted the salt blocks and pocketed the brightness and puddled the dry, dry ground. All three of them stood outside the tower, and they let the rain drive itself refreshingly into their faces. Afterwards the clouds lightened and the air seemed clean enough up there to cause nose bleeds.

Mrs McCarthy came over with food for him this afternoon. Roast spuds and a big breast of chicken. Don't know what drives her to bring the odd dinner to the old man – nobody else in town could care less. Some sort of Christian charity, I suppose. She was a bit surprised to see me, but she brightened up soon enough and asked me if I was going to mass on Sunday. Gave her a bit of a wink and told her I'd be there the following week, come rain, hail, or shine.

The old man surprised me when he stood up and took the plate from Mrs McCarthy, announced with a flourish of his hand: 'I'm so hungry I could eat a farmer's arse through a hedge!'

He sat in the big chair and the gravy tumbled down his chin. Later, Mrs McCarthy came back grinning and brought a plate for me too.

'God bless ya,' she said to me, looking around the kitchen, 'I see you've done a spot of cleaning for him.'

He went fishing until nightfall, six hours of ferocious stupidity, for nothing this time, not a bite. It was cold when he came in and went up to his bedroom, said he didn't want to fall asleep in the chair, it's giving him a backache, there's a draft coming through the window. I made him a hot whiskey, lots of sugar, but no cloves in the cupboard. Brought the whiskey up on the old silver tray, draped a white towel over my arm for a joke, swished my way through the door, shouting 'Room Service!' and he was squatted down, by the dressing table, naked, bent over a handheld mirror, examining something on his backside. His legs came down, spindle-like. There was a small chain of blood on the inside of his buttocks, dried there. He was staring at it and he had a washcloth in his hand, about to wipe the blood away.

'Oh Jesus, sorry,' I said, backing towards the door, and he rose up, some pleistocene beast, grunted, lunged towards the door, stopped for a moment, perplexed by himself, one hand gripped on the frame, peering around it.

'What do you want?'

'Nothing, nothing.'

'Get the hell out of here,' he said, bringing his trousers up from around his ankles.

'I'm sorry.'

'Go on now and get the fuck out of here.'

'Are ya all right?'

'I'm marvellous.'

'I was only –'

'There's a door to knock on, isn't there, man?'

'I wanted to surprise –'

'Well, ya did that.' He walked back through the room – it was almost comic the way his feet moved in the dropped trousers. He cupped his hands around himself even though his back was turned. 'Ya surprised me all right,' he said. 'Now leave me alone.'

'What's wrong with ya? Are ya sick?'

He looked at me, squinted: 'I've a nose bleed in me arse, what d'ya think is wrong with me, for crissake?'

'I don't know.'

'Ah, go away, son, for Jaysus sake.'

I placed the tray at the bottom of the door, went downstairs, grabbed my jacket, sat on the outside stoop, stared at the agitated Mayo sky, clouds skidding along across the gibbous moon. The marmalade cat came up and crooked herself in the inside of my knee and I stroked her. The wind whipped across the yard, the wheelbarrow by the barn rocked a little from side to side, even the river might have been moving. Some ashes flew out of the firepit. I heard the old man rumbling in the kitchen, bashing around in the cupboards, and after a while the high whistle of the kettle broke through. I pushed open the bottom of the door and went inside. The button of his trousers was still open at the top. He was staring at the fire stain on the wall, some hot whiskey in his hand. But he had forgotten the metal spoon and a crack had formed down the edge of the glass, the whiskey streaming out on to his fingers. He stood there as if he didn't feel it.

'I thought I better tell ya,' he said.

'What?'

'It's only the grapes of wrath.'

'What?'

'The grapes of wrath.'

'Steinbeck?'

'Haemorrhoids,' he said.

He kept staring at the fire stain on the wall and I didn't know whether to laugh or not.

'Must be Mrs Mc's food,' I said.

But he acted as if he didn't hear me and just stood there,

licking his finger for some reason and smearing it against the fire stain on the wall, turned around and put his arm on my shoulder, rubbed along it, quite tenderly.

'I want to be on my own for a while, Conor.'

I gave him his space. Walked down the full length of the river, the banks widening, a few ox-bow lakes created by its meander, all the way along the reedy edge towards the graves of the Protestant ladies, cleared away some of the gravestone weeds, hunkered down, looked out towards the river as it emptied slowly into the sea. There were lights out on the ocean, boats bobbing away in the rough water, bits of phosphorescence on the waves. Enough nothingness, I said to myself. Enough of this half-emergence. I scrambled down to the beach, hopped around on the sand for a moment, took off my clothes, stepped to the edge of the water, waded slowly up to my thighs, dove in, came up laughing and freezing, and I swam for fifteen minutes until it felt warm, suspended myself in the float, let big waves carry me in, caught glimpses of a satellite in the tremendous shrinking of the night, felt strangely light in the holiness of silence as the water lapped over me – the light hitting my eyes might have come from a star long imploded – big salty crests of water pulling me down and shoving me upwards, throwing me about, exhilarated in the darkness. Nothing wrong with being romantic, I said to the sky. To hell with the curse on sentimentality. I felt alive at last and the long grasses were bowing on the shore and the wind brought an invigorating chill and the moon sprayed out light and I thought I heard two old women laughing along with me, raising white parasols to the sky to stop the raindrops, and saw the vision of one of the women, Loyola, appearing along through the waves saying: *Don't be so hard on him, he's about to die,* and I said, No he's not, no he isn't, it's only the grapes of wrath, and laughed maniacally to myself at the ridiculousness of it all, went on swimming, saying hallelujah to the stars, rave on, rage on, flapping my arms, roaring stupidities at the night, thinking he's a cantankerous old bastard, my father, always has been, always will be, submerged myself once more, seawater stinging my eyes, came up chuckling, swam around the shoreline, let waves carry me in. Clambering out of the sea, I ran along the beach to get warm, my hand cupped over myself until the wind picked up stronger, and it got so cold that I could hardly see and my teeth began chattering and I dressed hurriedly, hopping on the sand, and ran my way along the riverbank towards home, making paths and swaths through the rushes, knocking them backwards with my hands, and they bent for a moment, then rebounded. Back in the house, I pulled a blanket around myself, shivered in the kitchen. He had left the bottle of whiskey on the table for me, and I drank two glasses in his honour and said to myself, shivering: I might even miss the old bastard when I leave, although I doubt it.

# SATURDAY

## *a burst of blue herons*

Went to town – smell of sea salt still in my hair – and bought my train ticket to Dublin, got him some haemorrhoid cream in the chemist. He was embarrassed by it when I gave it to him, retreated his way up the stairs, humming a bit of a tune.

'You have to sing every now and then,' he said to me from the top of the stairs, 'it's the only way of pissing on doom.'

He waved the little tube of cream in the air.

I laughed and went out to the barn, started nailing down a few of the stray aluminium sheets that have popped through the rivets over the years. The barn's in terrible shape, looks a bit like my cabin. Won't last another winter. Used the ladder to climb up on the roof. I was there an hour or so, switching a couple of the metal sheets, turning down the jagged ends, putting in new rivets. Some of the beams were a little soft and woodwormed, the nails sank right into them. The sky was the colour of old jeans and I sat back to watch a ziggurat of geese make their way through it. They flew over the house and my eyes followed them. Leaning against the ladder, I caught sight of the postman's van driving along the lane, Jimmy Kiernan from school at the wheel. He parked his van, rang on the doorbell. Trash metal blasted from a ghetto-blaster on the passenger seat. I could have called out to him, over the music, but Kiernan was one of the last people I'd have wanted to speak to, and I just let him ring away.

Kiernan had a bit of a paunch and his silver lightning-rod earring caught the light, his pasty-white skin like the flabby underbelly of a herring. He banged on the front door.

The curtains at the old man's window were open and I saw him walk across in his vest and open the window latch, lean his head out.

'Package,' said Kiernan.

'What's that bloody racket down there?' the old man shouted down.

'Package!'

'That's grand, leave it there.'

'Ya have to sign for it.'

'Sign it yourself.'

'Jaysus!' said Kiernan, leaving the small brown parcel on the doorstep. He wheeled around and I'm sure he must have seen me, but I leaned further into the ladder and looked riverwise, laughing to myself at the old man's stubbornness. Kiernan stood for a moment, clicking his fingers, climbed into his green van, and left with his arm propped up on the open window, the music fading off.

My father came out, still in his string vest, carrying a wooden tray. The cat came up and rubbed against his calves, but he leaned down and pushed her away gently. He sat on the doorstep, put the box on his lap, opened the package. There were a few small things inside, plastic packages that looked like dimebags, others like matchboxes. He took them out deliberately and placed them in the wooden tray, put the invoice in his pocket, knocked the empty cardboard box with his hand, rolling it against the drainpipe. He took a bare fish-hook out, put it between his lips – maybe remembering his Mexican fishing days with Gabriel – and walked across the yard to the barn with the barb of the hook sticking out of his mouth.

I had one of the metal sheets off the barn, could see down below – an old lawnmower, shovels, a turf-cutter that has never been used, a few potato sacks. He shuffled into the barn and dragged a seat across to a counter that he must have built when I was away. Motes of dust settled down around the barn as he sat, some of them flicking upwards to be caught in the shafts of sunlight coming through the roof. He left his hat on the far corner of the table, took the hook from his mouth, reached down and petted the cat. Placed the hook in a vice grips on the edge of the table and, like a surgeon, began arranging things in front of him.

'Making flies?' I shouted down.

He whipped his head around, shifted the chair.

'Up here,' I said, sticking my head through the hole in the roof.

'Christ, you'll be the death of me yet. Where, in the name of Jaysus, are ya?' I whistled and he looked up.

'Who d'ya think ya are – Michel-fucken-angelo?'

'You're making flies?'

'Dressing flies,' he corrected.

'When did ya start that?'

'Ah, years ago.'

'Really?'

I've never seen him do that before – when he first started fishing he bought all his flies from a tackle shop in town, came back with dozens of them in his hat. I watched as he rubbed his hands up and down his bare arms.

'You're not cold?'

'Not a bit. I could do this in an icestorm. Love it

altogether.'

'Should put something over that vest,' I said.

'Ah, go away out of that.'

He turned the seat again, tightened the vice down on the hook, and rearranged the material in front of him, meticulously. Looked up at me once more, removed his glasses, and went to work. Took out some purple floss, rolled it between his thumb and forefinger, began trying to wind it along the shank of the hook. But his fingers were shaking – like hummingbird wings about to lift – and he kept dropping the thread, lifting it again, staring at it. He placed his trembling hand down on the table, glared at it, maybe telling it to stop, then suddenly thumped the back of his hand with his other fist. It stopped and he chuckled to himself. He finally got the thread started around the hook and the shakes in his hand seemed to quit altogether and there was a quiet content there, an acceptance of the slowness of time and the art of making a fly so simple that it would cause a fish to want it, something naturally belligerent and real, something that would whizz through the air with two pairs of wings and maybe three sets of eyes, something with an incoherent longing for motion. He began humming and looked happy – pissing on doom in his own peculiar way. I reached across the barn roof for the metal sheet, placed it over the hole, hammered it in, descended the ladder, went to the house and got him a shirt and his overcoat – he would have frozen down there otherwise, the length of time I knew it was going to take him to make that fly, with all its colours, all its trapped motion.

Bus stations are among the saddest places in America. Everyone looking for a way out. Slinking around. Looking for lost children. Keeping eyes glued on nothing in particular, waiting for life to happen.

In San Francisco a young girl howled about Jesus. Her arm was long with a string of watches. She said she was waiting for the Second Coming. A boy beside her hustled to carry suitcases and bags. He had a sign around his neck that said: 'HIV Positive'. A man in a Rasta hat tried to sell me a leaflet for the deaf. He played out some sign language in the air, wrote on a piece of paper, scribbling that I could use the leaflet for commercial breaks between the books I was reading. I bought it, and he thumped me playfully on the shoulder, said he wasn't deaf at all, went sauntering off. I shoved the leaflet down into my backpack and it was only then I noticed that Cici had put the bear's-claw bong in the top compartment, under my jeans. I went to the bus-station bathroom and washed the last of the resin out, just in case my bags got searched.

It was a two-day trip to Wyoming. A road-rattle through high deserts and mountains, on interstates with giant rest areas, and stopovers in cities with grey afternoons hanging above them. When I finally got to Jackson Hole I found myself walking around in a stupor until I got to the Million Dollar Cowboy Bar. I negotiated some dope from a man in a black stetson, went down to the Snake River, filled the bear's-claw pipe, got a little stoned.

In the morning, when I woke, two blue herons burst their way over the banks of the river, wings flapping hard enough to break a man's arm. Washed my face in the meltwater rush brought down from the mountains by late summer.

I went back down to the bus depot and looked around again. My parents had been there over thirty-five years before. Cici had told me about it. I reconstructed the scene in my head. Mam had stood, nervously, cheekbones daubed with rouge, her lips coloured with a delicate red, a crimson scarf languid at her neck. She feared the moment when the bus would belch out smoke from its exhaust. Cici waited beside her, laid a hand on Mam's forearm, ran a fingernail through some fluffy arm hair. Mam put her head on Cici's shoulder and stared down the road, out the length of the town and beyond, into the late fifties, the unsure distance of the future. She let the crimson scarf fall down around her shoulders.

The old man was there, too, his back to them. He was shoving luggage in the bottom of the bus, arguing with the driver. There was some oil in the luggage well and he wanted the driver to clean it up. 'Ain't my job, mister.' My father threw his arms up in the air, opened his suitcase and took out a pair of underpants, mopped the oil. He thought about burning the underwear, a totem to the summer, decided against it. He didn't want to get kicked off the bus. The driver let out a huff, climbed behind the steering wheel, beeped the horn. An announcement was made over a loudspeaker. Cici took Mam's face in her hands and they kissed each other, flush on the lips. My father was busy at the luggage well. 'Good luck,' Cici whispered in my Mam's ear. They were hugging. Red lipstick was smudged on Cici's upper lip.

Behind them my old man shouted: 'If ya don't get your arse in gear, we'll miss the fucken bus, woman!'

Cici ran her fingers along Mam's face. They kissed again – on the cheek this time – and then my parents were gone. The old man was drumming his fingers on the seat in front of him, a jazz beat. He didn't look back as the bus took off. He said 'yeah' over and over again in a slow saxophone way. It was as if New York clubs already existed in his throat. 'Yeah, yeah, yeah.' He kept on drumming and he didn't give a second thought to it, the leaping tears on my Mam's face as the driver crunched through the gears and down another road, another long road in the roll of themselves, leading them to New York.

I moved away from the vision, walked through Jackson

Hole. There were tourists in abundance. A gunfight was being re-enacted as theatre down near the market, little red eyes of video cameras blinking around it. In the distance, trees ran on one another's backs all the way up the mountains. Birds sang out, marking their territory. I knew the search for Mam had become hopeless and, besides, I would soon run out of money. I found a cabin to rent on the road near the Snake River. Weedy and tumbledown, a few wild cats perched on orange crates in the yard, parts of an old windmill, an engine block on which wood had once been chopped. At the back of the cabin I wore a trail in the grass, all the way to the water's edge. It was so high above sea level that satellites could be seen making paths, clusters of stars shuttling and winking, and once an eclipse which gave the moon an incredible penumbra.

I forged a Social Security number and found a job cleaning swimming pools, diatomaceous clay under my nails, leaves lifted out from filters, blue-ribbed vacuums used after shocking pools with chlorine. In the winter the ski lifts made caterpillar-shapes up the slopes and I sold tickets. More than three years were spent like this, patching my cabin, fixing water pipes, climbing hills, walking, rafting rivers, watching birthdays pass, still wondering about Mam.

Kutch turned out to be my neighbour. Short black hair and a face that could have come from a gargoyle, full of stitches and welts – he had once been involved in a dam-bombing accident. He and Eliza lived in an abandoned railway carriage. For a living they fashioned benches out of fallen logs and sold them to trendy stores in Cheyenne. Mother and son together, I envied them their closeness. Eliza worked on the benches, chiselling, carving, long brown fingers moving softly over wood. Kutch learned from her, imitated her patterns. Sometimes they went out driving and chopped down billboards together, spiked trees, destroyed bulldozers, left red fists on them. Red fists abounded. Even on the fire tower – which Kutch showed me that first autumn – they had painted a mural. Boysen-berry red, the thumbnail intricate and dark, the wrist sidling off into an arm, lofting its way over the trees and the mountains, thrusting up amongst the circling hawks. Beneath it the words, in a black oval sweep: 'No Compro-mise in the Defense of Mother Earth.'

I sometimes drove Kutch and Eliza around in their pick-up as they did their eco-guerrilla stunts. I never did anything myself, never drew any fists or poured sugar in any tank, paralysed by my own inaction.

They chopped down a row of billboards in Utah, a long line of advertisements with a ridiculous painting of a penguin on them, miles and miles of inanities that scarred the land. I sat waiting in the driver's seat, parked on the verge, and we got chased by an unmarked car, a red light flashing on its roof. Eliza and Kutch jumped in the back bed of the truck, the acetylene torch still flaring, and I sped off. Through the rear sliding window, Eliza put her brown wrinkled hand on my upper arm and squeezed tight until we drew away safely, in the dark. When we got back to Wyoming she kissed me on the forehead and said I was welcome anytime to come live with them in their railway carriage, that they had a spare room. But I liked my solitude. I've always liked my solitude.

Eliza showed me how to work on benches, told me old legends as we worked. With a chisel I carved out intricate patterns in fallen trees, her tales swirling around me. She made tea, and we listened to old flute music – it seemed to lift the cabin into the air. I sometimes stared at her for a long time as she worked, beads at her neck, furrows of concentration in her brow. She returned the look, silently.

I was out walking in the late-winter snow when I found the two dead coyotes hung on the fencepost. I stared for a while, then hurried back and got Eliza and Kutch. They pulled on their coats as they walked down the trail after me. Eliza clipped the coyotes down from where they hung. Carted the bodies back to her cabin. She took their teeth out and made some bracelets – one set of teeth was old and gnawed down, the other young and sharp. Afterwards she and Kutch brought the stiff bodies up to the forest, laid them out on the ground, left them there to manure themselves back into America. Eliza told me the old legend about the birth of the universe, the yammering-in of the world. I trudged home under the blanket-black night, the snow reflecting off the ground, went back to my cabin, took out my photo album, flicked through it. It had become a habit of mine, looking at the album.

I would rise from my chair, step out the door, look at the Wyoming sky, the thump of creation, and then I'd take another step forward on to the edge of the porch, and I would walk my way slowly into old photographs.

The first of them is a street, a Bronx tenement street, hermetically sealed at the end of the 1950s. The street loops itself into a red-brick cul-de-sac. At the end of the road there's a commotion. It's a summer's day and boys are wearing bathing togs and running back and forth through a geyser of water erupting from a broken fire hydrant. Their hair is very short, their bodies scrawny and white. One teenager, with a few tufts of hair in bloom on his chest, is in the middle of a huge leap through the water, arms held out wide, his fingers spread, a roar on his lips, eyebrows arched, rack of ribs exposed. The girls aren't allowed to put on bathing suits – this is a Catholic street – but some of them run through the water anyway, in long dresses which cling to their thighs. Along the side of the street a football is in mid-motion, heading towards a girl who looks shocked. A woman with a face like a trout peers from beyond the edge of the spray.

In the far background of the photograph a group of men and women are gathered on the steps outside a house. Only by walking into the photograph, going beyond the rim and up very close, can you make out their faces. They are Irish immigrants. Their clothes and expressions tell you that. Flat hats and grey trousers held up with suspenders. Some of them are sharing cigarettes, laughing, breaking out a melodeon, peeling labels off bottles that come from jacket pockets. They are fetching Galway and Dublin and Leitrim and Donegal from the bottom end of these bottles – and toasts are being made, or have been made. A toast to new arrivals who come hugging their suitcases with ash-wood hurleys strapped on the side. A toast to strange billboards that flash out new neon signs over the Bronx. A toast to a boxer who puts away journeymen heavyweights. A toast to the fire hydrant and the leaping boy. And maybe a toast to the big grey figure of Eisenhower, who will soon put a big chunk of metal up high in the air.

They have no names when I walk up to meet them, these immigrants. But I know their jobs – a list which, when converted to spittle at the edge of a tongue, could fill a keg – mechanics, maids, doormen, waitresses, line cooks, roofers, plumbers, garbage men, dishwashers, furnace foreman, doughnut maker in the morning, security guard at night, pint-puller, scrap buyer, dogcatcher, junk seller, shoeshiner, secretary, policeman who doesn't ticket his own, fireman with a sprig of plastic shamrock in his helmet, landscaper, taxi driver, peddler, telephonist. They are watching their children play in the water. 'He's a wild one, that same fella.' 'Wouldn't she break your heart?' 'Look at the head of hair on him.' The men remember a time when they were boys. They made footballs from the bladders of pigs, but the shape of footballs has changed in this country, no longer round. Their sons often come home in colourful high-school jackets and it's a strange language that they speak, quarterbacks and sackings. The men are wondering whether the ball, in its mid-flight twirl, will be caught. The women watch their daughters down by the fire hydrant and worry about how high their skirts are being lifted. The new leather shoes might get damp and unshape themselves. One mother is worried that the ball is heading towards her daughter, and maybe a joke rises up in her mind that her daughter is so clumsy that she hasn't even caught the measles yet, how could she catch anything else?

Mam is wedged in between two rather fat women. Her blouse is white and opened down to the fourth button so that a man in a flat hat above her is leaning over, trying to peep down into the cleavage. It might be a bit bony for his taste. She has lost a lot of weight in the Bronx. She has a tendency to sit at the dinner table and push the food around on her plate, the fork clanging tinnily. Her arms are cartilaginous. A hip-bone juts from the dress. Her neck is a brown stalk of rhubarb with its long striations. The dark hair is pulled back, ribboned in red. She is on the bottom stoop with her hands placed carefully in her lap, one over the other. They are hands that have been doing laundry all day. She works with a family from Tipperary who still keep the letters 'CHINESE LAUNDRY' over the door, inspiring jokes about the slanty eyes and yellow skin of the Irish rednecks. Mam's eyes are drawn down to her hands. Long and water-wrinkled, they have been scrubbing for many hours. Remnants of white washing powder under the nails. The tops of the fingers are puffy and the skin is loose from so much water. It is strange the patterns that are made in her hands. The fingerprint lines seem to become much more prominent, so that the rings at the top of each finger are bigger to the eye. Maps on her fingers. Far away, a boy named Miguel could lodge dirt in the fingernails and make a work of art from it. Mexican earth, the good earth.

A salesman has called earlier that evening, selling hand cream. She has bought a bottle of it. Salesmen are always calling at their door, at night. They have very short hair and perfect trouser creases and fabulous pitches in their voices – selling vacuum cleaners, knife sharpeners, wireless radios, kitchen tiles, kettles, ironing boards – and a lot of notes change fists. A great street for salesmen. People here talk a lot about new kitchen machinery. The lemon scent on her hands rises up to her nostrils, and she is glad that she bought it, although money is fairly tight these days. Money is like that flock of birds that arrived last night just as an old Hoagy Carmichael song jumped out of the radio. The birds arrived on the very first strain of 'Ol' Buttermilk Sky,' flittered through it, left when the song ended. When they took off there were a lot of bird droppings on the ground outside the door. Money is like that flock of birds, Mam might think. You notice it when it's not around. But if you have enough money you can get away, fly off, as many do.

Removal trucks sometimes arrive, and many jealous stares follow the lifting of the furniture, off to a street in a wealthy part of Brooklyn, or Queens, or Long Island, a road lined with trees and motor cars, where there might be a few Italians or Jews as well. Or even some of her own.

Mam is just about smiling as she looks down at her hands. It is not an unhappy smile, just a little lost on her face. Maybe she's wondering what she's doing here. Wondering what has led her to this. Wondering if life is manufactured by a sense of place, if happiness is dependent on soil, if it is an accident of circumstance that a woman is born in a certain country, and that the weather that gives birth to the soil also gives birth to the unfathomable intricacies of the heart. Wondering if there is a contagion to sadness. Or an entropy to love. Or maybe Mam isn't thinking this way at all. Maybe she is wondering about the sheer banalities of her day, what she will cook for dinner, what end of the kitchen table she will do her ironing on, when she will get time to wash the white tablecloth, if she should put some aloe on her husband's hands, hands that are now out of the photograph, pressing down on a button that will open a shutter.

The old man is hot-roofing these days because he cannot make enough money from his photographs for them to live on. He hates the job, but it's all he can find. The Wyoming photographs come back from publishers with courteous notes, not even signed. Mam doesn't like the idea of him being on a roof. Brutal work, carrying buckets of hot tar. She doesn't like the man who runs the company either, Mangan, a sly-eyed man who drives around in an old Ford truck, ladders jutting from it. The company is called Koala-T Roofing Company, with a picture painted on the side, an impish koala holding a bucket. Mangan doesn't pay very well and when my father comes home she has to scrape the globs of dried tar from his forearms. 'Koala-T, me arse!' he shouts. Sometimes he curses and slams his fists down on the table – 'I want to take photos! Not do this shit! Do you understand me!' and she must soothe him and sometimes get in front of his camera. She is wondering if perhaps he will take more photographs tonight and be happy for that. I stand in front of her and ask: Are ya happy, Mam? She doesn't reply. But there is something in her that says: Well, yes, I am happy here, I suppose I'm happy, but I'd be happier elsewhere.

I drift off from the group again and hear the leaping boy still screaming in delight by the fire hydrant.

Not a lot is going on in Mam's life. Sometimes, on a day off from the laundry, she goes into New York City on the subway and tries on red hats in the Fifth Avenue department stores, wanders around through acres of perfume and cosmetics and fineries. The ladies behind the counter soon realise she isn't buying and leave her alone. She moves gracefully through the stores, fingering things, acquiring them for the briefest of moments, lays them down again, moves out into the street, where she walks through the traffic to sit in the rear of St Patrick's Cathedral. In the silence she reincarnates herself – nothing too romantic, a grackle maybe. She settles down on a telegraph pole in her hometown, looks around. Swoops down and takes the host from the mestizo priest's fingers. Takes off again into coloured winds. Revisits a house. Darts along dry streets. Strange to be a bird. Strange how hollow your bones become.

And how curious it is that she hasn't heard from Cici in so long. The last time Cici wrote, she was on a train heading west, slamming through flatlands. She scribbled from a boxcar, where light filtered through in slants, and a mad red-faced hobo shared Spam sandwiches with her. It was a short letter and Mam read it so often that she began to incant parts of it in her mind like a church prayer: *I miss you very much, Juanita, keep smiling, it paints the world well, I will see you very soon.* There is something about Cici that makes the world worth living. Mam thinks about her often – it's not so much that she wants to kiss her again as just simply see her, reassure herself that Cici really existed, that there was a time of such splendid happiness, that there might be one again.

Most of Mam's other times are spent in quiet exactitude in her apartment, cleaning, arranging, putting things back in their proper places, meticulous, proud. When she talks she has the strangest lilt of half-Irish, half-Mexican accent. People seem to enjoy her company. She has stories to tell about chickens and a far-off country. And another world of fires and a tower. Yet the secret part of her – the photos in their bedroom – is well hidden from view, behind lace curtains on the third floor, where pigeons sometimes nestle at the windowsill. The only time that her husband seems to be truly at peace is when he's taking those photos. They're not obscene, not in any way. They make him content. It's a small enough price for Mam to pay, and it's an attention of sorts. He is still in love with her. He still makes a temple from her body – even though it's much like a minaret now.

She remains looking at her hands as I ghost my way through the photograph and try to say things to the people around her. They are busy with their bottles and their dreams of appliances, so I step back through the shot and up the street. For time immemorial, that boy will be leaping. And I will never know if the ball was caught. And the trout-faced woman will continue to stare.

I move on down towards the end of the cul-de-sac, nod to my father as his fingers press on the shutter button, but he doesn't nod back. I step out again, on to a black rim and into a night scene.

It is 1960, and a few young men are dancing with my mother. There is a radio set up under a windowsill and an Elvis Presley song is swivelling from it. It is apparent in the euphoric movement of the young men's hips that a new decade is just under way. They have the beginnings of copycat quiffs on their heads. A boy with a harelip purses his mouth, as if he might kiss the moon, my mother dancing just a few feet from him. The boy wears drainpipe trousers, a purple shirt, pomade in his hair, and he is twirling imaginary hula-hoops around his groin. She is clicking her fingers. All along the cul-de-sac, bunting is up for the election of a man whose portrait sits on virtually every wall, green, white, and orange ribbons hung underneath his chin like a colourful goatee – John F. Kennedy with his perfect teeth, vying on the walls with the Pope and the Sacred Heart of Jesus. It must be a happy night for Mam, because her cheeks are flush with alcohol and her face is made-up, eyelashes curled, mascara carefully applied.

Her eyes are open very wide and brown. Her thin body is in the middle of a twist, so that one shoulder is lower than the other and her chest nudges up against her blouse. I walk out there to go dancing. It's hot and muggy, a humid night in late autumn. I twirl my hips, too. I move with abandon. She says to me: When are you going to get rid of that stupid earring, Conor? I take it out and give it to her, and she smiles.

I ask and she says that nothing much has changed. The laundry has grown bigger and new employees have been taken on. Other girls doing the scrubbing now. My father is still on the roofs, and the tar docks itself under his fingers. His forty-second birthday was spent above the Bronx – jokes being made about Marilyn Monroe and those who like it hot. Cici has written to her, raving about marijuana, but she hasn't visited yet. Cici would like it here, out moving in the night, with moths flaring around under lamplights, dancers in a bouquet around a radio, the grind of hips, the swivel of words. It's her sort of place – except Cici might be aware that there's even newer music on its way, runnelling along over the continent, newer ideas, newer dances. Mam has a bead of sweat on her brow. Maybe she will wait for it to negotiate its way down her face to where she can tongue it. Or maybe not. Maybe she will wipe it off with a quick flick of the hand. Or maybe it will stay there eternally, a bead of sweat to say: I was dancing once, when I was thirty-three years old, and I didn't have a care in the world.

Outside the photograph, my father is slickly dressed in a white shirt that smells of barsmoke. His dark tie is open and the long end of it reaches past his waist. Hair is quite thin now, furrows of it across his scalp. He is glad to watch his wife dance. He is afraid that life is becoming staid, he doesn't like the roofs. There are days when he goes searching for other jobs, something in a press syndicate, or a newspaper, but all he ever gets are a few freelance shifts. He just wants to take his photographs, but there's not much opportunity for that. The world rotates on an axis of what-ifs? What if we were somewhere else? What if we sauntered off and just didn't come back?

But, for now, he enjoys the music coming from the radio. The men on the roofs sometimes sing Presley, their favourite being 'Heartbreak Hotel.'

While he stands to take this particular photograph his foot is tapping, but he has to stop so as not to jolt the camera. A million light cells have just burst from the flash. I walk through them, packets of light swarming around me, and out the other side, back into the nineties, where the sun is going down over the Teton mountains. I cannot help this wandering backwards. It is my own peculiar curse.

Their apartment has a bedroom and a living room – but it is in this bedroom that all the living is done. I feel queasy about stepping into this private domain, a voyeur, a Peeping Tom. The room is painted mauve. It is two years on. Mam is in a white summer dress and she is lying on a *chaise-longue* that they've rescued from the rubbish. The *chaise* has carved feet that curve and bend and give it elegance, but the material is ripped and tatty, bits of stuffing come out from it. She lies, as if on a throne. The dress is purposefully off the shoulder. It falls down and exposes the top half of a dark nipple. The shot is loaded with more sexuality than almost any of the others – something to do with its casualness. Despite the skinniness, she looks good. Her feet are stretched in front of her and it seems like she is contemplating her toes. She is chewing on the end of a pen and a sheet of paper is propped up on her stomach. I imagine that she is writing to Cici. I step over to see what she is saying on the page: *I miss the fires. Don't you?* The last letter that Mam received was very strange – Cici had been exalting marijuana, going into rhapsodies about acid. *What does marijuana make you feel like?* Mam might be writing. *I have heard it makes you sick, true?* The end of the pen is so well chewed that it looks as if she simply sinks her teeth into it, but in this photo she is kissing it, lost in thought, thick lips pursed upon it. She wears no jewellery, only her wedding ring. Her body sweeps away from her in the photograph, along the *chaise-longue*, a sheet of paper flying in the breeze.

He likes the pose, my father, he is enjoying the capture of it. He is up on the balls of his toes, shouting, Perfect! Perfect! Hold it right there! He is fresh from a shower and feels good about the world. This will be one of the best shots. He sweeps his fingers over his balding scalp and shouts, Hold it! Maybe he will put on a gallery exhibition in an avant-garde place, he thinks, show her to the world. Fifteen years of Mam – in Mexico, in Wyoming, in New York. He is very excited about the idea, which will never come to fruition. But for now he is happy with the vision of it.

Her lips are kissing the end of the pen, and she's glad that her husband isn't throwing a fit and that there is something quite smooth and secretive to the grey light that is filtering its way through the curtains, the rays seeming to bend as they hit a dusty mirror. She won't remain in this apartment for ever, she thinks, but at least it isn't too bad. The cream is still working on her hands. It has given them a certain softness. There is a small amount of money in the bank. Things she had never dreamed of – toasters and televisions – have begun to fill the empty spaces in the apartment. Even some Spanish speakers have come to the street now, from near the Atacama Desert in Chile. She spends time with them, looks after their baby. There are still some days when my father whispers that he will bring her home to Mexico. She is sitting back, relaxed, writing her letter, and I leave her there, in that peculiar peace, my father shouting, Here we go, Juanita! Yeah! Yeah!

I move away from them, out of their bedroom, and into a

print given to me by Cici.

It is 1964. The camera must have been held out by Cici at the distance of an outstretched arm, because it is a lopsided close-up. It shows only their faces and the tops of their clothes, their cheeks touching against one another. Cici has hitch-hiked all the way across the country from San Francisco. She looks exhilarated, her pupils set high in the rims of her eyes. The acne crevices have been darkened in from her spell out on the open roads – in the nudist camps, the psychedelic buses, the growing lines of war protests, last year's march to Washington, the hailing-to-the-sky of Martin Luther King.

The top of a bright t-shirt peeps out from the bottom edge. Mam's hair is loose on her shoulders. Disembodied, I float in. The kitchen is full of sparkling pans. Some water boiling on the stove. The Rolling Stones on the radio. A familiar smell drifts up from the table where Mam and Cici are sitting. I am amazed to find myself staring at a joint, burning itself down in the ashtray. Cici has been smoking. Maybe my mother has, too, but I doubt it. A tumble of words from them – Cici asking Mam to join her for a while, even just for a holiday, that they'll caress the road, maybe meet up with some Sonoran gypsies, eat peyote, go down over the border together.

'Come with me, man,' she says.

'Why you call me "man"?'

'Why not?'

The offer is tempting. This touching of hair, this touching of cheek, this apparition of Cici again in her life.

'And Michael?'

'What about him?'

The joint is held between lips and there is an uproar of laughter. Cici's head is jerked towards the fridge, which up until an hour ago Mam had been proud of. But Cici has quoted a novelist talking about 'dumb white machinery,'

145

and the fridge is not quite so magical to her anymore. Cici says that the dope has made her hungry, and again they laugh. There is a hand laid on a hand and the two of them look at the camera.

Cici says, 'Cheese!'

But there is a secret behind all of this and, afterwards, when I extend the rim of the photograph and follow them into the living room, Mam tells her about it.

'I am going to have a baby,' Mam says eventually, smiling, 'Michael and I are going to have baby.'

Cici tugs hard on the joint.

'That's lovely,' she says, and suddenly a serpentine sweep of roads rises up in her mind, away from here. Her hands are shaking a little. 'I'm very happy for you.' She goes outside and sits on the step. Mam stays in the living room. The baby's been there for three months. I can imagine her running her hands very lovingly over her stomach, talking to the child that hasn't even begun to move within her yet, waiting for the faint soothing thump of life against the wall of her womb. When Cici comes inside, her face flushed, she finds Mam in the kitchen, making bread.

'Come with me.'

'Michael will be back soon.'

'He can come, too, man.'

'I told you, I am going to have a baby.'

'You want a baby to grow up in this shit?' Cici's arms fly towards the window.

'No.'

'Then, come on.'

'Later I will ask to Michael.'

'Aww, man.'

Mam watches from the window as Cici leaves that afternoon, the photograph tucked in her pocket. Cici carries her belongings in a grey duffle bag. Mam moves from the window, and maybe she turns on the television set to watch a famous game show, or maybe she kneads more dough, or maybe she stares at her hair in the mirror, thinking it could be the last she will see of Cici.

The baby follows Cici's example – comes far too late, leaves way too early. On an evening of torpor, Mam loses the child. The old man is coming back from the roofs. He carries an apple tart up the stairs of the apartment, the smell wafting around him. He is happy, for once, with his day's work. When he opens the door she is lying in a pool of blood on the bathroom floor. He drops the apple tart. His feet slide in the blood. She is unconscious with her head slumped against the wall. He lifts her to her feet, whispering, Sweet Jesus, sweet Jesus. On the way down to the street a dark patch of red insinuates itself into the front of his shirt, where he carries her. He brings her to hospital, and the dead child propels them on to a year of misery. She comes home from the hospital, hand held to her belly. They don't talk much. A lethargy hangs in the air. Some nights my father finds that she has disappeared from the apartment and he pulls on his belted overcoat to go searching, finds my mother down at the maternity ward of the hospital, staring in through the glass window at babies, with nurses trying to gently steer her away. She spends money on baby clothes. She carries a soother in her purse. Sometimes she is torn towards going to find Cici. Mam writes a letter to her friend: 'Regretting is expensive, sometimes I wish I had gone with you.'

The old man stays on the roofs, but they both know that they will have to move on. And they do move on – towards the west of Ireland. He suggests that it will be a good place for Mam to recover, that there may still be some money left over in the bank, he can get a job easily there, he can take photographs, there is some land that was never sold. They can try again for a family. They will have a child, maybe two, maybe three – whatever she wants. After that, he says, they will make their home in Mexico.

'Promise?'

'I promise.'

'Ireland is far.'

'I know, love.'

'We will be all right?'

'Of course.'

'And then we come back to Mexico?'

'Of course.'

When they leave the street, the old man relishes the triumph of it. He sways his way down along the pavement with the suitcases in either hand. He has arranged for the taxi to meet them at the end of the street. There is more drama that way for the old man – walk the full length of the street.

He wears a grey tweed jacket in the airport, a white dog rose in the breast pocket, the hat devoid now of its rabbits' feet. Mam has bought a brand-new strawberry dress. She is radiant on the airplane, a stewardess marvelling at her accent. They move onwards and backwards – always onwards and, for the first time backwards – to a place where some wisps of grey De Valera mist still hang, although it is the winter of 1966 and all over the country other mists are being dispersed. They have difficulty in Shannon because my mother doesn't have a visa, but my father bribes the immigration official with a twenty-dollar bill. He is home free. He is walking gigantically again. A great swagger out through the airport, arms swinging, pushing the suitcases on a trolley with his foot. Mam beside him. They take a bus to Mayo. There's some money left in the account, but no land, and they must take out a mortage to buy an old farmhouse – Guinness bottles among nettles in the garden, windows cracked in the shed, an old bathtub in the courtyard, wisteria growing upwards with the years. Mam settles down in much the same way as their new bathtub – a shiny anachronism. She is the dark-skinned one, the one the drunks in the town square call Senorita, the one who never cuts her hair even when it becomes long and brazenly silver. She wears a scarf over her head as she goes to mass in the red-brick church. Letters to Cici are returned, unopened. In America the war protests are in full flight, and Cici is rampant around the country with a flower on her cheek, elephant flares covering her sandals, hypodermic needles stuck blithely in her arm. But Mam knows nothing of this, and she waits for letters.

Mam lingers in the farmhouse, eyes to the bog, spending years this way, slow as Sundays, longing constantly for a child's movement in her belly. I am to be born four years later, when she's forty-two years old, and as a precautionary measure the doctors slice open her belly for a Caesarian section. The old man waits in the hospital corridors, gently tapping his heel on the floor, hat propped on his knee, bobbing.

An array of equipment neatly lined in front of him – silver tinsel, purple and golden floss, blue chatterer feathers, some yellow seal's fur, a hot-orange hackle, tiny golden-pheasant feathers, some black thread, very black, riverblack. He pointed each one out to me, hand hovering over them. Most of it had arrived in the package this morning, from an angling shop in Dublin.

He told me that brighter flies work better in dark waters, that the salmon will rise at the sight of colours.

Curious thing, though, he said that salmon don't eat when they're in rivers, they're just conditioned to respond – if you catch them they've nothing in their bellies. And when they leap it's not out of any happiness, it's just to move up fast water or to get rid of sea lice. But they're clever bastards, he said – they know the real thing when they see it, and a badly made fly is about as good as a Hail Mary in an air raid.

I pulled up an old crate and sat down, the deep lengthy smell of him around me.

'Ya don't overdress it,' he said, pointing at the hook, 'otherwise it collects too much water. But a big fly means a big fish, it's all about balance.'

He was having difficulty with a knot.

'D'ya need some help there?'

'Nah, I'm grand, I could do this with my eyes closed.'

He wound two small chatterer feathers back to back. 'For the tail,' he explained.

I noticed how much bigger his hands were than mine. They had stopped shaking and worked with precision. He reversed the hook in the vice and leaned down into it, sometimes with his glasses on, sometimes without, a bit frustrated. 'Fucken hell's bells,' he said, 'here,' and he handed me a slim pair of scissors, got me to cut off some of the excess thread. 'Get in here now, closer.' I was surprised to see that he didn't smoke at all.

He made the body of the insect, wound on a long slender feather, and then he worked on the throat and the wing, put some golden-pheasant feathers on each side. He stacked the hairs so they looked wing-like. 'Ya give the fuckers as much life as possible,' he said. I handed him the hackle pliers, the scissors, and the tweezers. He enumerated each one as we went along. He had a large darning needle stuck into a sherry-bottle cork for the bodkin. And a thimble made from an old lipstick container that must have belonged to Mam. Each time I handed him something he nodded up and down, wheezed, approximating a thanks. But the rest of the time his breathing was still and even, in full and splendid concentration at the making of the fly – it was turning out something like a miniature Indian headress, threads and feathers and tippets. I thought of Kutch and Eliza, maybe bringing one of the flies back to them as a present.

When he finished the first one he gave me a thumbs-up. 'That'll do,' he said, 'we'll see if the bastard can resist this.' He walked around the barn for a while, the coat on, strutting around, sniffing at the air, wiping his hands.

He hummed a tune, rubbing the air against his lips. Sometimes he stopped to place the feathers in his mouth, or asked me to wipe bits of glue from the fly, or catch a piece of waxed thread coming through a loop, pick up dropped pieces from the floor, clip and taper, wind some floss around the shank. He pursed his lips into the melody again, the rise and fall of it around us as he showed me a few little tricks, how to tie in the tinsel tags, merge the colours into one another, make the head of the fly with black thread. Time moved with the rhythm of an insect wing – it struck me how a second of an insect's life might be a decade of ours, the whole world shattered into prisms of vision, the concentrate of living, the vitality of each instant – and the old man could have been creating both the brevity and length of time. The hum became immutable so that I forgot it was there, sunk down into soundlessness.

It was evening when he finally stood up, put the last fly in his hat, donned it, said, 'I'm fucken starving, young fella, come on, let's go.'

He put the other flies in the tray and closed the lid. We went up to the house and there were midges out – he used to be able to dress up a midge, he said, but they're too small and difficult for him nowadays.

I cooked some spaghetti and sauce. 'Do I look bloody Italian?' he said, but he ate it with relish, talked about flies, an assembly line of chatter coming from him. Told me that some old guy in Donegal a hundred years ago was the first to make colourful ones, butterflies, made himself a fortune doing it too. He used to put feathers in donkey piss so they wouldn't lose their dye. Could tie them with one hand behind his back. Someone even brought him over to London to lecture on them. There was genius in making colours for dark water. My father rattled on, intermittently stopping for a cough or to blow his nose, the words flowing from him again. At one stage, over pasta falling from his fork, he pointed at me sternly: 'Tell ya what though, the only mark of a good fly is when ya catch something. That's the long and short of it. Ya can make pretty ones until the cows come home, but if ya don't catch you're just taking a lash in the wind.'

After the food we had a few cups of tea and his hands started a little bit of the tremens. Went up to the room, said he'd fish the big one tomorrow.

When I followed him up he was trying to tie himself another fly in bed, but he needed the vice, and he just laid the wooden tray down at the edge of the mattress.

The flowery sheets were drawn around him. He started hacking up into an old handkerchief, which he folded very precisely after each spit into it. Turned it over and rubbed along it with his fingers as if he were enclosing a very important letter. Mucus oozed out the side at one stage, and he opened the hanky and re-folded it, twirling up the edges. He seemed fettered in by the room, turning his eyes to both walls, the ceiling, and back to the walls again, which seem to have buckled under the weight of the house. I sat by the bed.

'Did ya hear that?' he said.

'What?'

'There was a knock on the door.'

'No there wasn't.'

'Go down and see who's at the bloody door,' he said. 'Maybe the postman again.'

'At this hour?'

I went over to the window and lifted it, stuck my head out.

'Nobody there.'

'I could have sworn I heard someone,' he said.

'Nobody.'

'Maybe it's Mrs McCarthy,' he said.

'No, nobody.'

'Go on down and check, for fucksake.'

A smell filled the room and I knew straight away why he had been trying to send me downstairs. The smell suffocated its way through the air, blocking out everything, the acridness of his breath, the unbathed effluvium of his body. He had some matches by his bed and he rolled over and struck one, coughed on it to blow it out, but I knew what he was doing, and even after the sulphur filtered off, the odour remained, hovered, mocked him with its pungency.

'Leave me alone,' he said suddenly.

He lay back in the bed with an almost theatrical gesture of labour, but I told him that I just wanted to sit there for a while. He gave a quick flick of his head as if bothered by a real insect this time, reached across, flipped on his bedside radio. It gave out a steady diet of foreign wars and dying. He cursed and turned it off, leaned into his handkerchief, brought up another ream. His forehead was wrinkled in pain, and he put his hand on mine and said, 'Conor.'

I said: 'Yeah, Dad?'

It's the first time in years I've called him Dad, but he didn't seem to notice.

'That was a grand time, dressing the flies.'

'Yeah,' I said.

He shifted his body in bed and asked me for a smoke.

'Don't think you should.'

'Look, I'm all right, okay? Haven't had one all day. That's a record.'

'They're killing ya.'

He coughed again: 'Wonderful. Let them kill me so.

They're over there by the bedside table.'

I reached across but the packet was empty. He told me there were some downstairs, under the sink, he hides a few packets away for emergencies. Said to make sure to get the ones that were fresh, some of them had been down there since time immemorial and might crackle to the touch. I don't know why, but I went down and got a packet, they were tucked way in at the back of the cupboard. When I came back upstairs he had propped himself up against the pillows – 'Lovely, oh lovely, now you're talking' – and I turned one upside-down in the packet, the way he does for luck, handed him one. He never smokes with the wedding-ring hand, always keeps it in the right one, perched between his fingers.

'Sure, a puff now and then does nobody any harm.'

I waited until he had finished, in case he fell asleep and brought the house down with him, another fire, another echo. He pushed himself back against the bed and I heard him letting go again, but I pretended nothing had happened.

'I'll get Doctor Moloney out tomorrow morning,' I said.

'You will not.'

'Why not?'

'It's Sunday tomorrow and, besides, I won't have anyone shoving anything up me rectum.'

I laughed.

'What's so funny?' he asked.

'Oh, nothing really.'

'I heard they do that in San Francisco these days,' he said.

I was a little startled and thought for a moment of Cici in her whitewhite city. 'Do what?' I said.

'Shove strange things up beyond.'

'What d'ya mean?'

'Gerbils and the like.'

He chugged on the cigarette. 'They said it on the TV. I

was up at all hours one night, watching.'

'You watch TV these days?'

He took a moment to reply, held his hand to his temple, scratched the bald spot. 'Times have changed.'

'You used to hate it.'

'Every now and then in the winter.' He scrunched up his eyebrows.

'How about a glass of hot whiskey to make you sleep?'

'Nah,' he said, 'I'm content with this,' dropping the ash into the cup of his hand, then letting it fall out on the floor.

I stubbed the butt end out for him and, just before he lay over to sleep, he sat up and leaned his head against my shoulder. I moved in closer to him, put my hand at the back of his head. When he pulled back from my shoulder there was a little bit of phlegm on my t-shirt. I didn't want to move, but he saw it and, using the handkerchief, he started to wipe if off.

'Jesus Christ,' he said, 'ah, Jesus.'

He rolled over to the far side of the bed, pretending he was sleeping. I picked up the wooden tray with all the flies in it, worked away at one of my own for an hour or so, trying to wind some thread on the shank, but couldn't find the knack, kept dropping the damn thing. It seemed impossible, so finely tuned and delicate. I looked at the flies he had made during the day. They lay there in waiting, ready to burst into flight, and I took two small chatterer wings and flipped them together between my fingers as he dozed off.

# SUNDAY

## *lord, i remember*

He woke early this morning, rummaging around before the sun rose. Heard him as he opened up his window, spat down into the grass, went to the bathroom and pissed in the sink. I went downstairs after him and he gave me a nod.

'How ya feeling?'

'Like a million dollars,' he said. 'Look.'

He had the tray out open on the kitchen table and he was admiring one of the flies in particular. 'Isn't that a beauty?'

Jazz bucked from the radio and he moved over to fiddle with the dial, fine-tuning it. He pecked rhythmically at the air with his head. Hair stuck out where he had been sleeping on it. He ate a little cereal, some toast with jam, said he felt great for fishing today. Reached for the fly once more, held it up. 'You and me both,' he said. I thought he was asking me if I wanted to go fishing with him, but then I realised he wasn't talking to me at all, that he wanted to be on his own, him and his fly, so I let him be.

He wore a baggy green crew-neck jumper and a fat red tie knotted up to his neck, mashing up over the top of the sweater. His head looked skeletal above it.

'All dressed up?'

'Yeah,' he said.

He gave me a shrug.

Before he left for the river I asked him – for a bit of a joke really – if he was going to go to mass, that Mrs McCarthy might be expecting him, down there in her rosary beads and headscarf. But he shook his head sharply and all he said was: 'The Lord's my shepherd, I shall not want him.'

We stood at the door and I told him that I've never been much of a man for mass, either. A bit too much like a spiritual suppository. He cocked his head sideways in agreement, opened the door handle, turned around to face me, looked at the rods, switched them back and forth, touched the inside lining of his jacket where he had placed one or two of the new flies. He reached out to shake my hand, then drew it away quietly before I had a chance to shake. I was going to ask him why he wanted to do that, but he just turned away. He picked up the rods and left, shuffling slowly through the yard.

It was strange the way he walked, stopping every few yards to catch his breath, hitching the back of his grey trousers, shuffling along, contemplating the sky as if he might try to reach up and shake its hand, too. I just went outside and sat on Mam's wall and celebrated the lack of rain – it was a beautiful bright morning.

Lord, I remember. Mornings back then, in the mid-seventies, before it all tumbled down around them.

Mam was building the low stone wall along the lane. She wore a yellow rain jacket, her silver hair woven back into a braid that touched the small of her back. She would kneel down at the half-built wall as if in prayer, sometimes singing a bit of a Mexican song. The wall wasn't very well built, but it broke the land in a splendid way. Holes in it like rheumy eyes staring out at the fields. It threatened with topple – because she was always failing in one way or another, making it too high in places, too low in others, a little lopsided, a touch drunk. But she loved the building of it. She would start work when breakfast was finished, shortly after the morning swim. She stood and watched as my father and I fought the current, but even then you could tell she was itching to get started. Long thin fingers cracked against one another. As soon as we emerged from the water, she'd put her hand on my lower back and hustle me up to the kitchen, jogging alongside me, leaving the old man there. As I ate she pulled on her blue garden gloves and, just before my father breezed his way into the kitchen with his head wrapped in a towel, she'd lean to me and whisper: 'Now, *m'ijo*, I will begin.'

The wall ran two hundred yards from the house to the main road. It was anywhere from two to four feet high, serpentine, almost coiling by the time it reached the road, as if she wanted to extend it further and further, but could only make it loop into itself. It looked like an ancient set of grey teeth. Birds sometimes nestled in the gaps between the stones. Mam was forever dismantling sections, putting it back together again, replacing larger stones with smaller ones, juggling, shuffling. Men rode past on bicycles and hailed her with a giant 'Senorita,' and she quickly corrected them. '*Señora!*' she'd shout. They'd wink: 'Whatever you say, Missus Lyons.' She'd bend down to the wall again, cramming in a flat rock, or chiselling the side of a sharp stone. She covered her eyes with a brown arm so sparks didn't jump up at her when she worked. At lunchtime the men would stop again, and instruct her on the building of the wall. She'd make them cups of tea in large white mugs, listen closely, nod her head, braids swinging, then wave them off and continue as before, stubbornly, steadfastly. It was her wall. It belonged solely to her. She made it the way she saw fit.

She spat when working – a continuation of the habit she had picked up working with the chickens in Mexico, when dust got in every pore.

The wall made some sort of crease in her boredom – there wasn't much else for her to do, the washing fluttering out over the bog, dishes piling up in the sink, ham and cheese sandwiches to be made for my school lunchbox. She was in her late forties by then. The world was growing older. The wall helped her whittle away the days until she could return to Mexico. They argued a lot, she and the old man. They stood in the kitchen and waved their arms, pointing fingers at each other. Shouts rang around the house. Sometimes he thumped a fist into the cupboard – a little row of indentations appeared like puckered stabwounds in the wood. He saw no use for the wall – except as a place to crouch down to light a cigarette, or to take a quick clandestine piss. Maybe they were still in love, but it was a different quality of love than I imagine they had in the beginning – a pathic love, a brusque love, no magic there. When he was away on photographic jobs, a great grey silence descended around the house, and Mam sat me down and told me things. If she began in her native tongue, which I didn't understand, she'd reach up to her grey hair and sweep it back, begin again in English. Bits and pieces of stories that began to mesh and merge for me, stories told to a child in a childish way, and Mexico became a country just down the road.

In the kitchen she scrubbed pots and pans, watched the passing of the world through the window. Cars trundled by, women in headscarfs on their way to coffee mornings, the postman's van eddying past without stopping, herds of cattle driven along with sticks.

Her only friend was Mrs O'Leary. Mam went to her pub a few afternoons a week – it was a ship-pictured pub, old and creaky at the joints, much like its customers. Sometimes, in the summer months, she took me along. Mrs O'Leary kept chickens out the back, about a dozen of them pecking around. And Mrs O'Leary was not unlike an old chicken herself – with a great red face, a long beak of a chin and a wizened wattle abandoned underneath it. She must have been eighty years to heaven at that stage, a gigantic woman in chalcedony-coloured dresses, huge billows of breasts, a deep voice, always on the verge of a laugh. But her eyes were giving way, so that she could hardly recognise the labels of bottles anymore, sometimes mistaking Jameson's for Paddy's, Bushmills for Irish Mist, causing an uproar of universal sorrow among the men who stuck to whiskeys like limpets to sea-rocks. She couldn't see the clock moving on the wall, walked into doorframes, could only read the headlines of the *Irish Press*, which served well for moppinig up brown spills on the concrete floor. What devastated Mrs O'Leary most was that she could hardly tell the sex of a newborn chicken anymore – a skill that required the eyes of a hawk, the patience of years, an awareness of the whimsical vicissitudes of nature. She sauntered up to our house one summer afternoon and said to Mam: 'I hear you have a way with the nether regions,' and, after a moment's explanation, they both burst out laughing.

Mam said: 'Of course, I will look at the chickens.'

Mam filled in for Mrs O'Leary, examined the undersides of the chicks. They would sit together on wooden stools at the back of the pub, feet swinging beneath them, chatting, laughing. Their cackle rose up and swung its way through the bar, where the men pounded their fists every half an hour to the chime of the headless cuckoo on the wall: 'Another glass there, Alice, make it snappy.' She sold the eggs to the men, who lay like dormant rags on the bar counter all day long, staring at the dusty mirrors, a musty smell pluming up from their jackets, handkerchiefs peeping from trouser pockets. But Mam and Mrs O'Leary ignored the men most of the time, sat out the back and whiled the time away, swapping bits and pieces of their lives, José with the Sewn Lip, Rolando, Miguel, fires in that far-off place, the peculiar Cici, the chicken opera that had developed in my grandmother's yard in Mexico.

After a while Mam and Mrs O'Leary began to invent their own opera, using the men in the bar as their actors.

They were a curious bunch – men scared of living, even more scared of dying, afraid of ghosts that rose up and tiptoed through their kidneys. One sported a walrus moustache and wore shiny grey trousers, and he often slid off the end barstool, finishing his Guinness while sitting on the floor, a hedge of white cream above his lip. There was a misanthrope with a face like an oven-fresh roll, taking tenpenny pieces from behind his own ear. One man smelled of vinegar when he sweated. Another slumbered in the slop-house of his own giant Smithwick's stains. All of them seemed to cough together in a choir, blowing their noses into the palms of their hands, bleary-eyed over newspapers, exhausted over whiskeys. 'Who in the name of Jaysus stole the racing page?' 'Give us another jar there, Alice.' 'How about a lift home?' 'Well, there's cars in the family but they're all in America.'

From what I can figure out, they treated Mam fairly well at first – the odd swoop of the hat when she walked in, the shadowy wink, the quiet suggestion of lechery with dentures moving up and down in their mouths, a hailing of her new dress, a compliment on the shade of lipstick. But there were whispers of curiosity as well, and soon rumours abounded like storms. Storms, too, brought in strange birds – hadn't a peregrine falcon arrived all the way from Nova Scotia once? She was a former lover of Che Guevara. She was Jack Dempsey's girl. She was an orphan from the slums of Central America. She had failed in Hollywood.

She was a daughter of Franco. She was in flight from a revolution. She had once owned a hacienda in southern Mexico, lost it all in a game of bridge. Or maybe she was a model for the old man's camera, perhaps even posed for him, nude. The latter rumour – the one they eventually embraced – may have caused a peculiar quickness in their dentures, the shaky lifting of a glass to the mouth.

I came to the pub late afternoons, after school, swinging my satchel. Mam's eyes were decked out, rocking back and forth in a curious sort of happiness that I didn't recognise from home. Looking back, I can see that they could have been sisters, she and Alice O'Leary. They could have been in love with one another – sometimes sitting with a hand laid on the back of a hand, Mam's mud-coloured fingers on Easter-lily white. Mrs O'Leary would run her fingers over my face. 'He's the spit of you, Juanita, feel the head of hair on him.' Occasionally a gargantuan bottle of stout passed between them as the chickens pecked around in the garden. Mrs O'Leary would miss her lips with the drink, and a necklace of black would spill down the front of her apron, 'Ah, Jaysus now, I couldn't hit a barn door, used to be I could pee through a wedding ring, and now I couldn't even hit a bucket!'

The Angelus was always Mam's cue to go home and make dinner for my father. When it sounded out in the pub smoke, a rat-faced comedian began a recitation: 'Holy Mary, mother of God, pray for us drunkards now and at the hour of eleven, amen.' We walked home along the narrow roads together, Mam and I, seagulls over the bog, rainbows, winter stars rising early in the first darkness of the east. She was always wondering what to cook for him, and she'd stop by the wall, lodge in a few more rocks before she went to the kitchen, sometimes muttering quietly to herself.

The old man was freelancing for some agricultural

magazines. His life had whittled down to fields of barley, gleaming red combine harvesters, cows with splatterings of shit on their tails, formal committee meetings, product launches, brand-new packages of bacon, shots of serious men in grey suits shaking hands at conventions. Banality at its finest, it meant little or nothing to him, it had no art, but it held him here. He took the sort of shots that appeared in the unread sections of newspapers. Or the type of images so indistinct that a byline underneath them embarrassed him. The world had come down to this – he was a father growing middle-aged and bored in a grey Mayo farmyard, patient as a draft-horse for a new season of grass. His wife built walls and spent afternoons in a strange pub. She talked and dreamt constantly of her homeland. He would slump his way through the front door in the evenings, smelling of old milk and cigarettes, sigh, kiss her brusquely on the cheek, ask her how much stout she had drunk in O'Leary's. He'd wander around the table, put a hand to the back of my head, rub my hair: 'How's my young fella today?' I'd tell him that I'd scored a hat-trick in a schoolyard football match. He'd put his hands into the pocket of his waistcoat and say: 'Good on ya, lad, good on ya,' and then lean his head down to his plate of food, every now and then looking up and winking at me, saying, 'Hat-trick, huh?' Moments like that, I loved him hugely, admired his bigness, but Mam sat at the end of the table and said nothing, all the time knowing that I hadn't played football after school at all.

He kept a notebook with him, wrote the accounts in it. Sometimes he read the financial situation aloud at the dinner table, promised that soon there would be enough for us to make our great trip to the Chihuahuan desert. 'Yes,' he'd say, 'just a few more months and another big job, we'll be on the pig's back.' Mam's lips would give a small twitch as if Mexico was sitting there, at the edge of her mouth, as if she might just be able to taste it.

But instead he built his own darkroom. He wanted to use the old cow shed, but it let in too much light, so he created it from scratch. Hired a JCB and dug out the foundations, sat me in the plastic swivel seat, pretended to let me steer the huge yellow digger. He drained the foundation holes with an industrial hose-pump and put in pipes, dropped the cement in by himself, let me draw my initials in it. He contracted a couple of men to help him on odd days. They called him 'Boss,' in an almost derisory way, and they went into exaggerated raptures when Mam brought out tea and slices of fruitcake. 'Missus Lyons, ya make the best cup of tea in the county.' 'Jaysus, Missus Lyons, I'd put some of this on me head and beat me brains with me tongue trying to get at it.'

Once, when the old man was gone to town for sand, I heard a wolf-whistle as Mam bent down to work at her stone wall. She stood up and smiled, waved at them, and the men hung their heads and went back to work.

Out there with his shirt off in the cool drizzling summer, my father strutted around. His chest had begun to sag just a little so that he would sometimes pinch at his nipple to make it look hard. I remember now that he sucked in his belly and put his hands over the side of his love handles to seem slim. There was still a drama to him. Up on the roof the hammer was raised high, an arm cocked histrionically to show a muscle. Flamboyant with the electric drill, his finger wagged when he showed me how it worked. He had begun to comb his hair across, to cover up the large bald spot, but it was still impossible to control. It was long enough that it sometimes blew out and fell to his shoulder. He licked his fingers and pasted it back.

The building was modular and neat, made of cinder blocks, with two rooms separated by wood panelling, no windows, a flat roof, carefully insulated, mindfully monitored so that no light leaked in under the doors. He drilled bolts into the wall for file cabinets and shelves, ran in electricity and water, jerryrigged a phone line. He called it 'The Gulag,' a nickname that could have been a premonition. He had a string on the knob of the second door, which he kept locked, so that, when he pulled it, it would flip the lock and open the door. I would go out at dinnertime to call him in. Some shuffling around before he opened the door, a sound of papers moving, drawers closing, lids going down on boxes. Then he'd pull the string to expose the small banalities of his world. Rows of photos hung under a string of red bulbs, a contact sheet of Friesians or an advertisement for cheese. He'd wipe his hands on a piece of red towelling and ask me: 'Is it chips she's cooking again, tonight?'

It was a familiar phrase.

Early one morning I heard the old man thunder down the stairs. I followed him. A fire in the kitchen, the chip-pan ablaze. Mam stood in the middle of the floor, staring at it, eyes effulgent above her gorse-coloured dressing gown. She didn't even look at him, kept staring at the fire as it leaped. 'I only wanted to cook something,' she said, 'I couldn't sleep, you see that I cannot sleep lately.' The old man wrapped the flap of his string vest around the handle of the pan. He moved through the kitchen, muttering some surreptitious obscenity, stormed outside to the yard, where he threw the pan into long grass for the night dew to seal it. The last few sparks were spectral in the grass. He came back inside, a burn on the inside of his palm, licked at it, chopped an orange in half to soothe the wound.

'Are ya off your fucken rocker, woman, who wants chips at this hour of night?'

She was by the stove, still motionless beside the tea kettle, not unlike a tea kettle herself, one hand bent out spout-like, her face silver, slowly beginning to move on the balls of her feet, but lucid, a whistle in the voice – 'It was just a little mistake, Michael, we all make mistakes'. He looked at me, his eye-whites slashed through with twigs of redcurrant, fingered at a bit of sleep in one of the corners, then scratched at the cavern of his belly button, looked like he was trying hard to remember something that wasn't important anyway. He moved the tongue around his lips: 'And you, young fella, isn't it time for all good children to be in bed?'

He guided me to the hallway, kissed me on the forehead. I hugged him, ascended the stairs in a confusion of love and hatred. Don't worry about it, son,' he said, 'your Mam's just a little tired.'

That night I heard them arguing downstairs, and after that, when I called him in from the darkroom for dinner, he'd say: 'Is it chips she's cooking again, tonight?'

On television there were programmes where men came up behind women at stoves, wrapped their arms around their waists, even helped them stir whatever was in a pot – and I wondered why the old man didn't do that with Mam. Slumbering in their own solitude, they didn't even saunter to mass together, as other parents did. On Saint Valentine's Day I gave them identical holy crosses made from reeds, left over from Saint Brigid's Day. They came up to my bed at separate times and thanked me, my father with a pound note, my mother with a cup of hot chocolate. They were in different worlds, impossible to bridge. I imagined them swaying through the house, the open jacket of my father's pyjamas not even touching against the jumpers that Mam wore over her nightdress, the two crosses placed in different windows at opposite ends of the house.

Weeds grew around the bottom of his darkroom. I tried to break in, but he had locked it tight and there were no windows to get through. Once, when he was travelling for a week, I tried to dig a tunnel for myself at the back. I imagined myself as some gaunt-faced prisoner breaking into his gulag, war ribbons dangling from the holy medal at my chest, using a trowel to scrabble away at the mucky mess, him high above me in a watchtower with a rifle. All I hit was foundation stone. When he came back he asked me about the hole. I told him I'd seen a dog back there, digging. 'You chase him off with a big stick next time you see him, right, son?' I gave up after that, though there were still times I rifled through the pockets of his trousers, unsuccessfully looking for the key.

The old man made friends with a big-shot who owned a meat-processing company in Swinford. O'Shaughnessy was the sort of man who had bottles jangling in the pockets of granite-grey suits. He had a bulbous nose and a huge belly, drove expensive cars that rolled down our lane late at night and beeped very loud for the old man to come out drinking. Mam hated O'Shaughnessy, avoided him when he came to the house – he was always trying to touch the sleeves of her blouses, planting Continental-style kisses on her cheeks. Sometimes, when he visted, she went out and did a few bits and pieces of work on her wall, even at night, in the dark. The old man and O'Shaughnessy would come home when the pubs closed and they would sit in the living room together, loud guffaws rising up through the house.

Once or twice Mam came into my room and sat by the window while they were downstairs. She said nothing, just looked out the window, watched the pattern of weather outside. The thing that got her most was the cold, the more or less constant lack of sun, the way it would seep downward into her marrow. She often wore two or three jumpers over one another. In the morning, while she got the fire ready in the living room, she kept the tea kettle beside her, warming her hands over the steam, even wearing gloves while she cooked breakfast, teeth chattering. Still amazed by snow, in winter she would watch my snowmen dribble down to a carrot and eye-pebbles, hugging herself into a coat, stamping her feet on the ground, watching the clouds made from our breath. The whips of winds shook her to the core – she was a watcher of storms. Huge billows lashed in from the Atlantic, carrying spindrift, causing the river trees to kowtow to the ground, litter to animate itself. One storm was a peculiar blessing for her – a sandstorm from the Sahara, carrying dust, red dust, all the way from North Africa, depositing it on the land so that tiny particles covered the windshields of cars, the roofs of houses, gates, walls, boots, the leaves of flowers by the front door. She didn't wash the windows for weeks, enthralled by the revisit of red dust to her life. She ran her finger along the window ledge and held it up for me to see, 'Isn't it nice, *m'ijo*? A red wind.'

O'Shaughnessy and my father began to take trips abroad, mostly Belgium and France, something to do with EEC beef deals. Pictures were taken of O'Shaughnessy at conventions, wearing his fat gaudy ties. They'd be gone for a fortnight at a time, and Mam would fall asleep in a wicker chair by my bedroom window, three blankets pulled around her.

And then one evening the old man arrived home from France with two cardboard boxes. It had been a particularly cold day, frost on the ground, all the windows of the house locked tight, robins frantic over bits of bread in the yard. O'Shaughnessy dropped my father off at the front of the house, blew my mother a kiss as she stood at the window in her jumpers. She turned away. The old man lumbered the boxes and his suitcase out on to the porch, shuffling his feet precisely over the ice. He sat there for a while, the boxes at his feet. Mam asked me to call him in for dinner – this time he said nothing about chips. He breezed his way into the house, threw off his coat, just a white shirt underneath, combed his hair across his pate, pasted it down with spittle, and put his suitcase down against the kitchen table. Mam was bent over some eggs with *salsa* sauce, rubbing her gloved hands together.

'Two shakes of a lamb's tail,' my father said, and he stroked her tenderly on the side of the face.

She looked up, surprised. He went back outside and lifted the cardboard boxes from the porch. Despite the chill, two large ovals of sweat formed on his underarms. He laid the two boxes on the kitchen table and nodded up and down, turned and told me it was time for me to take my swim. 'He will be frozen,' said Mum. My father winked: 'Nah, he'll be fine, he's a big man now.' There was a strange look in the old man's eye. I went upstairs and got the two sets of togs. At the front door I waited for him to come with me. I held the togs up, but he motioned me away with his hand, told me to go on my own. He took out a knife and began cutting the string from the cardboard boxes. I waited at the window.

'This is a present for your Mam,' he said, 'you go on down and I'll join ya later, take your coat, wrap up well when ya get out.'

We had often swum in the cold before, but always in the morning, the initial shock of climbing in disappearing, a feeling that another skin had developed over my body. I had become better at going against the current, didn't have to hang on to the poplar roots any more. I swam for maybe ten minutes, let the water push me backwards, went to the pool at the side of the river and pulled a hollow reed, went underwater, breathed through it. It was a strange green world down there, immense and fascinating and slimy, until I was so far down in it that water poured through the reed and I let it go, and my breath left me at the same time, bubbles rising up, and I sank, felt like I was swimming blind, the pressure thumping my chest, pushing arms outwards. I sat on some riverbottom stones until the pain became almost peaceful, a barrage of it in my lungs, and I shunted myself up, resurfaced.

The meat factory had only just been set up and none of the offal floated in the water yet, although I had begun to notice a little bit of a smell. I paddled around the river for a while, saluted a duck, got out and pulled my anorak around me – the zip was broken – put a towel around my neck. When I came back up from the riverbank Mam was at her wall in her big coat and three sweaters, and the old man was nowhere to be seen. I walked up and stood beside her, my hair dripping wet, a chatter in my teeth, wanting to tell her about my swim, but she told me to go into the house and towel myself off. She was looking down at a place where her wall had given through, one of the teeth fallen from the grey gum of it. She looked at it long and hard, knelt down, picked up a field rock, tried to wedge it back in, tried very hard but couldn't, broke a fingernail, said something in Spanish I didn't understand. It sounded as if there was custard in her mouth. I thought she was just cold. Her body began to tremble, quietly at first. 'I thought it would support,' she said to herself, 'it's so easy thing to do.' She tried to wedge another rock in, but it jutted out and her fingers shook. She pushed her knee against the rock, but it still didn't budge. She stood up, shivering.

'I always thought it will be better than this, *m'ijo*,' she said suddenly. 'I always told myself it will be better than this.'

And I – ten years old – thought she was talking about the hole in the wall, and said: 'It'll be all right, Mam, we'll give it another shot in the morning.'

The ancestry of act – every moment leading up to haunt that one particular moment. Instead of Mam's own body breaking itself down in the slow natural entropy of motherhood and age, it became something else altogether – destroyed for her in a strange sort of way. It wasn't even a vagarious thing, or a whim, or an impulse on the old man's part – it might have been easier that way. But he had planned it for a long time, I suppose. He wanted a memorial of some sort, an epitaph for himself, a packet of light to emerge and print itself indelibly on his life, to say: *I was once great, look at these great photos I took, look how perfect they are, look how I once lived, I was alive!* Maybe he laboured over that book, maybe he pored over all his contact sheets with a singular intensity, maybe he truly believed that it would reinvent things, or maybe he thought it was a gesture of love – that she could look in its pages and remember herself. Or some vision of herself.

But something other than her life was on display – it was the moments of her body. Her neck and breasts and stomach and legs and spine and moles and pubic hair and ankles and eyes and raven-dark hair under mosquito nets, near fire towers, in a pine-pole camp, in a dark Bronx bedroom, screaming out for some sense of place, lost between the cheap covers of a book.

The night of the carnival in Castlebar. Eleven years old. The old man was still broad and big-boned, but heavier. A summer evening, and a gulf of men stood around under a marquee of lightbulbs, in white shirts, grey waistcoats, and gigantic red ties, chatting. They ran their fingers through wild emigrating hair. Some of them gazed longingly at a girl in a chartreuse jumper and blossoming lipstick who was selling toffee apples at a stall. Other men stood by and played darts at another stall, keen on the ace of hearts, which might have won them a tiny bottle of Paddy or an ashtray leaping with flowers. Their wives roamed around with plastic bags full of goldfish about to suffocate. From the big wheel – which, in retrospect, wasn't very big – boys my age were sending down jets of saliva through the gaps in their front teeth on to the onlookers below. I wanted to be up there with them, but Mam had told me to stay with her.

She and the old man had been arguing again. He was walking around, fulminating under a flat hat, taking pictures. But after a while he came up to us, camera across his shoulder, and asked Mam if she wanted to go for a spin on the chairoplanes. She nodded and smiled. I was stunned by the smile. There'd been a long period of silence in our house. Mam had stopped eating at the table with him. She was sleeping in the guest room. When they talked, the old man would give a shrug of the shoulders, like a twitch. She spent most of her time at the wall. The huge dark bags had filled out under her eyes, and I suppose they just kept up a semblance of themselves, for my sake, nothing else tying them to one another.

Mam gave me a few pence to get a toffee apple. The girl at the stand had cheeks white as Styrofoam. I watched as the old man launched Mam on the chair, rocking and twirling the seat every time she came around, leaning into her, saying something. For a while she was actually laughing, I couldn't believe it. Her skirt was flying upwards in the air. A chiffon scarf leaped backwards from her neck, a few silver strands of hair were in view from the scarf, a gasp of teeth all caesium-white. The chairoplane was moving in a circle, faster and faster, a spinning top. Each time she went past, Mam leaned out and said something to him, smiling. He was chuckling as he pushed her. But suddenly she didn't lean out anymore.

A group of older boys was gathered down by one of the tents, pointing at Mam. Her skirt was billowing and her thin legs were licking outwards under the billow, exposing her underpants. She blanched and shoved her fists down into the skirt to stop it from blowing upwards. As she went around she leaned outwards from the chair, towards the old man, and perhaps there was a bouquet of bile from her lips – *¡Vete al diablo Michael Lyons!* – and the old man suddenly moved away, the chairoplane bringing Mam outwards towards a malachite night, around again to a muskrat-muddy ground where footprints ranged, around, around, around, gradually slowing, her skirt tucked and held between her knees now. The boys moved off, laughing, and my old man went down by the strongarm machine, with a cigarette stooping like a ladder down to his chin, the long sideways swish of his hair Brylcreemed down.

Mam climbed off the chairoplane, smoothing the back of her skirt, hitching up some pantyhose at the knees, her voice a loom, interweaving with carnival notes, spinning out once again. 'Come, Conor,' she said to me. I pretended that I didn't hear and tucked the toffee apple under my jacket so the lads on the wheel couldn't spit down into it. The moths flared away under carnival lights beneath a massive burlesque of stars.

I saw the old man walking towards the strongarm machine, a giant loping stride as if he'd just stepped out of an advertisement for very strong cigarettes, like he always walked – even when I hated him I loved him for the gigantic way he walked – shoulders swinging, everything in a loop around him. Mam went the other way, moving through the tents and the broken brown bottles. I stood there between them, by the toffee-apple stall, listening to a man play a concertina. I walked towards her as she moved through the sea of shirts and gypsy-fed eyes and faces lacquered with alcohol and – even before I was beside her – the hand, brown and slender, reached out backwards to take mine, a well used reflex. I took her fingers. The spindrift of carnival seeped outwards to further-strung lights of the town. Behind my back the old man was standing by the machine with the giant hammer in the air, against the backdrop of a red and white tent. The carnival clamour wilted as Mam and I moved towards the edge of the car park, and I was wondering if my father was the one sounding out the trilly muscleman bell as we tramped down weeds at the side of a field, Mam and I, circling around, waiting for him to drive us home. From the tents I could still see the boys peeping.

She was famous by then.

The books were censored in Ireland, of course – at first they couldn't be found anywhere except in his darkroom, although O'Shaughnessy probably had some, too. Maybe it was O'Shaughnessy who showed them to people. Or perhaps they were found by emigrants in obscure European bookstores, sent back home in envelopes with fabulous stamps, young men stumbling across them in the corner of a Parisian stall, tentatively peeling back a cover, feeling the heart thump, looking over a thin shoulder, lifting the page higher. Maybe there were drunken miscreants in the backstreets of Liège who recognised his name on the shabby front cover – men with holes in overcoat pockets so they could reach all the way down to their articulate penises. Or curly-haired artists crazed against the sunsets of a plaza in Rome, denizens of vivacious dreams who loved the photos for what they were, sent them home, wrapped in brown paper to beat the censors.

I had seen a copy. The door of the darkroom had been left open, the old man was gone for the day, and twenty or so were stacked in a corner. At first I didn't understand that it was her. I just kept flicking the pages. A huge feeling of sickness rose up in me. I scoured quickly through it again, hands shaking. I remember feeling as if a big vacuum was sucking the air from me, dry-retching, a world churning in me, slamming the door, afraid to go home. I had a dream that night. The book was on the coffee table and my schoolteachers were in the house. They picked up the book and smiled, comparing different shots, bits of chalk circling around the pages, one teacher constantly circling her breasts. I kept grabbing the book and tucking it behind the pail of peat near the fireplace so that they wouldn't see a leg leap from the glass of the coffee table, or a nipple emerge from under a plate of biscuits, or a belly button give an eye from beneath a teacup. But the teachers kept tut-tutting at me, taking it back, some of them holding it up in the air. A giant bamboo cane was raised by the headmaster and I woke, tremulous, walked out into the landing and hunched down, inventing ways of killing my father: make him swallow his chemicals, thump him to a black and white pulp.

Copies got through to people in town, or the rumour of the book did, so that the whole place swivelled and the postman was famous and the telephone operator was abuzz. Father Herlihy flapped in his vestments and made a veiled threat, saying, 'Blessed be those who know the reasons for things, we must fling all filth out! Fling it out, I say!' Men in peatbogs who had heard about the photos hailed the heroic eye of my father, caps raised up over centuried soil. Workers from the abattoir, blood-splattered, shit-splattered, passed by our house, looking up at the bedroom windows for a glance which would never come. And the women in their coffee mornings surely set about whispering, lipstick on their teeth, slapping their tongues against the news.

'Listen up now, I heard they took photos in the bath.'

'Go away out of that.'

'Swear to God.'

'You're having me on.'

'I'm not.'

'Well, the water bill must be something fierce.'

There wasn't a whole lot of money in our house anymore – the old man had obviously paid to get the book published, and he never read from his notebook anymore. The silence at our dinner table doubled and redoubled itself. The idea of our trip to Mexico had vanished.

Mrs O'Leary still supported Mam. She still went to the

pub as often as she could – slinking through the bar quickly with her head down as barstools shifted and swivelled, out to the back garden where the chickens were. There were probably jokes made – 'There she goes, Mrs Public Hair,' the rat-faced comedian might have said, 'would ya look at the swish of her!' I figure that much, because Mrs O'Leary banned him from the pub. Over the bar counter she declared with a flourish of a fleshy hand: 'Leave her bloody well alone! I'd do it myself, go bloody starkers, only they'd laugh at me best and whistle for more.'

I continued to meet Mam at the pub after school, until one afternoon when birds were beating blackwinged against the sky and hay was on the wind and rain was dolloping through chestnut trees. I pulled the heavy door open, was met with curls of smoke. The man with the walrus moustache was sliding off his barstool, drunk. He looked at me as if surprised by my existence, curved his index finger towards me, 'Come here a second, you,' he said, 'come here,' leaning into me with a wink. His breath was stale with Woodbine, his eyes like apples just bitten into and discoloured, his moustache hairy over his teeth. He shifted himself on the barstool, looked around, reached forward, and out of his lunchbox on the counter, suddenly, like a rabbit pulled from a hat, came a picture of Mam which he held in the air and examined for a moment. He licked the hedge of Guinness off his moustache, rotated the photo between his fingers. He sighed, smiled at me, saying, 'Look at this, look at this, would you have a look at this,' and I looked, and she was there, staring out with sepia eyes from a bed overhung by a white mosquito net, beside an old lantern, beside a painting of flowers, beside a crack in the wall – Mexico – and the walrus man was twirling her in his fingers, incanting a low whistle over his lunchbox, and I stared at Mam, her breasts all soggy from lettuce and tomato sandwiches.

Mrs O'Leary broke out from the bar counter, a grey-hound from a trap, slapped the man with the walrus moustache, slapped him twice, so hard that his head moved, a wooden doll, side to side, the sound of it around the bar, 'Get the fucken bejesus outa here!' she shouted, then blessed herself for the blasphemy. 'Sorry, Father,' she said to the ceiling. She gathered me to her immense chest, held me there, turned to Mam, who had come in from the yard, and said: 'I suppose you'd be best off leaving the young fella at home.'

Mrs O'Leary wiped the topaz sleeves of her billowy dress across my face. She reached for a bottle of Guinness at the same time, took a slurp that dribbled down the front of her dress. Mam was fumbling at my anorak – trying to hold the steel teeth of the zip together to close it, hands shaking. Mam looked up and said sadly: 'Yes, Alice, I suppose I should leave the child at home, should't I?'

Geese out over the land, heading towards the sea. Long necks stretched, gunnelling their wings against the sky. They made a curious sound with their wings as they went overhead, like rifle fire. Spread their wings out to hover, settled down somewhere distant. Quite gorgeous.

I got up off the wall and went back to the house to make a pot of tea, then went down to the river to see if he was doing all right. By the time I got to the river some of the tea had spilled down on to the tray and soaked into one or two of the biscuits. I picked one up and ate it. It felt like a strange Sunday communion melting on my tongue. He was sleeping in the red and white lawn chair and the rods had fallen down by his feet. All the rubbish still lay unmoving in the water, the same piece of Styrofoam that was there last week, stuck in the reeds. I thought that maybe I should clean the river up for him before I leave tomorrow – but instead I just sat down and watched its colours change as clouds passed through the sky.

The old man was smacking his lips together – like Cici had once said, maybe he was eating his dreams.

But his breathing was somewhat irregular and I moved up close to him, felt his breath against my cheek to make sure he was all right. It came loud and patchy through his nostrils. For a moment I moved to wake him up, shake his shoulder, decided against it. I sat and sipped at the tea, ate a few more biscuits, had a bizarre and hopelessly ridiculous notion – maybe I would feed him a damp biscuit while he slept.

Mam started buttoning up everything very high, even when we went to the beach, especially when we went to the beach. A long stretch of clean yellow sand, edged by rocks, studded on the ten good days of summer with deckchairs and bathtowels and coloured balls floating on the air. Men with farmers' tans shoved the top end of matches into the ground, exhaling smoke generously to the sky. Older boys stood with binoculars on the dunes, itchy with lust for the sight of a porpoise, or a ghost ship, or a drowning, or a daring bikini.

Along the hard edge of the beach a middle-aged gypsy whom I had seen in town was guiding a donkey. Beside him, on a motorbike, was Jimmy Donnelly from secondary school, older than me, going very slowly, no helmet on. Donnelly and the tinker nodded to one another, weaving in and out, hoof marks in a strange language amid the tyre tracks. A young girl stared at them, vanilla stream from an ice cream runnelling down the front of her chin. Dogs were unleashed and curious, and urinating by seaweed. A woman with toffee-coloured shoulders, wrapped in a towel, piled herself into a swimsuit, ballooning her breasts up with one hand. Mam sat on the blanket, wearing a white linen blouse buttoned up to the neck, a neck so thin and strained that when she took a cup of tea from the red flask and drank – sandflies jumping around on the rim of the cup – it looked as if it might be very painful to take it down, the striations furrowing down towards her bony chest. She rubbed cream on the smooth curve of her calf muscles where her skirt was hitched up, to the knee, never any further, not anymore.

The old man was walking along the strand in his poppy-red togs, his belly plopping out over the drawstring, lifting up a jellyfish with a small piece of driftwood, turning the bell-shaped body over and over, leaning down to stare at it, his stomach creasing. Mam took a kitchen knife, from the plastic bag because we couldn't find the hamper in the morning – he had stood by the door, shouting 'Are yez coming or what?', her fumbling, 'Of course we are coming,' him ringing the doorbell over and over, 'Well, so's bloody Christmas!' – and she held the knife and unscrewed the lid from the honey jar, smearing it very slowly, precisely, over some slices of bread. She smoothed it out to the edges as if everything somehow depended on it, long slow rolls of her hand, stopping only to whip the stalks of hair back from her eyes. She wiped her fingers on the edge of the blanket. The motorbike beeped and Donnelly raised his arm in a gesture of glory, left a plume of smoke around the donkey. But the wheel got stuck in the soft sand. He toppled, looked up ignominiously from the ground. The tinker, riding bareback, reared in laughter. Donnelly suddenly started laughing, too, and pushed the bike through heavy sand to the applause of some old ladies.

Donnelly and the gypsy started shouting, so that everyone looked up and listened, 'Fivepence for a trot, ten for a canter, come and get it!'

I moved down to the hard edge of the strand. Donnelly's companion smelled like campfire and cider. He held the rope in brown fingers, leaned across, eyes green as silage, looked at me and said, 'Are ya right, so? Where's your money?' 'I don't have any money,' I said. 'Well, fuck off, so.' Donnelly started whispering something in the tinker's ear. The man whipped his head back with laughter. 'Come here,' he said to me, 'd'ya want a go on the donkey?' I said, 'Yeah.' 'Fair enough, get your old dear down here to give us a blowjob.' 'What?' 'Your old dear, she gives us a blowjob, we'll give ya a trot.' Donnelly began laughing. I edged away from the donkey, and the tinker started whispering something in the animal's ear, giving it some form of benediction. Is that what he means? I thought. I was eleven years old.

I ran up the strand to where Mam was headbent staring at the ground, and the old man was standing with his arms stretched out, like Jesus crucified, arguing about no butter on the sandwiches – 'Ya want me to eat these fucken things dry?' – so I sat on the edge of the blanket and watched Donnelly and the tinker roll down along the beach again. A sandwich was laid in my lap.

'Mam, what's a blowjob?'

The old man suddenly slapped his knees uproariously. 'Ah, Jaysus, even I've forgotten that! Even I've forgotten what that is!' Mam's face drained slowly, plucked at the tassels on the side of the blanket, 'I don't know, *m'ijo*, ask me later.'

Donnelly and the tinker were down the beach now with two girls on the back of the donkey, another man alongside them with his handkerchief knotted on his head, trying hard to keep up, with a plastic bucket and shovel in his hand. My father grunted and walked down to the water's edge, pulling lint from his belly button. After a while the beach slowly began to clear. It was Mam's time – I had seen it before – she was stretching her legs out along the edge of the blanket, her arms moving up to massage the back of her neck. Donnelly and the gypsy moved off from the dune, cigarettes held furtively. Along the length of the beach the other blankets had been lifted, Dunnes Stores bags tumbled, a Fanta can rolled towards the dunes, a cigarette butt bumped into a jellyfish. The sun gave a bow to the sea. Soon there was nobody left on the strand except the tinker, who was pulling his donkey up towards the cross where the life-belt was, red and white. The road curled like a rope away through stone walls built to last an eternity of storms, unlike hers. Not a soul was left save us and a few glad seagulls, bragging with crusts of bread over the sea.

She took off her blouse, unbuttoned it slowly, underneath was her purple swimsuit, like an anemone around her, sea-bound. 'You come?' she said. 'Course I'm coming, Mam.' The cavernous hollows in around the throat, smokeblue, lines criss–crossing each other moving upwards to a strange smile, aware of her body, tentative, ashamed, and maybe the tinker staring back at us, but she was suddenly cantering ahead of me like a purple tenpence towards the ocean, the old man absorbed by the sight of jellyfish, while her swift skinny arms made butterfly shapes in the shallow edge of the Atlantic, her spraying me with water, leaning in conspiratorially, saying: 'Conor, I will explain to you that word when you are older.'

That night she stood in the kitchen under the fluorescent lights and pushed her fork through an uneaten plate of food.

I came home from school the next day and she was down by the firepit. She was wearing an apron from Knock shrine, a gift from Mrs O'Leary, the picture of the Madonna with a bit of homemade *salsa* on her nose. Along the lane on the bicycle, the brakes squeaking, I pulled up to where she was standing.

'What ya doing, Mam?'

She swung around, a little startled. 'You are home early,' she said, wiped her hands on the face of the apron.

'What're ya burning, Mam?'

'Nothing, *m'ijo*, come on inside, I have something special for you.'

She took my schoolbag from my shoulder as we walked to the front porch. A parcel sat on the table from Dublin, brown and crinkled. She handed me the scissors with long lean fingers – 'Go on now, hurry quickly.' The parcel produced a brand–new blue anorak. I laid it on the table but she told me to put it on. It was still hot outside, and I didn't want to wear it, but I zipped it up quickly to try it on. She was happy then over the *salsa* pot, looking out the window. I said that I was just going outside for a moment, took the anorak off and left it sitting on the table.

Out in the firepit she had burned herself, made a pyre of her past, a giant cardboard box of books with the ends of flame around it, licking the edge of herself in the same way that the mountain fires did, a wale of fire upridged on the books. I poked around the flamed edges with a stick, around the mosquito net that the walrus man loved so much, around a dozen different bedrooms, around a tumult of skin, a dressing-table photo unburnt, a grove of trees ashy at the edges, a leg prominent from the knee down, a bedsheet disappearing. Suddenly she was shouting at me from the porch, with the coat in her fingers.

'Come here, come here right now!'

I ran through the farmyard.

'What are you doing there? You don't like the coat?'

'Oh, yeah, I like it, yeah.'

'You don't use it?'

'Don't want to get it dirty, Mam.'

She nodded her head and beckoned me with a large wooden fork covered in red sauce. 'Come here and taste my *salsa*, tell me if it's good, maybe there are missing peppers.'

But I leaned against the door and placed my muddy foot on the black and white linoleum and said: 'I hate him, too, Mam. I hate him, too, he's a bastard! I hate him!' I had found out in school that day what the word meant – *Hey lads, Lyonsy doesn't know what a blowjob is! Are ya thick, Lyonsy? Everyone knows what a blowjob is!* – and I had come home, detesting my father for the enormity of what he had done.

But Mam spun around and pulled me quickly to the chair – with surprising strength – and laid me down over her knee and slapped me, hard, six times on the back of my legs with the fork, sauce splaying around. 'Don't say that again never, don't make me hear it again, don't say that again never!' I couldn't understand her. The back of my legs were stinging, and, afterwards, at the kitchen table, she said: 'Your Papa should hit you himself, but he never hit anybody in his life, you should be thankful, he never even hit a fly in his life! Your Papa never touched anybody!' Later that afternoon, with a scarf of dusk coming down over the courtyard, and a smell of slaughter from the meat factory, I saw her as she strode purposefully back out to the firepit, arms swinging down by her side. She finished the job off – burning the books with a small splash of petrol and a match that took ages to light. They were damp and they snapped when she struck them. She didn't throw much of a shadow anymore.

He woke up from the lawn chair, unaware I was sitting there, reached into his pocket for his packet of cigarettes. Before he lit up he reamed up from his chest and let a gob out towards the river. It landed near the bank, close to where I was sitting. The spit was strung through with blood. 'Jaysus,' he said, noticing me, 'I must have fallen asleep.' He saw me looking down. He was silent for a while, then he breathed deeply again through his nose.

'Too much raspberry jam on me toast this morning.'

I felt a foul revulsion and love for him.

★

183

Us in the kitchen. Her hair thrown back behind her in long rushes of tungsten. She looked up at him as he took a plastic lighter from his shirt pocket, a pack of Major. 'Living with you is like living with the ashtray!' she shouted. He rose up from his chair, scooted it along the floor, cigarette between his teeth, pointed at her, shouting: 'And it's well you'd know about bloody ashtrays, isn't it, woman?'

It was the morning after the books had become ash themselves, the wall of the firepit scorched, an aurora of herself amongst it. 'You and your chip-pans and your books and your fires,' he said, softer now, 'would ya ever get a grip on yourself?'

He bravadoed his way out the door, camera bag slung over his shoulder in a motion of boredom – off to take pictures of some cows, corn-fed for the meat factory. He closed the car door, beeped the horn, lifted his finger wearily from the wheel.

Mam stood in the kitchen, awash in thought, by the stove, perhaps recalling fires of such spectacular magnitude that looking at the chip-pan or out at the firepit simply made her shake her head. She wiped her suds on the pocket of the holy apron – 'Okay, *m'ijo*, I have been looking at this for a long time,' staring at the stain above the stove. 'How do we take it off the wall?' The car moved away towards the road. Flies landed on the sticky yellow paper hung from the windowpane. I propped myself up on the stove, scrubbed with a Brillo pad. We leaned into the wall, but the mark wouldn't come off no matter how hard we tried, it had its own stigmata. She stared into space, reached down and twirled the knobs on the radio. After a while I climbed down from the stove, said: 'Mam, I should go, I'm going to be late for school again.'

She stared at the fire stain for a second. '*Quitate*,' she said, smiling, 'I will take care of this myself.'

She wiped a smudge of black from above my eyebrow,

kissed me gently on the cheek. 'Your new coat looks great.' She shoved a bar of chocolate into my pocket. I went outside into the spindrifty air, past the mound of ash in the firepit, hopped on the bicycle, pedalled furiously, brown puddlewater skipping up on to the back of my coat. At the meat factory my father was chatting with a man who was leading half a dozen fat cows out to be photographed – later to be butchered and hung on hooks. Two of the cows were simultaneously letting dung out to splatter on their tails. Crows flew in behind the cattle to feed on the disturbed insects in the hoof marks. I watched my father for a moment, leaned my head down to the handlebars and rode over the hump-backed bridge to school.

Later that week the old man was off in Europe again, and Mam was at home waiting for Mrs O'Leary to come in for lunch. It was the first time that Mrs O'Leary had come for a meal. Mam had cut flowers. I thought that she might even eat something substantial that day, she had prepared tortillas. Jittery, she ran long fingers over one another.

At noon, a taxi swanned down the laneway. Mrs O'Leary sallied up to our door, feeling her way with a walking stick. The taxi driver carried tins of paint, and rollers and brightly coloured vases and a host of exotic flowers – 'A small gift for you, Juanita,' Mrs O'Leary said. It was all laid down on the floor of the living room. The driver took off, tipping his flat hat to Mrs O'Leary.

'Right,' said Mrs O'Leary, 'let's decorate.'

The three of us dragged the old furniture from the living room to the farmyard, Mrs O'Leary cursing about her eyes. The yard looking strange to me with its tables and chairs standing lopsided on the rickety stones. Inside, we put old plastic bags, newspapers, and bedsheets on the carpet, painted the living-room walls with a very light pink, like flesh. We stood the vases on the mantelpiece and the flowers were carefully moved from corner to corner. 'I think we should put the plant on the far corner, don't you?' said Mam. Some music erupted from the Victrola. We stopped early in the afternoon for a tea-break and Mrs O'Leary produced a bottle of Guinness from her handbag. She asked Mam if she liked the new look, if it was Mexican enough. Mam said, 'Yes, it is very real,' and then she whispered as if in a trance that it was the happiest she had ever been in her life, but her fingers were still rubbing over one another, and talk was sparse at the table, the tortillas having grown cold, Mrs O'Leary wondering how her stand-in was doing at the bar.

Two days later, when the old man came back from France, he gave a generous nod to the room and said, 'Not bad, not bad at all.' He laid a box down in the centre of the floor, lit a cigarette. Mam's cheeks went gaunt in the kitchen as she bit them. He took the box of books from the floor and put them out in the darkroom, padlocked the door. 'You won't be burning these,' he said. He wouldn't show them to her, but I found out, years later, that it was a different book, a completely different one, using the shots of his early life in Mayo, when he used Loyola. He must have paid a fortune to get the book done. Mam left soon after, and my father made a pariah of himself – with me, and almost everyone else – his only occupation in life being the whisk of a fishing line in the air, Mrs O'Leary avoiding him, O'Shaughnessy gone on to other things, only Mrs McCarthy's car tires crunching on gravel as she brought the odd Christian meal down to him.

I felt tense when evening rolled around. We were still sitting in the same spot. He was dozing, hadn't fished all day, even with the new flies. I noticed a couple of old Spar bags tangled in the gorse, got up, picked them off, and started cleaning around the river. Went down to the footbridge first, the planks loose and rickety, creaking away as I leaned over. Used a stick to drag in the piece of Styrofoam to the bank. The ripples reached out, aspiring to one another. Plucked the Styrofoam out with my fingers and put it in the bag, used the stick to lift the plastic bags from the reeds. The sun was low on the horizon, and the geese had gone from the sky, only a few swifts out. I walked down along the far side of the bank, picking up a sack, a length of rope, some paper.

A drizzle began.

'What ya doin?' he asked when he woke, the wind-blown droplets on his face.

'Just picking up some litter.'

'Why's that?'

'Something to do.'

'I suppose it is.'

He stood up to go to the house. I watched as he went through the bushes and over the stile. He was gone for a long time and I thought he was sheltering from the rain, but he surprised me when he came back carrying a large black plastic bag.

He walked to the edge of the water and stood, the flanges of his hair blowing out, saluting the sky. The drizzle was lighter now. He peeled open the top of the big black plastic bag, shook it up and down to belly air into it, ballooning it outwards. I came across the footbridge and we started picking up more litter from the banks, a crisp bag, a soggy newspaper decaying near the reeds, a giant meat-factory syringe, a paper sack full of nails on the bank, a few small wine bottles shoved into the ground in a circle. He flipped one of the bottles towards me to catch, laughing, shuffled around and stabbed at the litter with his stick, dragged it, leaned down slowly to pick it up, filled the bag half-full, every now and then stopping to hum himself a bit of a tune, or look at the sky, or to run his hands along the side of his face.

I was about twenty yards away from him and he was staring down into the reeds. I drifted over, curious. An unrolled condom was lying in the small brown pool beyond the reeds, and he was staring at it – 'Fucken litterbugs, the lot of them,' he said, pointing towards the town, 'up there.'

He picked up a dead branch from the side of the river which curved at its bottom end in a V, like a divining stick. He stared at the branch for a moment, twirling it in his fingers. A small smile appeared as he nodded down at the condom.

He took a red knife out of his pocket, used the fingernail of the thumb to take out the blade, fumbled to whittle the branch down to a sharp point. 'What're ya doing?' I asked. He shrugged again, let the smile crack some wrinkles around his eyes. I heard a car trundle by on the distant road. Bits from the branch fell down at the side of the river as he carved with slow precision.

'Ah, Jesus, Dad,' I said, 'leave it there.'

He shrugged and bent down to the reeds, holding the stick, balancing himself with it. I took a grip of his arm so he wouldn't fall in. He leaned further, caught the condom on the sharpened point, where it teetered for a moment, fell again.

'Ah, fuck it.'

'Leave it be,' I said.

He moved his arm out of my grip, put his hand down on the muddy bank, shifted his way down into the water, up to the rim of his wellingtons. He lifted the condom on one of the V ends, and suddenly burst into laughter as he raised it in the air, dangling it absurdly.

'A million fucken fishes in that thing,' he said, 'and I'm not even using me rod!'

He held the condom on the end of the branch, twirled it for a moment, chuckling and coughing at the same time, opened the black bag, shook the condom off inside with the rest of the litter, flung the stick away down the riverbank. I reached down and gave him a hand out. 'We should get those trousers of yours dry,' I said. He put his arm around me, told me he was knackered. He hung the bag over his wrist and we came back to the house, the evening sun semaphoring off puddles as he stepped right through them, chuckling to himself. In the house I put on the kettle. He took a seat in the armchair, pulled off his trousers, hung them over the fire grill, sat there in his underwear. 'Some Goldgrain with the tea!' he shouted as he picked up the marmalade cat and stroked her. It's been a while since I've seen a flush in his cheeks like that – they were forge-red as if, at last, he had done something spectacular with his life.

'A million fucken fishes, son,' he kept saying, until he went upstairs, steam churning from his teacup, feet creaking lightly on the stairs, still in his underpants.

'Dad,' I said, at the bottom of the stairs. 'Can I tell ya something?'

'Course ya can.'

'I'm a bit embarrassed.'

'Why's that?'

'Well, I'm heading off tomorrow afternoon.'

'Yeah?'

'And I think . . .'

'Ya think what?'

'I mean, the bath.'

'What's that?'

'You're a bit ripe, these days.'

'For crissake, Conor.'

'I was thinking that maybe I'd run the water for you.'

'Ah, for crying out loud. Go away out of that. I don't need a bath. The last thing I need is a fucken bath. What would I need a bath for?'

'Okay.'

'The bath can wait.'

'Whatever you want. Okay. Okay.'

'Ah, Jaysus,' he said.

He was switching his weight from one foot to the other. He went to his room, closed the door softly behind him, but popped his head around and looked down at me, lifted his eyes and closed the door again. I felt that it was some sort of invitation. I followed him in. He had one foot in the bottom of his pyjamas.

'You're an awful man for barging in.'

'Yeah, well.'

'What's going on?'

'Was only kidding about the bath,' I said.

'Fair enough.'

He climbed in under the sheets. He didn't even reach for his cigarettes, just pulled the sheet up as far as his waist. The tea was growing cold on the bedside table.

'D'ya remember?' he said, and then he stopped.

'Remember what?'

'Ah, Jaysus,' he said, 'I remember nothing at all these days.'

'Why's that?' I asked.

'You're better off that way. Remembering nothing.'

He reached over to get the cup of tea.

'You know what someone once said to me, Dad?'

'What's that?'

'They said memory is three-quarters imagination and all the rest is lies.'

'That's a load of codswallop, that is. That's horseshit taught by flies. Who said that?'

'Just a friend.'

'Talking through his arse.'

I sat on the edge of the bed. I surprised myself when I just summoned it up. 'Listen, Dad, why did ya do that to Mam?'

'What?'

'You know.'

'What?' he said. He moved a little.

'Why did ya let that happen?' I said. 'With the photos.'

'Ah, Jaysus, is that what this is all about?'

'I'm just asking. Why did ya . . .?'

'Can't a man forget?'

'Don't think so.'

He was quiet for a moment, looking at his teacup. 'And ya know what someone once said to me?' he said, pointing his forefinger at me. 'Don't know who the fuck it was, but he had it right – he said that, when you come into a rich man's house, the only place to spit is in his face.'

He ran his hands over his face, waiting for a reply, then said: 'So what the fuck happens when ya come into an old man's house, huh?'

'I don't know.'

'Ah, bollocks,' he said. 'All I'm looking for is a bit of peace and quiet. Go away. Let me sleep.'

He turned his head towards his pillow.

'You know where I was, Dad? Those first few years when I was away? You know where I was?'

'Where?'

'I was looking for Mam.'

He sat up and stared at me with one eye closed, and the life drained away from his face, came down to whiteness. 'What were you doing a stupid thing like that for?' he asked.

'Just because.'

'Just because what?'

'Because.'

'Ah, Jaysus.'

'Couldn't find a trace.'

Silence slinked its way around the room. The tea was almost finished but he was draining the last drops of it, holding it up in the air and waiting for something to come out, watching the brown runnel form along the side, licking the drop from the rim of the cup. He held it out in front of him, ran his fingers in amongst the leaves. He started flicking the tea leaves off the end of his forefinger.

'For Jaysus sake, Conor.'

'I'm in Wyoming now,' I said.

'What the hell are ya doing in Wyoming? Nothing but trees there.'

'That's not what you used to say.'

'Ah, to hell what I used to say.'

I told him about cleaning the swimming pools, the ski lifts, Kutch and Eliza, the fist on the tower, about how, every now and then, I take off on foot, go wandering. 'I like it there,' I told him. He gave me a nod and started humming 'Hit the Road, Jack' – I couldn't tell if he was asking me to leave the room, or if he was just lost in his own little world. He said nothing more about Mam, just kept on humming and I was left there on the side of his bed, thinking of those words, hit the road Jack don't you come back no more no more no more no more. I wanted him to say something more, anything, anything at all, and I stared at his face as if I could carve an answer out of that, but I suppose what he was suggesting to me is that you don't spit any differently in an old man's house than you do in a rich man's house, that it all comes down to the very same thing.

# MONDAY

## *leave a man in peace*

When he woke me it was still dark outside. I was curled up at the bottom end of his bed. During the night he must have put a blanket over me. It was folded all the way in under my feet, and a hot-water bottle had grown cold by my toes. He had taken a pillow and propped it in under my head. The marmalade cat was curled in with me, the saucer-ashtray full on the bedside table. He told me that he'd make breakfast for me, that I'd need something for the trip to Dublin. Rubbed his chest and went out the door. I took the saucer full of cigarette butts and went to the bathroom, flushed the fag-ends down the bowl, had a shave – my first shave all week – washed out the sink, had a quick scrub, went downstairs.

I had to laugh when I saw the sunnyside eggs he had ready for me.

He sat opposite me at the table, wearing a white shirt dotted with bits of egg. He was still rubbing his fingers over his chestbone, deliberating the rising of the sun out the kitchen window. And then he opened a button on his shirt and his fingers moved in further around his body. For a moment he shoved them in under his armpit, closed his arm down on them, kept them there for a moment, took them out, almost Napoleonic in the gesture. He held the fingers up to his nose and sniffed them, scrunched up his nose and chuckled.

'You really think I need a bath?'

'Yeah, I suppose you do.'

'I'm a bit on the smelly side, amn't I?'

'A bit.'

'I noticed it last night,' he said. He coughed deeply, went to the kitchen sink and reached across for the bottle of washing-up liquid.

'What's that for?'

'No shampoo in the bathroom,' he said.

'Of course there is,' I said. 'I have some in there.'

'You don't need to pack it?' he asked.

'Not really, I can do without.'

'Are ya all packed?'

'Sort of.'

'Didn't have much time to talk, did we, really?'

'I suppose not.'

'Sometimes you have too much time. Then you figure that too much time isn't any time at all. Know what I mean?'

'Not really.'

'Come on up, then. You can chat to me from outside the door.'

He walked out of the kitchen and I backpedalled in front of him, punching him lightly on the shoulder, until he told me that he'd deck me if I didn't stop, that he still has it in him to throw a good punch.

Headlights swerving down the narrow road towards our house. New territory for the fire department – they had run this road many times before on fire drills for the meat factory, but never this far along the road, so that when one of the trucks tried to thread its way through the laneway a wheel got caught in a rutted ditch and it slid sideways and blocked the entrance. A chorus of obscenities rose up from the men.

Mam was rocking back and forth on the front porch, her head into the blue crucible of her dress. The old man was trying to connect the hose to the tap at the front of the house, shouting 'Jesus fucken Christ!', with the hair outshooting from his pate in brusque surprise, 'Jesus Christ!' The hose sprayed around the tap – a tiny hole had developed in it, which he told me to hold my finger over. A rainbow spectrum arising against the wisteria on the wall. The hose was hardly long enough to reach. My father thumped himself vigorously on the side of the head – 'Ya fucken bitch, ya fucken bitch!' Twelve firemen in yellow jackets were using a winch to take the truck out beyond, others running down the lane, bellies jogging, one of them still in his pyjamas so that his penis leaped out from the gap in his pants. As he ran he pulled on his yellow jacket top, stuffed his penis back in his pyjama bottoms, and moved along with one hand held over his groin, as if wounded. Well into middle age, they breathed like freight trains when they reached the end of the lane and were temporarily immobilised at the sight of the low squat darkroom aflame.

Smoke was coughing out from the bottom of the blue door, moths and midges careening in the sky above the smoke. The men quickly leaned towards my father, asking him something. He grabbed a bucket from the barn, a red bucket, swinging it around and shoving it into the fist of a fireman. 'Where's the fucken fire truck?' he shouted, cursing out more against the lustrous night. He was frantic with movement, lifting his arms up imploringly, then grabbing at the bucket again. The firemen tried to calm him down, drag him back from the flames, hysteria in their voices: 'Hey, this one's rocking, boys, watch the bloody beams don't crash.' A couple of hand-held extinguishers sprayed out frugally against the power of flame. My father was screaming about chemicals that might ignite, but the fire truck was unstuck now, coming along the lane with lights flaring like the carnival whirlywheel, red against the walls. The old man was watching the truck, waving his arms and pointing, stamping his feet up and down on the ground. I looked around at Mam clutching her blue dress, wiping her hands back and forth on the cloth, drying something off her hands.

A sharp crack issued into the night with violent accelera-tion, a joist swinging down in a graceful arc, and then the whole roof came down with a huge splintering sound, sending sparks yawing out over the courtyard, ecstatically fizzling out towards the countryside, caught on the air in somersaults and plunges which extinguished them, up-wards in petition to the sky, then down in greyness to enrich the soil. Other sparks lisped sideways to fade away towards the river. The boom sounded out. Maybe there was a communion of beetles and spiders in uproar in there, a chainwork of scuttle among ripples of negatives and prints and lenses and slides and paper and half-eaten sandwiches, a litany sounding with the boom, 'Ya fucken bitch, ya fucken bitch!' The fire truck was working now, four frenzied men at the giant hose, all of them shielding their eyes from the wild up-burn. Mam was curled like the limb of a heavy orchard tree, bent down, staring at the ground, finished with the rocking. 'Are ya all right, Mam?' She didn't even look up and I noticed the fringe of her hair was singed and the wisps on her arms were fizzled down to stubs. I sat down beside her, insane with pride, but all she said was: 'Bedtime, *m'ijo*.'

I found myself drifting off towards a small crowd that

had gathered, waiting, watching. A slew of cars rolled their way down our laneway for a gawk that was a million times better than any television show – 'Oh, come quick, look, Lyons' darkroom is up in blazes.'

An irate fireman shooed the crowd backwards, out to the lane. Shouts rose up from the men, faces varnished at the sight. Women stood in dressing gowns and hair rollers, toothbrushes still wet in their fingers. An owl-faced man I had never seen before went down on his hunkers in front of me – 'It's all right son,' he said, 'everybody's safe, there's nothing to worry about.' Suddenly a massive flab of arms came out of the crowd and negotiated its way past the stranger and gathered me in to Guinness stains and stale smoke – Mrs O'Leary, somehow aware that it was me, taking a hold of the front of my t-shirt, 'Where's your Mam?' Another roar came across the courtyard – 'Watch the sparks don't make the house catch boys!' Smoke was overcrowding the flames, bits of it shoaling around us so that Mrs O'Leary took out a handkerchief and told me to place it over my mouth, the waft of washing powder pouring into me.

Doctor Moloney, young and slim as a hurley stick, broke his way through the crowd behind us and sprinted over to the firemen who were moving around the darkroom wasplike in their jackets, muttering amongst themselves, some of them looking backwards over their shoulders at Mam, who hadn't budged from the doorstep. The old man was being held back by firemen, two of them on either side, clamping his arms, his legs moving furiously beneath him, shouting something about a Leica lens and a certain roll of film. But he was held back from the smoke-throwing building as if pinned back against the world, an insect in a tray. Mrs O'Leary bent her chest over Mam and, with soothing words rushing forth, combed her hand over the tied-back hair.

'There there, Juanita, there there.'

She told me to run to the kitchen and get some whiskey. 'Quick, lad, before she goes into shock!' But Doctor Moloney was suddenly hovering and holding me back with a hand on my shoulder – 'It's not whiskey she needs at all.' Together they lifted Mam by either shoulder into the living room, which, after their decoration, was a commotion of colour – the vases, plants, amulets, tumultuous paintings, red coffee cans with flowers – and they sat her down in the giant armchair and lingered over her. It might as well have been a peaceful Sunday for the hush that had descended outside, except for the red light of the siren that seeped into the room in swirls from the eastern window. Mrs O'Leary had the kettle on in the kitchen, where the radio had been left on with a gospel song – *Lead me on, precious Lord, through the ripening sun, lead me on, precious Lord, gonna get a glass of buttermilk before the day is done.*

Mrs O'Leary snapped the radio off brusquely. Doctor Moloney had a white washcloth held across Mam's brow while she sat placid in the chair, staring straight ahead without even the suggestion that she had ever learned to speak, fingering at the burnt fringe of her hair. 'Don't make the tea too hot!' shouted the doctor. 'And plenty of sugar in it!' Mrs O'Leary came into the room, feeling her way delicately. She was blowing on the tea, dolloping some extra milk and sugar in it, when the door banged open behind her. My father stood there as huge as an ancient elk exhumed from the bog, shouting, 'Let me smell her hands! Let me smell her hands!' and two policemen came behind him, removing their hats as they crossed the threshold. 'Let me smell her hands, I said!' One of the policemen reached out and grabbed my father by the elbow. The old man looked around and stared at him, pivoted again. Then suddenly, gracefully, swanwise, sad, my father, seeing Mam's face, turned his whole body around and ghosted his way through the policemen and back out into the night.

Outside in the courtyard the whole world had gathered to watch the darkroom stand in a shell of nothingness, hard and broken and brick-high without a ceiling and roamed around by figures quietly shaking their heads at the audacity of flame. Rumours were whispered into the palms of hands.

'Isn't it horribly sad, all the same?'

'They say she burnt it.'

'Torched it good-oh.'

'Go on out of that.'

'Well, that's his comeuppance, I suppose.'

Boys my age were flinging stones at the gutted structure and edging their way closer, always closer, until they were swatted back by the adults, who themselves moved in for a better look. It was the most spectacular thing that had happened in years. I muttered to myself: I will never go to school again in my life, I will never go anywhere ever again. And, at the kitchen window, I watched the old man walk his way around the building, slowly following two firemen through the kicked-down door to emerge with his hands clasped to his head. Some firemen were dragging out the filing cabinets. In the living room Mrs O'Leary was saying, 'It's all right now, Juanita, I'll stay with you the night,' and she ran her fingers over Mam's brow, all the time still incanting 'there there there.'

Mrs O'Leary, withered down into herself, said to me: 'You and your Mam are coming with me, she needs a little rest, she's awful tired, you know. You'll be staying with me for a few days until she's better.' And outside, my father, in a stained grey shirt, combing through the ashes of his darkroom.

From outside the door I could hear the bath running and the old man fumbling with his clothes. There was a loud bash against one of the cupboard doors and I pulled at the handle of the door to open it. It was locked tight. 'It's all right,' he said from inside, 'I'm only taking off me shoes.'

Mrs O'Leary felt her way to the end of the counter to pull pints for the firemen. She had set up an empty Guinness keg for me to sit on, gunmetal grey, old beer gone sticky around the rim. The men in the bar were arranged in a stonehenge of themselves, chatting darkly and seriously, one of them coming up from the ring to collect the row of pints. They wiped their hands across their brows, whispering: 'Bychrist, I'm ready for a pint. That'd put a thirst on a Bedouin.'

I sat on the keg and made a wigwam out of toothpicks, gazed at the names of All-Star hurley players on wall posters.

Mam was upstairs in a dusty and crucifixed room, guided there by Mrs O'Leary, a look of curious defiance on her face as she went up the stairs. Every now and then Mrs O'Leary went up to check on her, whispering prayers as she went, following the chiselled-out track that she'd made in the wall. I sneaked in behind the counter and, with shaking hands, secretly poured myself some beer in a 7-Up bottle, watched the men in their circle. They glanced furtively over their shoulders at me, one of them saying: 'It's all right now, lad, it'll all be grand in the morning.' I held the bottle to my lips – I wanted to be a fireman, I wanted to be outside all of this, looking in at myself, conjuring up mutterings and sympathies and inanities.

'Time for bed for you too, young man,' said Mrs O'Leary, coming down and placing a hand on my shoulder. 'But don't be disturbing your Mam.'

'I don't want to go to bed.'

'Come on, now, you'll be okay.'

I looked around at the row of bottles along the counter,

200

sitting there like capstans on a pier, and I reached for a bottle of whiskey, took it by the narrow neck, hid it quickly behind my back and stuffed it into my waistband, untucked my shirt over it. The bottle was cold against my skin. I took a couple of steps around Mrs O'Leary and she said: 'Don't do that.'

'What?'

'Leave the bottle there.'

'What bottle?'

'Come on, now, Conor.'

'I don't have any bottle!'

'Ah, now.'

The firemen had turned around, cigar smoke above them.

'I don't have any fucken bottle!'

'Give it to me.'

'It's only 7-Up.'

'Sure, you're just a bit upset. It was a bad accident.'

'It wasn't an accident.'

'Ah, now, of course it was.'

I brushed past her and my shoulder hit against her and she stumbled back a little, reached out and steadied herself against the counter. A fireman moved towards me with his arms outstretched. He took the bottle from the back of my trousers, gently, and I was all of a sudden a whirlwind of arms, my fist thumped into his crotch, he doubled over, and I was running for the door when my arms were pinned back by another hefty fireman and tears leaped from me. Mrs O'Leary came across, the rattle of her rosary beads at her neck, saying, 'It's been a long night, we'll tuck you in.'

She pursed her lips, raised her head, told the firemen that it was time to leave, kept her hand on my shoulder as she came behind me up the stairs. The door was slightly ajar, and I saw Mam sitting upright in bed, spectral, with extra jumpers over her nightdress and she was looking in a little mirror and putting make-up on her face. I couldn't believe it. I had thought maybe she'd still be rocking, but there was a small brown circular pad in her hand and she dabbed it on her face precisely, as if with love for what she might have come to terms with in the mirror. 'Say goodnight,' said Mrs O'Leary, and I did, from the doorway. Mam looked up and smiled at me, said she was sorry for all the ruckus, she'd make it up to me the next day, maybe we'd take a trip together. Her voice was perfectly even.

'Goodnight, *m'ijo*.'

I said nothing.

Mrs O'Leary leaned across me: 'You can sleep in my bed.'

'I don't want to sleep in your bed.'

'Go on, now, give your Mam some rest.'

Her room was curiously bright and colourful, some paintings on the wall, Saint Lucia glaring down from a wooden frame, beside it a wallhanging with peacocks in strut. Mrs O'Leary knelt down and said some prayers by my bed – 'There are four corners to my bed, there are four angels there lie spread, one at my head, two at my feet, one at my heart my soul to keep' – and all at once I felt vacuumed and angry and repeated them after her, a litany of uselessness – even then, at twelve years old, I thought how useless it was, that praying. The exposed hands of a clock moved and I pretended to be asleep as she pulled the sheets around me, folded them back. 'Be a good lad, now.' She leaned down and kissed the top of my head, tiptoed from the room. I didn't want to be tucked in. I ripped the sheets out from under the mattress, made a puddle of them down at my feet. Later I could hear her downstairs in the pub saying: 'Right now, gentlemen, I think it's time, don't you, I've said it's time a million times, they need their rest, have yez no homes to go to at all?'

I got up and looked out the window – cars were leaving

202

the pub, a horn going like the cry of a sick curlew, the fire-engine lights not twirling anymore – and suddenly voices came from down the landing, and I jumped back into bed.

'Are you okay, Juanita?'

'I am fine.'

'Shall I stay here with you?'

'I am okay, Alice, I am okay.'

'I'll stay with the boy.'

'Thank you, Alice.'

'Are ya sure?'

'I am sure, *gracias*.'

And then the shuffle along the landing, and the knob turning and Mrs O'Leary coming to bend over me, moving to a chair that she had by the window, kicking off her shoes, breathing out a sigh in the cold, bringing a coat out of her wardrobe, slowly closing the buttons, a twist of a bottle and a small slurp, settling down into the flesh of herself, sighing deeply again before I fell asleep. When I woke up in the morning, Mam was gone and there was a make-up kit sitting on the bed where she had been, everything silent outside, a small mirror catching the light.

The bathroom lock clicked open and he stuck his head around the door, said: 'Come on in, for fucksake, before I freeze me jewels off.'

He still had his shirt on, but his shoes and socks and trousers were off. He had put on his swimming togs, the old red ones that he used to swim and prance around in on the beach. Pulled the string tight until the material valley-rippled around his waist, but even then they were miles too big. I was almost afraid to think of him rubbing the sponge against himself. See him turn to dust. Maybe crumple in his own fingers. His hands were shaking when he fumbled with the bottom buttons on the shirt. Strange how embarrassed he was by the nakedness, even with the togs on, using the one good hand to cover himself.

I went to put my arm under his shoulder but he brushed me away, slowly steered himself towards the bath, tested the water with his toes. 'The water's too fucken hot,' he said. 'I can't even remember how to make a bath!' But I tested it with my fingers before he got in and it was simply lukewarm. I was sure he had lost some sense of feeling. The way his whole body gently shook. He went clawing for the soap after it fell in under his left leg. I was going to reach in and get it but he just shook his head. 'Go on, now, I'm not a fucken invalid, I told ya a million times.' Left the soap disintegrating away beneath his leg.

'Right,' he said, dangling his arm out the side of the tub, like it didn't belong, a pantomime prop. 'So tell me about all this travelling,' he said. 'Ya almost gave me a fucking heart attack yesterday.'

'I just wanted to know some things.'

'Like what things?'

'About the past.'

'Christ, couldn't I have told ya that, Conor? Didn't I tell ya everything? And you wouldn't even look me in the eye. Isn't that right? Didn't I tell ya everything?'

'I don't think so.'

'Well, I did.'

'Maybe.'

'No maybes about it.'

'Let's not fight.'

'I'm not fighting. Am I fighting? Do I look like I'm fighting?'

He raised his hands from the bath and turned his palms in the air. I turned away and picked his trousers up from the floor, placed them on the radiator to get them nice and warm. She used to do that for me when I was very young, five or six, clacking her way through a hum or a rhyme, neatly folding them first in the crook of her brown arm, weaving out a hand underneath them, smoothing them out, placing them on the radiator, always very precise, afterwards reaching in the cupboard for special soaps, leaning over.

'I mean,' he said, 'it's all so long ago now.'

'It's not really.'

'We make our mistakes.'

'We all do,' I said.

'Then we move along.'

'We do.'

'You learn finally that some things aren't meant to heal.'

He said it without sentimentality. His voice was as slow as syrup. He let his head loll against the back of the bath and clacked his teeth together, sighed. Outside, through the hazy bathroom window I thought I could see the movement of some birds. I turned back to the bath. I must have looked at him too long and hard, because he turned his head away and then looked back at me again.

'Conor,' he said after a moment, raising one hand to scratch at his forehead, 'd'ya think there's any way you could put some of that shampoo on me hair?'

'What's that?'

'My arm is sore here. Can't reach up properly. Gives me a bit of a stab here.' He rubbed his shoulder. 'Maybe just help me wash it, you know.'

I stood.

'What's wrong with ya?' he asked.

'Nothing, nothing.'

'Ah, it doesn't fucken matter,' he said, putting his hands back down into the bathwater.

'Sure,' I said, 'sure I will.'

'Good man.'

I reached into the cupboard, fumbled around, and got out the shampoo, my hands shaking. He laid his head underneath the water, a boat of bones sinking, got his hair wet, resurfaced, reached his fingers up and ran them through it, still greasy and tangled. 'Phhhhfffff,' he said, shaking his head.

'Are ya right?'

'Right so. Go easy on it, there's not much of it left, for fucksake.'

I put a small dollop of shampoo on my hand, told him to wet his hair again, rubbed my hands together. 'Ya look like a bloody executioner there,' he said as he rose slowly out of the water. I sat on the edge of the bath and leaned over. 'Out with the electricity, son.' He hunched himself up, held on to the handrail, the veins stark and blue. The hairs on his back ran all the way down to the red togs.

The soap piled up at the back of his neck and he gave out a little contented hum as I massaged my fingers into his scalp.

'She wasn't in Mexico.'

'No,' he said. It wasn't a question, the way he said it.

'I thought she'd be there.'

'Well, now, you can never be sure of anything.'

'And she wasn't with Cici.'

'Why would she be?'

'Why not?'

I kept massaging the soap into his scalp, around the age spots.

'I miss her,' he said.

'I know ya do.'

'No, no, you don't understand, I really miss her. I honestly miss her.'

'I know, I can tell.'

'Ya can't change the past. You know, you try to change the past, but you can't.'

He let out a long whistle and closed his eyes, and my fingers worked themselves into the soft spots on his head and he almost pushed his head back into my hands and I thought how easy it would be to hurt him, just by mashing

206

my fingers into his head.

'And Cici, what's she doing with herself?' he said after a while.

'This and that. Nothing really.'

'Like the rest of us. Still writing poems?'

'Says it's not worth a damn.'

'She's dead right.'

'Why did ya give up the photos, Dad?'

'Jaysus, now, that's a stupid question. Don't be rubbing my hair away, now! For fucksake!'

'Take a dip.'

He took a long time to position himself so that he could go down into the water again.

'Once more,' I said. 'One more shampoo.'

'Christ, it isn't that dirty!'

'Hold still there, now.'

'And yourself, I mean, are ya making a living?'

'A few bob.'

He closed his eyes: 'Ah, this'll do me for years. I'll have the cleanest hair west of Waterloo.'

I had put too much shampoo on, and some of the soap fell down from his hair and on to his neck. I reached to scoop it up, left my fingers there, began to wash his neck. His head went forward at first, a little shocked, then laid back into my hands. I felt curious knots in his neck. It was like rubbing cheese. It had that peculiar texture, not hard, not soft. He didn't budge while I massaged, and maybe his body was relaxing, maybe he was calling things back, because I could feel some sort of melting-away, washing along his neck tanline. The soap bubbled over on to his shoulders and I rubbed it down and over the top of his back, along his shoulders, until I was using both my hands, my fingers converging on his spine – thinking that if I pushed too hard I could crack his whole nervous system – and time seemed to be effortlessly drifting from us, rolling along, until he pulled away and bobbed down into the bath.

'Soap was getting in me eyes,' he said.

But I knew what it was and he turned his face away from me, said: 'I'm grand, so. Leave a man in peace so he can take off his fucken togs.'

I pursed my lips together and nodded: 'I'll be outside if ya need me.'

He pulled at the string of his togs as I closed the door and moved as if he was going to take them off.

'Conor,' he said.

I peeped back through the crack in the door. 'What?'

He still had his hand on the string of his togs.

'I really have no idea.'

'What?'

'About your Mam.'

'That's all right.'

'For all I know she could be in Timbuktu.'

'I don't think I'll be going there.'

He made an attempt at a little laugh.

'Just walked out from there,' he said. 'Didn't even know she'd left until Mrs O'Leary came around and told me. I was knocking the rest of the darkroom down with the big hammer. Turning it to mush. Played it over and over in my head ever since. Thought she'd be back. Swore it to myself. Didn't give it much thought until a few hours later. Then a day. Then two days. Three. Sometimes I even think she could have walked her way down to the river beyond. She was awful depressed, you know.'

'The river?'

'I don't know. Anything's possible, isn't it?'

'You mean she walked her way into the river?'

'Maybe.'

'When?'

'Maybe that night.'

'Are you sure?'

'Ah, you can't be sure of anything, can ya? You can be sure of nothing. That's the only thing you can be sure of. Nothing. But I miss her. I miss her more than anyone thinks.'

He picked up the washcloth from the shelf and dunked it in the bath, lifted his armpit in the air and began to scrub as vigorously as he could. The water must have been getting a little cold because he shivered a little when he did it. Droplets were dripping from his hair on to his shoulder. The rims of his eyes were red.

'I'll get the hairdryer,' I said.

'You won't catch me using that fucken thing,' he muttered, 'no bloody way.'

I closed the door to let him take off his togs and scrub himself down. I sat down on the top of the stairs. 'The river, Dad?' I said from outside, but he mustn't have heard me, the bathwater gurgling down the drain.

Water is what we are made of. It has its own solitude. A storm blew in and the search was called off for a few hours. The rain filled the ditches with flow, hammered down on the roof, made small lakes in the roads, the lane impassable. The old man stayed outside and watched as it rifled down. Doubt sunk itself into the searchers, and the rumours were again rife. She had gone to Chile, where she had fallen in love with a military dictator. She had been seen in Dublin with nasturtiums behind her ears. She had taken a boat out into the storm. She was in the mental hospital in Castlebar, behind the big yawning gates. But for me she was home where she belonged – and a letter would come for me one morning.

One of the searchers, a young girl, handed me a gold earring, told me it was for luck and I believed her, went home with it shoved into a jacket pocket.

'She's just disappeared for a few days,' my father said. He

slept on the floor outside my room that night, and for the next eighteen months, stories coming from him each evening, like hallucinogenic prayers, magnificent dreamscapes, while I – brutally young – waited for a knock on the door, twirling a gold ring in my hand. It was a couple of years later that I came home from school wearing the earring. He had begun his fishing then, every day he would go down to the river. 'Take that piece of shite from your ear,' he said to me on the riverbank, 'or I'll give ya what-for and no doubt about it.'

'Ask my bollocks,' I said. From then on, that was one of the few things I ever said to him.

After he towel-dried his hair he pulled on two jumpers, the warmed trousers and the overcoat. Even got some clean wool socks. He stretched himself out and gave a sniff at the air. 'Jaysus, haven't smelled this good in years.'

He told me that the morning midges and other insects are attracted to sweet fragrances, that if he went outside he'd be besieged after the amount of shampoo I had put in his hair. But we went out anyway into the dawn and I didn't notice any more insects than usual. They made their normal congregations around the bushes, and a few of them hovered around us, grey smudges. A drizzle broke, stopped, fell again.

'See, I told ya,' he said as he attempted to clap his hands on a few of the midges in the air.

We shifted our way around the farmyard and he made a crack about the wheelbarrow and pushing him around in it. Even gave a little kick at its wheel, a swipe that missed. I noticed the flap of one of his wellingtons was coming undone and told him about the old man in Mexico whom I had seen dance, in his collarless shirt and his holey shoes. 'Nothing better than an old man for dancing,' he said as he shuffled over the courtyard towards the pathway. We went out beyond the yard. Clouds were out, swifts following them. A breeze blew over our heads. It was too early for the factory smell. He negotiated his way over the stile and through the gap in the bushes down towards the water. The river was as dead as ever.

I tucked my jacket in under me and took a place at the edge of the riverbank. He took to a fit of coughing in the lawn chair, then stood up and started collecting a few cigarette butts that we had missed yesterday. I started helping him, put two butt ends in my jacket pocket. I was standing close to him when his arms flew out.

'Look at that!' he shouted, 'Look!'

I looked around and there was nothing, absolutely nothing, not even a ripple.

But I know what he saw. Caught in mid-twist in the air, the flash of belly shining, contorted and unchoreographed in its spin, reaching out over the surface so the skips were alight in the air around it, fins tucked in, tail in a whisk throwing off droplets, making a massive zigzag of itself, three feet over the surface, mouth open to gulp air, eyes huge and bulbous, a fringe of water around it – place and motion caught together, as in one of the old photos – reaching up, the whole surface of the water in a frenzy beneath it, so that the flow jiggled and freed itself from its home within the reeds, went down towards the sea, the grass itself bending to the movement, until his salmon hit a zenith and it retreated headfirst into the water with a magical sound, a chorus of plops, erupting like weather, and the water knew something about itself and became all at once quiet and there was joy there, I felt it, marvellous, unyielding, and he leaned his shoulder against me and said: 'Fucken hell, amazing, wasn't it?'

He slapped me on the back and asked me to go to the house and get his fishing rod and the flies, which I did. I opened the wooden box and brought him the colourful one he had made the other day. As I came back down, he was nodding away on the riverbank, clapping his hands together and laughing and shouting at the magnificence of his fish. I walked up to him with the rod and said to myself, and to the swifts that flew around, and to the midges that they fed on, and to the clouds that were sauntering along, I said: Let this joy last itself into the night.

He tied the fly on. He was whispering, 'Did ya see it, son?'

I looked over and said to him: 'Yeah, I saw it.'

He gave a grin, fixed the fly, adjusted the reel, stood away from me, just a few feet, spun out some line, caressed the length of the rod, all the time whistling through his teeth as he whipped the rod back and forth above his head, fluidity to it, the swish and swerve, casting away as if there was no tomorrow, none at all, just casting away with all his might.